Monarch of the Square

Middle East Literature in Translation
Michael Beard and Adnan Haydar, *Series Editors*

Monarch
of the Square

An Anthology of
Muhammad Zafzaf's
Short Stories

Translated from the Arabic by
Mbarek Sryfi *and* **Roger Allen**

Syracuse University Press

∞ The paper used in this publication meets the minimum requirements
of the American National Standard for Information Sciences—Permanence of Paper
for Printed Library Materials, ANSI Z39.48-1992.

For a listing of books published and distributed by Syracuse University Press,
visit www.SyracuseUniversityPress.syr.edu.

ISBN: 978-0-8156-3369-3 (paper)   978-0-8156-5296-0 (e-book)

Library of Congress Cataloging-in-Publication Data

Zafzaf, Muhammad.
[Short stories. Selections. English]
Monarch of the square : an anthology of Muhammad Zafzaf's short stories /
translated from the Arabic by Mbarek Sryfi and Roger Allen. — First edition.
pages cm. — (Middle East literature in translation)
ISBN 978-0-8156-3369-3 (pbk. : alk. paper) — ISBN 978-0-8156-5296-0 (ebook)
1. Zafzaf, Muhammad—Translations into English.   I. Sryfi, Mbarek, translator.
II. Allen, Roger, 1942– translator.   III. Title.
PJ7876.I4A2 2014
892.7'36—dc23   2014030648

Manufactured in the United States of America

Contents

Acknowledgments

We would like to thank Professor Jilali El Koudia for taking the time to provide us with his helpful comments. We would also like to express our particular gratitude to Hassan Najmi for his insights and encouragement.

Thanks also to Hèdi Jaouad for providing permission to reprint the stories "The Clinic" and "The Locust," previously published in the journal *CELAAN*, spring 2008.

Mbarek Sryfi and Roger Allen
University of Pennsylvania

A LATE NIGHT CONVERSATION

(1970)

A Late Night Conversation

$\mathcal{F}$rom a spot directly opposite the small café the man kept staring, his eyes riveted in that direction. It felt as if his every nerve was an outburst of blazing fire. Over his head there hung a picture of a mythological being. Outside the café, a square opened up. Lights shone from the tall building across the street, colorful and brilliant. The wind was blowing across the square and weaving its way through the side streets, which were completely empty apart from the light.

"But that was years ago," he said without any preliminaries, as he leaned over.

"I don't know," the doctor said, "I was hungry when I learned how to do that job. I had to walk ten kilometers to get to school. How about you? You'll learn easily enough. You'll work out how to earn a living."

The short man kept rocking backward and forward, over and over again. Staring hawk-eyed at the square, his gaze seemed distant, strange, and frightening.

I peeped from behind the newspaper and watched his body rocking back and forth. He had a round head that looked somehow out of proportion with the rest of his short, pathetic frame. There was a smile on his lips, but it, too, looked different, unusual. He continued rocking back and forth. "The man's crazy," I told myself, "mad!" I kept looking at the round head, the rocking body, and the unusual, broadening smile.

In the square there were groups of mischievous homeless children who kept bickering with each other. From where he was standing, the short man glanced over at the milk bottles arranged on the shelf,

3

then lowered his head and hitched up his pants. He stared at the torn seams on his homemade shoes.

"'You're a disaster,' she told me when we were at the public market. Then it happened, an atrocity."

"And why weren't you ready for it when she told you?" I asked.

"I didn't know."

"You should have been ready."

His eyes were fixed on the newspaper. He couldn't read, of course, but he evidently knew how to sleep until late under the hotel stairs.

The café owner wasn't listening to him. It was a well-known story, oft-repeated. The café owner's eyes were fixed on the square, where dirty puddles reflected the light. I could smell the early odor of rain, and so could the café owner. Paying no attention to the nonsense the short old man was spouting, he reached for the radio switch.

"I sleep under the stairs at the hotel."

"Aren't you afraid of the police? They're quick to pick up people like you."

"They've often taken the money I've managed to collect one way or another."

"And they let you go?"

"Yes. . . . Dirty sons of b—. . . . It was a woman."

He held his pants, pulled them up, and kept on talking, rocking back and forth.

"Did you love her?"

"Of course I did, but she didn't love me."

"You said she wanted you."

"That's right. But, if a woman wants you, it means she doesn't love you."

"Perhaps."

I pretended to be reading. It was getting late. Earlier I had walked through the maze of streets, in the all-embracing darkness, and had ended up at this café. I couldn't afford a hotel room and admitted to myself that my own destiny was similar to his. The only thing was that he knew the city, and I didn't.

"When do you close?" I asked the café owner.

"We're open 24 hours," he answered.

"Great."

The short old man kept scratching his belly and back. I could imagine layers of dirt caked on his aged body. That made me start scratching too and rubbing my belly. "Where did you know the doctor from?" I asked him.

"Here, in this city. It was in 1930, and I knew the woman, too, at about the same time—'30, '32, some time around there."

I folded the newspaper, lit a cigarette, and offered him one, but he refused. The café owner was cleaning some glasses, then went through a small back door toward the radio. Suddenly an irritating sound could be heard. My eyes were heavy with sleep, and I badly needed to rest.

The short old man came inside the café. Without a word he turned and walked back to the square, which by now had been dampened by early rain. He kept moving, his short body tottering like a turtle. As he walked in that specific direction, his image was silhouetted against the towering wall. Before his small, silhouetted image disappeared, a small flame suddenly sprang up; he was smoking.

I looked at the newspaper again, then glanced toward the front of the small café. I spoke to the man standing across from me behind the stone bar, who had been totally indifferent to my presence. He was very short with me. I asked him about the old man, and he replied that he knew the man; he was a regular. I tried to keep the conversation going, but his answers were terse. I sat back on the chair, relaxed, and put my elbows on the table. My eyelids felt heavy and tired; I wanted to get some sleep. I assumed that at such a late hour they would arrest the short man. At the same time, I presumed that they would let him go if he had any money. I fumbled around in my pockets, looked up, and kept staring at the square, which was now full of small, dirty puddles. I began to smell the odor from the early rain.

The Path to a Lighted Room

The frigid sunshine was pouring down on the street, driven by the wind.

I was walking along the sidewalk. Even though I was wearing white wool socks that clung to the hairs on my legs, my feet still felt cold and numb. Mathilda and I were walking in step; our joint tread sounded like pebbles being thrown into a stagnant river, or, at the very least, like the echo of somebody beating a drum—sad and remote, resounding beyond gloomy, distant forests, limitless labyrinths.

I watched my black shoes and Mathilda's sandals forming strange shapes as they moved along the asphalt; I found that exciting. While the wind was blowing straight at us, it managed to turn Mathilda's blond hair into something from a fable, like the hair of a lonely fairy on a desert island.

"The fairy's been waiting for a long time in the jungle," I told myself, "and now I've arrived on my small boat to rescue her and take her to safety."

The whole crazy idea made me laugh. I wanted to tell Mathilda the fable about the fairy with mythological hair, her very own story, but then I was afraid she would just laugh at me.

"It's getting cold," she said as she stared at an ad on the wall. "We're going to freeze tonight."

I looked at her hair flying in the breeze, but said nothing. Instead I looked at her black coat with its wide collar turned up. She was holding it tight around her marble neck as she continued to stare at the ad.

Now she looked straight ahead and pressed against my thin body. "Look," she said, "there are some wonderful things in Lillian's shops."

I stared at her through my cigarette-smoke. "They're of no value to anyone," I said, throwing my cigarette butt away.

Mathilda looked at me calmly and stared until I too turned toward Lillian's shops.

"Let's just have a look, okay?" she said with a smile, her hair covering part of her lower lip.

Tugging me toward her, she led me as we both walked down toward the shops. I kept stumbling because it was so steep. Finally, at the bottom were Lillian's shops, hidden behind clean display-windows that glistened in the sunshine. As we browsed among the various items and clothing on display, it kept getting colder and colder. Mathilda was shivering, and put her hand in my pants pocket.

"Look, there are wonderful things for kids inside," she said, looking at what was beyond the display-window.

"Toys?" I asked.

"Yes, toys. Tractors, trucks, and . . ."

"That bike would be good for you," I interrupted with a chuckle.

She eyed me, her hand still clasping mine inside my pocket. "Okay then," she said with a shrewd laugh, "I'll choose a toy for you, too!"

I squeezed her fingers inside my pocket and pulled her back toward the main street again. By now the sun was looking pale and sickly. "No way!" I said to her.

"Come on," she begged "Let's go inside."

She kept tugging, and I had to control my temper. Once we were inside the shop, we found that everything was arranged in an attractive and captivating fashion.

Mathilda drew my attention to a black scarf. "That scarf would suit you," she said as she walked over to it.

"And you too . . . but it's expensive."

"It would suit you more. You're wearing black pants and a white pullover. It would look beautiful around your neck."

"It's too expensive."

We kept browsing in the shop, and eventually we discovered the back door. I asked Mathilda to leave with me, and she agreed nonchalantly, as though it didn't bother her at all. Once outside, I wanted to kiss her in the empty, forked street. She put her cheek against mine, and I felt her soft blond hair playing with my face. I put my lips on her hair.

"Can we see the Ibsen play tonight?" she asked as she took her hand out of my pocket.

"We don't have enough money."

"I think I have enough on me. Besides, I'll get my weekly check tomorrow."

"Your boss will apologize to you, just like last week."

"This time, I don't think so."

"Are you sure?"

"Positive."

"Positive. So, are we are going to see the play, or what?"

The pale sun was still brightening our autumnal stroll. The yellow, shining trees kept reflecting the light and seemed high up in cold space. We were heading west. Mathilda loved autumn; in fact, she adored and even worshipped it. She liked to wear this coat, pants, and light sandals. In spite of it all, when the wind disheveled her hair, it never seemed to bother her. It seemed to be able to arouse within her a shiny past, present, and future as well. I watched Mathilda chewing something. I assumed that she was thinking about my being there by her side, because her eyes kept darting erratically between the walls, display windows, and passers-by. I veered to the left, but Mathilda still held me tight.

"Look there!" she said with a loud laugh. I looked where she was pointing, and saw an old man urinating on a clean wall. Some children were laughing at him while a few grown-ups were acting disgusted at his obscene behavior.

"Why are you laughing?" I asked, with feigned annoyance.

"Oh, sorry, I didn't mean to," she said. "Aren't there any public toilets?"

She clasped my hand and kept looking at the old man. Finally she looked away. I was staring at the display window to our right, which reflected the image of the two of us close together.

"It's getting very cold," I told Mathilda.

"You'll catch cold," she replied, "and we won't be going to the theatre."

Going upstairs, we met the janitor on the second floor. She greeted Mathilda and ignored me. When I pointed that out to Mathilda, she told me that the woman was simply jealous. I said that she shouldn't be; she was old, and we were young. Once inside the warm room, Mathilda took her coat off and hung it up, then went straight to the kitchen.

She made coffee while I changed. As soon as I opened the window, the sunshine came in and lay down on the bed and floor. I lay down on the bed, too, and leafed my way through the daily newspaper, which I hadn't been able to read in the morning as I usually did. Mathilda brought in the coffee. Her hair was now neatly arranged.

"Listen," she said, smiling happily, "I've something to say to you."

"What is it?" I asked.

"Why don't we get married?"

"Don't you think we're better than married?!" I replied immediately.

For the second time she kissed me, then raised her cup to her lips. I got out of bed, walked over to the window, and stared at the sun's pale, sickly face.

The sky looked like a sad slate, and gray clouds were trailing away somewhere.

"Come on," I told Mathilda. "Let's watch the sunset. The sun's nearly gone."

Sipping my coffee, I turned to call her over, but she was already by my side, her eyes reflecting the colors of the sunset.

The Sun Rises Once

[1]

I waited for a long time by the café counter, feeling at once sad and happy. The faces around me looked as pale as death. My coffee was getting cold. One customer was sipping his juice, but I wasn't drinking. I had been waiting for a long time, so I couldn't share other people's happiness. Faces looked pale. Just a few yards away, the clean shop-windows reflected a tableau that edged towards silver. . . . Four p.m. . . . I let my coffee get cold. "Maybe she's not coming," I told myself. The coffee no longer tasted good; it felt weak on my tongue . . . it had lost the zing I was used to . . . that wonderful sweet bitterness. I started telling myself that everything is subject to change, even the heart of a woman who pretends to be faithful.

But I was wrong. My sweetheart did come, her eyes colorfully bright . . . rhythmic melodies. . . . Then, . . . then the world turned into a happy child who knows nothing of sorrow.

I left my stool and walked toward her.

"Will you sit with me?" I asked as I blew both happiness and cigarette-smoke in her face.

"No, I can't," she replied

"Why not?" I said. "You can do anything."

"You're wrong, but thank you for thinking so."

"Let's go somewhere else," I suggested. "That may be better."

We sat on a wooden bench in the park where children were playing.

"Do you like children?" I asked my sweetheart.

"Yes," she replied.

"Do you want us to have children?" I asked.

"Our relationship wouldn't allow it," she replied.

"Why not?" I asked. "Don't you love me?"

"No, I admire you."

I said nothing but stared at the children. . . . As I waved my fingers in the air, I watched her hair being blown by a slight breeze. I suggested that we get up and stroll along the wide street. . . . People's faces still looked pale, and store-fronts no longer reflected the sunlight. . . . Could such tall buildings ever reflect sunshine?

I said goodbye to my sweetheart and walked away, heading down toward the suq . . . and enjoying the display of human stupidity.

[2]

"I love you so much," I told my mother that evening. "You're wonderful . . . you're a saint."

She gave me a kiss and hugged me. I was touched.

"My son," was all she said.

I used to love my mother so much. It never occurred to me that someone could change my love for her . . . but things are always changing. . . . I had the impression that my sweetheart, who, as she put it, didn't really love me but only admired me, was in control of my feelings. She was throttling my heart (even so, my sweetheart, I'll still worship you for ever and ever . . .). She has managed to replace my mother in my heart, but now my mother is going to reclaim her place. That very evening, I expressed my long-suppressed feelings to her, the loving, unspoken relationship I had with her. My mother is wonderful; she can control the world with her finger. So often she has told me that she couldn't live without me. Her husband still loved her even so. He isn't my real father, but she thought she would be able to compensate for my own father, who had been snatched away by the darkness. What a kind mother! Yes, I love you too; I can't live without you. Look up at the sky and stare at the pale moon; that's where our gazes will meet, and you will find out just how much I love you, the way a child loves his mother. . . . Don't you realize that you are the most precious thing in the world? Please believe it . . . !

That night I stared at the moon longer and longer; the geometrical pattern in the sky kept moving toward the east, but I couldn't detect any motion. Yet my imagination was too strong to be defeated: I loved my sweetheart, I loved the moon, I loved the night, but I didn't love my stepfather. He reminded me of the Jewish character in Jean Anouilh's play, *Invitation to the Palace*. Too many speeches and declining values. . . . What's the value of money compared to gaining the love of a companion? A woman may be impressed by her boyfriend's wealth, but she will never love him (I don't think that my mother loved her husband for his money, but he certainly loved her *till death did them part*. And let's bear in mind that women have only recently acquired the right to fall in love). Sweetheart, I don't want to be admired; I want to be loved . . . Never forget that the world functions only on the basis of love. Without love, the moon will never shine. I will keep waiting and waiting. . . .

That night I slept better than I had ever slept before. . . . I felt totally shattered, and yet I had the sensation of loving the whole of humanity the same way.

[3]

Next day I walked along dirty, garbage-laden streets, the kind where children eat their own snot. I needed to go there. Narrow, dirt-encrusted eyes stared at me. . . . I paid no attention and went into the nearest house. . . . When I left, I was feeling sadder than ever before. . . . My imagination took over. I was bound to get syphilis . . . but I would still go on living, even if I caught the disease. . . .

"The world can go wherever. . . . Nobody can change its direction . . ."

Once I found myself on wider streets, I collapsed on to a chair at the nearest café. . . . I ordered a black coffee and then started staring at all the pale faces. . . . For a long time I waited for my sweetheart to pass by so I could ask her if she still admired me or had moved on to the stage of real love. I could put on a brave front and take whatever she had to say; to hell with feeling down. I waited for ages, but she didn't come. Syphilis kept threatening me with a lingering death. But, in spite of it all, I still love humanity. I shall return to the back streets where the encrusted, narrow eyes are to be found and children feed on snot . . . and the Jew will have to learn how to be happy with his money. . . .

State of Mind

I actually like fog, with its grey hues. That's not what's making me feel so bored. True enough, I'm angry and morose, but the fog has nothing to do with that. Cold weather affects people, especially people like me who don't have warm wool coats. Well, how's anyone supposed to avoid feeling sad when his head is like a heavy bag stuffed full of scary talk and disconnected ideas?

I gulped down the hot coffee, realizing that it would burn the roof of my mouth and hurt a bit. Better to suffer a little now, I told myself, rather than the rest of the day. My wife used to love me and pretends she still does (although I don't believe it), but every morning she complains, and then starts nagging and insulting me. She pretends that she loves me, adores me to the point of worship. But it doesn't matter.

In the past she was a beautiful girl with long hair that reached as far as her knees. We fell in love. I asked her to cut it short, and she did. She used to love me, and her hair as well, but now she slaps me.

"What's the use of a man with no job?" she says "and with no money?"

She's absolutely right, of course. But how can I get a job? If she gets me a job, I'll show her. In fact, if any of you give me a job, I'll show you, too. I don't care what kind of job: garbage collector, carpenter, anything—even toilet cleaner. I want to have a job, to use my hands, like this (he waves his hands). I want to get rich so I don't have to listen to non-stop complaints that only manage to hurt and depress people.

I want a different coat. Mine is all ragged. Well, it doesn't matter. Actually that's not true, it does. The cold weather is definitely

14

making me more depressed this morning, the way it has done every morning since November arrived with its freezing cold. I thank God for bringing me into the world in what they say is a country with a temperate climate. I've been told that in other countries, people can die of being too cold or too hot. I've never heard of that happening in my own country.

At any rate, cold weather can be a killer. If this choking feeling I have gets any worse, it may well kill me. For some time now I haven't detected much movement in my body, and this condition may well consign it to a hole that's large enough for me, my coffin, and my shroud. I may be moving, walking, and eating, but I feel as if I'm dead. Those activities don't have the same meaning for me as they do for other people—even the idea of being sated or having had enough. . . .

That man may have been kind, but he was still shameless. There may seem to be a contradiction in what I'm saying, but in fact there's none. Absolutely not! He emigrated to a distant land and left me without a job. Everything he'd paid me for my job (or whatever you want to call it) disappeared over years gone by. Potatoes, tomatoes, and bread, they all leave your hands empty. The bread-basket, that's the real enemy of mankind. Yes, that's right! You fill it up, then empty it again; fill it once more, and empty it once more. It's as though you're trying to sift water or trap it in your fingers as it cascades in a silver stream from above.

He owned a field in the city suburb. Truth to tell, for all those years he'd provided me with vegetables and even clothes, so I didn't need to buy anything. He used to give me hand-me-downs, which I always managed to exchange for other things. This old coat I'm wearing is one of his donations; by now it's very ragged. All of which makes it very easy to compute the number of years he's deprived me of work since he left. When he handed it to me with a cordial tap on the shoulder, we realized that the coat was in fairly good condition. He asked one of his friends to look after me, but that person was crafty. He told me that I was going to work for him, and I told him that was fine, in fact very nice of him. I agreed, but then he hired someone else and totally ignored me without explaining why. I felt humiliated, as though my sense of dignity had been trampled underfoot in broad daylight—like a chicken that's been run over by a shiny car and left flattened on the road.

"It's not a problem," my wife told me. "Just look for another job."

I told her that I would try. In fact I did try, and I still am. To give her credit, my wife tried as well. Her cousin's husband belongs to the class a notch above ours, so she asked her cousin to help. She promised to help and still does. While she waits for me to find a job, my wife is dying of anger. It's as though some mythical fingers were transforming her mood from sorrow to tears and making her say things that sound like lamentations for the dead.

This morning she did it again. You don't have a job, she told me. Go and look for one. What are we supposed to eat? If things keep on like this, I'm going back to my mother's place.

She was in tears. I felt like crying too, but then I remembered that I'm a man; and men don't cry. What they do is think, although actually they are crying inside, crying and crying. . . . It's by no means the first time she's told me she's going back to her mother's; in fact it may be the thousandth or even more. Perhaps I haven't taken it seriously enough.

She used to show me her clothes. "Just take a look," she'd say "They aren't even worth mending."

She was right, and I had to agree. She had every reason to cry.

I like fog with its grey hues. It's just that this morning the cold weather's bothering me while I'm enjoying the lovely fog.

My coat needs mending, and so do my wife's clothes. I've no job, but I'm heading for the seaport warmth shining in my eyes. I'm reasonably content.

The Burial

Breathing so hard was very painful. Sweat was pouring from his pores, overworked not so much because of the searing spring heat, but rather from having to clamber up mountains. It was trickling slowly through his short, thick body-hair; in the silent world that enveloped him, it managed to sound like the ripple of a tiny stream flowing through a canyon. Nothing but silence, the lethal trickle of sweat, a blocked road, utter exhaustion, and a woman who was still unburied even though she had been dead for two days.

S. stopped climbing, panting even harder than before; he was totally exhausted. Being forced to use another route than the one that was blocked made for very tiring work. For two whole days now he had been climbing up and down other trails . . . but no matter how exhausted he felt, he could not stop or take a break. Back down there, his wife still lay inside the house like a bag of wet hay. By now her corpse may well have begun to smell bad; perhaps worms had started sprouting from her toes in search of exits to the world of light. The cemetery was still a long way away. The blocked road had made it even further.

One evening, exactly a week ago, while S. and his now-dead wife were having dinner, they heard a violent crashing sound and a loud rumble, which totally obliterated the combined noise of thunder and pounding rain. They had never heard such a sound before. The next day they discovered that part of the mountain had collapsed in a landslide, because the floods had eroded part of the ground. The road was now blocked. There it all stood, stubbornly defiant. From that evening on, S.'s house was totally cut off from the world, from the village and its shops two miles away.

S. was totally exhausted as he tried to get there. To get around the landslide, he had had to resort to his hands and knees—in fact, his entire body. Once he had reached the top of the landslide, he'd jumped down to a lower point, then back onto the blocked road.

When his wife had died, he'd thought about wrapping up her body, tying her to his back, and making his way over the landslide. However, he realized that that would be totally undignified for a dead person. In any case, he might not make it, and that would make him feel very sad. For two days now, he had been trying to come up with some other way of getting his dead wife to the cemetery, but the road was still blocked. It was the only road, and the cemetery was very far away. He would need to go around the mountain and get to the place where the shops and cemetery were located. Feeling desperate, he thought of taking an ax and burying his wife somewhere close to his house, but everything he tried was utterly futile. The ground was as hard as steel; digging just a few cubic inches took many hours. He had tried in other places too, only to confront the same firmness, obstinacy, and rejection from the ground.

But now he had found a solution. In the afternoon two men were going to meet him and help him carry the corpse. They would walk with him down the circular road to the bottom where the village, cemetery, and shops were located.

When S. reached the house, he paused for a moment. Utterly exhausted, he collapsed on the ground; even though it was actually cold and hard, it now felt warmer and more sympathetic. He stared off into the distance, relentlessly observing the curved line that separated earth and sky. A doleful tableau took shape before him: white houses, plowed land, shapeless, colorless trees, and far away a curved line separating earth and sky. From that scene he looked back at his own surroundings and focused on the lower part of the door. Still feeling stunned and ill at ease, he realized that behind that half-opened door lay the shrouded body of his wife. By now it might well be, indeed probably was, turning blue and covered with a layer of worms. In his mind he gathered together all the foulest smells he could imagine; it was the most repulsive ones that seemed to stick in his mind. A strange image occurred to him: what if wolves had sneaked in through the door while he was out and savaged the corpse? He imagined his wife, whom he had often hugged and embraced, being instantly torn to pieces. In his mind he tried to put the pieces back together and restore to his dead wife the tender body that had become so diseased in her final days.

Like a defective machine, he stood up slowly, placed his hands on his knees that were sagging under the weight of so much grief and bitterness, and rushed like a madman toward the house, chasing away the image of carnivorous wolves as he did so. No one deserved such a death, he told himself, especially someone who, during her lifetime, had been one of the most beautiful, kind, and tender of creatures. Divine care always attends such benevolent souls, protecting them from evil.

He scratched the nape of his neck; it was the sweat that was making his hair coarse and damp, not the rain. When he opened the door, his eyes fell on a serenely shrouded body, covered with a clean and plain cloth that his wife had kept locked away in a chest for such a day as this. It was painful for S. to find himself alone and isolated, facing the world unaided (but then death spares no one).

His wife had passed away one morning while she was chatting to him in her usual amiable way. She never worried about death or imagined it would surprise her, but now it had! Even if she hadn't been aware of the imminence of death, her life-partner certainly was, now that she had died. . . . Her husband was now fully aware of the fact that death can surprise you wherever and whenever.

S. could not bear to stare so helplessly at the serene corpse, so he shifted his gaze elsewhere to focus on things that reminded him of his dead wife's image. Slowly closing the door, he left the house and sat on a rock fixed firmly in the ground. Once again he could see the white spots on the horizon, the plowed land, and the curved line separating the kingdom of heaven from that of earth. He stayed there sitting on the rock till he heard the sound of voices floating on the air, which was as oppressive as a stagnant lake.

The two men arrived and followed S. into the house. They looked sad. Even though they themselves hadn't lost anyone so far, they were aware that they were supposed to look sad and mournful.

After awhile, S. tried to close the door. By now, he was even more upset, but somehow his exhausted frame managed to find some fresh, nervous energy. More than ever, he now realized that he would have to face the world on his own, without any help. While the three of them stumbled their way over the rocks on the road, a movie image passed rapidly across S.'s vision. In it, the circular road was not long, and he imagined it as having been asphalted, even though it was actually rocky, hard, and impassable. In any case, it led to the valley where the white houses, shops, and cemetery were. Far away, a curved line still separated heaven from earth.

He was feeling bitter and exhausted. Even so, he sensed an unusual burst of energy which he had never felt before. . . . At this point, his wife only seemed to weigh a few ounces (for sure, by now her soul would be flying toward that distant unknown place along with many others). . . . A tear fell from S.'s eye. The rough, twisting road seemed to grow shorter.

LOW HOUSES

(1977)

In the Middle of Nowhere

10 p.m. Outside, everything was white, and the snow was still falling. Inside the freezing cold café, Ahmad had managed to wrap himself up in his overcoat like a hedgehog. There were very few other customers. The glass windows were all fogged up, which gave the illusion of actual warmth even though the café still wasn't at all warm.

"There's no way of avoiding the cold," said the girl behind the counter. "This place is between mountains, and it's always snowing. Besides that, we can't afford to heat the café; it's too expensive, especially now that the number of customers keeps dropping."

"This weather makes the place look deserted and gloomy."

"Not entirely," she said. "Can I get you a drink?"

"Please, and pour yourself one, too, if you want to stave off the cold. It could well give you a bad case of flu."

"I'll have a whiskey. The bar-owner refuses to let me drink cheap stuff."

The café was pretty empty: just eight people scattered along the length of the bar or sitting on chairs to the side. The door and windows were shut and the lighting was dim. Through the kitchen door came the sound of plates clattering and glasses being washed. Once in awhile, the girl brought them out and stacked them under the counter.

Sitting in a corner by the door, a woman had lifted her veil, revealing a tattoo that covered her face in the Zammori style. She was drinking one glass after another. At the same table, the man who was with her was completely drunk. The edge of his turban dangled over his shoulder and forehead, and his lower lip drooped, as well.

23

"The whiskey's bad for me," the barmaid said. "But I have to drink it."

"Try red wine instead."

"I can't. Look at that woman over there. She only drinks red wine, and she's stronger than a devil."

"Her husband's gotten drunk just on beer."

"He gets drunk easily," she replied. "But he's not her husband. He's married to two other women."

"Lucky man! He must be rich."

"He sells cattle and owns two trucks. Even the *Caid*'s scared of him. His two wives know about his relationship with this woman."

The girl heard a cup being placed on the bar and went over to dry it.

Now two men came in, their hats pulled down firmly over their ears. Their hats and clothes were white, and their bodies were covered in snowflakes. One of them, his greasy face shrouded in steam, started rubbing his hands together and blowing on them. He was clearly a mechanic, while the other one looked like a truck driver. They both went straight to the bar, stood by Ahmad, and ordered two cups of hot coffee. They whispered to each other, drank their coffee quickly, then left, but only after pulling their hats down firmly and opening the glass door. A freezing cold draft blew in, which made the customers shift their positions and bundle up in their clothes.

Ahmad took a cigarette from his pack, thinking he could at least warm the space around his face. Emptying the rest of his glass, he tapped it on the bar. The girl came over, refilled it for him, then served herself. She said she might get drunk tonight; it was a really good idea, especially in such awful weather. "It is very cold," she went on in Berber, "Do you know Tashelheet?"

"No, but I understand you. Are you Amazigh?"

"My late father was, but my mother was an Arab from Doukkala. Sometimes I have to speak Tamazight because most of the people here are Amazigh."

"So why have you exiled yourself to this place? You don't seem to be from these parts."

"No, I'm not. That's a long story, a very long story. Anyway, I can't go back to my own city. He keeps threatening to kill me."

"Who?"

"Him."

"But what about the authorities?"

"Oh, I know all about that!" said the barmaid. "Might as well not even mention it. I'm living a fairly happy life here, in spite of the isolation. By now, I'm used to the place, but I'm afraid I may be spending the rest of my life here."

"Anyone else in your situation would dread the idea, too. Can you see the moon, high above the snow-capped peaks?"

"The window's fogged over," she replied. "I can't see a thing."

"Me neither. I only imagined it. Give me another drink. I'm extremely tired. I don't know where I'm going to sleep tonight in this freezing cold. You say there's no hotel here."

"That's right, there is no hotel. We only have three rooms, but tourists have already booked them for four days. Drink up, and we'll think of a solution later. I know, it's hard for you. The nearest city is eighty kilometers away. Not to mention the foul weather."

"Yes. Not to mention extreme fatigue. I can't drive my car now. Do you understand?"

"Very well."

She poured herself another drink, served another client in the corner, then with a cough she came out from behind the counter and went over to the jukebox. It started playing a tender American ballad. The man with the dangling turban woke up and started singing in Tashelheet. The girl told him to stop. It wasn't the right time, she told him, but promised that they would all listen to him later.

"Give us something to drink," the man told her. "Life is short. I've got to sell a whole truck full of cattle next Saturday. What a deal!"

"Don't assume that other people are begging," replied the barmaid. She turned to Ahmad. "He only brags about his money when he's drunk," she said.

"He's right," said Ahmad. "Life is short. It's freezing cold, and I need to get some sleep. How about me spending the night with you and paying you?"

"I don't know about that. It's never happened with any customer here before."

"So then, let it be the first time! Empty your glass. Life is short. Uuh, everything is tiring, even sleeping with a woman. Don't think I'm like the others. I'll just sleep. If you don't want it, I won't even touch you. Even so, it'll be better to sleep in the same bed tonight."

"You drink too much. Have you had anything to eat?"

"I ate some sardines and half a kilo of bananas, but that was hours ago."

"That's not enough. Do you want me to order you a sandwich? I need to eat before I go to bed, too."

"OK, just as you like. Pour me a drink. It's not so cold now; I feel warmer."

"But your nose is red."

She heard a customer calling her and went over to get the bill. Three men left the café, but he didn't even feel the wind that blew in again. He watched as the thick flakes kept falling in the light of the streetlamps. The empty street was completely blanketed in white. The glass door closed by itself.

"Are you a government employee?" Ahmad heard her asking.

"No."

"Businessman?"

"No."

"Oh, I see. A drug smuggler? They pass by here a lot."

"No, I'm not a drug smuggler, but I do other things in life. Do you work with 'Them'?"

"Drug smugglers?"

"No. 'Them.'"

"Who are 'Them'?"

"'Them.' Don't you know 'Them'? The police."

"Impossible."

"Why?"

"Because that's the way it is," she replied. "I've ordered two sandwiches. Can I get myself another drink? You're very generous."

"I just want to get some sleep."

"It's possible, but still difficult. You don't know the region. I can't take a client home with me. Tomorrow everybody would be talking about it."

"But it's just one night in your life here."

"I see. You'll have to wait for me for two hours or more till the bar's finally empty."

"I'll try. Will you take me with you?"

"I only have a small bed."

"That's even better."

The wine made Ahmad's head feel heavy. He closed his eyes and slumped back in his chair.

"Go and wait for me in your car," said the girl. "I'll join you when I've finished. That way, nobody will know."

He paid the bill, grabbed the sandwich, and walked out chewing. The wind was freezing cold, blowing in from far away. He was shivering all over and found it difficult to run because his legs wouldn't obey him. He fell on the snow, struggled back to his feet, and headed for the car. He closed the door and tried to eat the sandwich, but found it impossible. He felt his hands letting the sandwich drop on to his thighs, but could not manage to bring it back up to his mouth. As soon as he started to feel warmer, he started snoring loudly, head down. At the same time, the girl had started dropping glasses between her feet at the bar. There was just one drunk customer left.

Shrine Visiting Season

The truck stopped at the side of the road. Halima jumped up in alarm and so did her three children. Lhadi opened the door, got out, and slammed it shut behind him. That annoyed the driver, but he did not protest, or say anything at all. After checking to make sure no other car was coming, the driver opened the door and got out on the other side. Lhadi walked along the right side, while the truck driver walked on the left. When Lhadi reached the back, he called out to Halima, who quickly answered, stood up, and looked down at him.

"Wake the kids up," he shouted.

"They didn't get any sleep."

"Good," said Lhadi. "Get ready to climb down."

Lhadi watched the driver on the other side as he headed for the ditch. It was dark; there were no sounds, only the chirping of tiny insects in the trees. The driver went into a thicket of trees close to the road and started peeing standing up. When Halima saw him, she hid her head so Lhadi wouldn't slap her.

When the driver had finished, he turned back toward Lhadi. "Get back on the truck," he said, still buttoning his pants, "and make sure your wife, kids, and your things are out of the truck. I'm in a hurry, and it's a long way to Oujda. I have to be there by six tomorrow evening."

Lhadi put his hands on the side of the truck. He was about to get in, but then a thought crossed his mind. He could make his wife step down; that was not a problem. But who was going to help her get off the truck? When he imagined the driver putting his hands on her hips to help her down out of the truck, his stomach got in a twist.

"Halima," he shouted.

"Yes."

"Get down and leave the kids. I'll come up and get them."

Halima agreed. She threw down her *cherbel*, then grabbed the side of the truck and lowered first one leg, then the other. While she was suspended in mid-air, Lhadi reached up, put his hands on her backside and hips, and eased her down. She moved away and sat down with her back against a tree, but then she discovered that she was perched on a protruding piece of wood or a small branch. It hurt, so she changed her spot. She was panting hard, almost as though she had just run a very long way. Lhadi jumped quickly and nimbly into the truck. His three children were standing there, anxiously waiting for him in the dark. After talking to them first, he lowered them to the driver one at a time. They went straight over to their mother and squatted by her, watching what their father and the driver were doing. Lhadi started lowering blankets, piles of clothes, and a worn-out old suitcase to the driver below. Finally he handed down a pile of what must have been metal, because, when the driver grabbed it, it clanked. He also heard the sound of glasses clinking. This man had to be really crazy, he told himself, to put glass in a package without realizing that it would break.

The driver got back into his truck and switched on the ignition. The truck moved off. Lhadi stood in front of his wife with his hands on his hips. "In just a few minutes, it'll be daylight," he said. "Should we leave now or wait till dawn?"

Halima had no fixed opinion on the matter, so she told him to do as he wished. He sat down beside her and leaned against the trunk. The three children were half-awake, but eventually they fell asleep. The first snuggled in his mother's arms, while the second and third rested their heads on either side of her lap. Lhadi took out a cigarette and started smoking.

"You'd better finish this pack," Halima said.

"I will."

"Now, before daybreak. Your father shouldn't see you smoking or smell it on you. It's forbidden."

"I know. Anyway, I've only got five cigarettes left. I'll smoke them before dawn. I don't know what I'm going to do this week without being able to smoke."

"Why can't you behave like your brother, 'Abbas?" Halima suggested, as she wiped her nose on her clothes. "He doesn't smoke."

"I can't."

"You could if you were a man."

"I am a man."

"We'll see if you can survive this week without smoking."

He kept smoking, gazing longingly at the cigarette as though it were his last one. He would have to quit smoking for a week because his father would not allow him to do so. Even though his father didn't pray or fast very often because of his age, he considered smoking as much a sin as drinking. That was why, during this visit to the shrine of the holy man, Lhadi would have to stop smoking, just as he had had to do in previous years. It would be like a fast from smoking for a whole week. Even during the fasting month of Ramadan he would regularly smoke, but he did conceal it from his neighbors. If they had found him smoking, they would have stoned and cursed him, then recited the Qur'anic Sura of "The Kind One" [Al-Latif] in the mosque, which would immediately turn him into an undesirable person. Halima kept on warning him not to smoke in the daytime during Ramadan, especially on Sundays when he went to the airbase. But on other days she never knew how he managed not to smoke. She had asked him once, and he had replied that everyone smoked. It was exhausting, debilitating work; his body could not tolerate it.

Now Halima started thinking about this tricky problem. *"Will he be able to stop smoking for a whole week?"* Actually, he had never managed to do that; even here at the shrine for the last few years, he would go off with his friends and smoke somewhere. But at all events, he never smoked in front of his father. This week he would also shave his head and put on a red fez. His father could not bear to see him with hair like the Christians.

Lhadi stared into the dark, thinking about the day ahead. Insect sounds could still be heard from behind the trees close by. Just then,

Lhadi watched a truck as it drove by, an American military truck. Lhadi tried to get a look at the driver, but failed. The all-encompassing darkness was making many things difficult.

Lhadi took out another cigarette, lit it, and started smoking with great relish. He put his hand over his crotch and started scratching with his long nails. Even though he had gone to the baths the day before, there were still a lot of bugs in his pubic hair, which made him itch. As they grazed freely in the thicket of hair, Lhadi itched and felt the urge to scratch. He cursed the bugs, which in fact were neither lice nor fleas but tiny bugs that attached themselves to the roots of small hair; they only detached themselves when they had sucked all the blood out of the place where they had attached.

Halima was well aware that the bugs kept bothering him. "Are you still scratching?" she asked.

"Yes."

"Keep scratching then! I've told you thousands of times to shave that forest of hair and keep yourself clean, but you're stubborn. I've told you a million times to use a bit of kerosene, but you always refuse. You only ever listen to that impetuous mind of yours."

"You know nothing," said Ahmad. "The doctor at the American base told me not to shave my pubic hair. It enhances a man's potency."

Halima told herself that was not true; his vigor had certainly not increased recently. In bed he would turn his back on her and go to sleep without stirring a single hair. That was not the way a man with any virility was supposed to behave.

"What are you thinking about?" he asked her.

"Nothing. It'll soon be dawn. Do you think your father has set up camp before us?"

"As I recollect, the people from our tribe set up camp one or two days before the season starts. That's a good idea, because latecomers have a hard time finding anywhere to pitch their tents."

"This year do you think your father will have put up his tent near the dome?"

"He's done that for years; that's the only place he's prepared to put up his tent. He wants to get the holy man's blessing so that the crop yield will increase every year. But unfortunately the harvest hasn't increased for years. As you know, my father's a spendthrift."

"I know. I wonder how a man his age still insists on getting married."

"Me too. And now he's married that slut. She's much younger than him; she's even ten years younger than me. Sidi Lkamel doesn't come to the aid of any man who marries frequently and squanders money. Even so, his clemency is plentiful and vast."

While Lhadi was talking, Halima had already fallen fast sleep. He let her and the three children sleep on. For his part, he thought about smoking the remaining cigarettes before dawn. Afterwards he could chew some mint leaves, and that would hide the smell. Then, when he gave his father a hug, the latter would not notice the tobacco smell on him. Halima had not slept all night, so her body was now crumpled up in sheer exhaustion. She had tried to snatch some sleep on the truck, but it kept on swaying all over the road. Not only that, but the children had kept asking questions about a whole host of unconnected things. All that made sleep impossible. Lhadi was smoking, apparently competing with some imaginary ghost. He felt himself dozing off, too, even though he had assumed that the cigarettes would keep his brain alert. "Don't fall asleep," he told his wife. "It's nearly dawn."

"I haven't been asleep," Halima replied with her eyes closed. "Wake me up at dawn. . . . Let me rest my eyes."

"No, wake up now. You can sleep when we get to the shrine."

"We're already there."

"I mean, when we reach the tents. Once we're there, you can sleep for two whole days if you want."

"Be quiet and let me sleep. I'm here to visit the shrine, not to sleep for two days."

While they were talking, their eldest child woke up. He was thirteen years old, but was mentally disabled, so he could not understand what they were talking about. The child was abnormal. He started staring at his father's face, trying to make out his features, but without success. Instead, he watched the bright-red tip of the cigarette and was delighted whenever his father took a puff.

"Father, are we going to get to the shrine today?" the boy asked.

"Yes, very soon," his father replied "At dawn."

"Is my grandfather going to be there?"

"Yes, he's pitched his tent near the holy man's shrine. This year he's going to be able to stay right near the dome."

The boy stopped trying to make out his father's face. Turning away, he stared off into the vast expanse of darkness. Closing his eyes, he put his head on his mother's lap. His father did likewise until dawn.

Halima roused herself and woke the rest of them. Various animals were scattered around the neighboring fields. They discovered that the ditch nearby was full of stagnant water; tiny frogs kept leaping and croaking by the water at the edge of the ditch. Lhadi yawned, and so did everyone else. They all made use of the dew that had fallen to rinse their faces and heads.

Lhadi stood up, walked away from them, and stretched. The youngest of the boys joined his father and grabbed his khaki pants, which were old and had patches on them.

The boy seemed to like his father's pants. Once he had a hold of them, he could not take his eyes off them. Halima rummaged through the pile, took out some bread, divided it into three, and gave the children each a piece. She yelled to Lhadi and examined him from head to toe.

"Shall I go up and get a cart?" Lhadi asked his wife. "Or shall we just put these piles on our shoulders and carry them up to the shrine?"

"We don't need a cart," she replied. "Why waste money? The children can walk."

"We're still one and a half kilometers away."

"We can walk and take a break if the children get tired. Anyway, it would take ages for you to go up to the shrine and bring back a cart."

Lhadi put two of the piles on his shoulders and handed another to Halima. He told the children to get ready to walk for a while. The retarded child tried to help his mother carry the pile, but she refused. She told him to be careful not to trip on a stone and fall down. The child said that he would be careful and would walk as far as possible. The two other children said they would do the same.

"Do you think the slut has woken up by now?"

"The first question you should ask is whether she's accompanied my father to the shrine."

"Of course she has. What would she do in Bni Yessef if she didn't come to visit Sidi Lkamel?"

"I don't know. But that slut really wants to annoy my father. People have told me that she hits him sometimes."

"He's a man. If he chooses to give up his manliness, that's none of your business. Leave him alone. Let his wife do what she pleases with him."

"But he's old," he said, swiftly adjusting the two piles on his shoulders. "He can't do a thing with a stubborn mule like her. You know how my father is, don't you?"

"But he's the one who decided to marry her," Halima said. "I am his daughter-in-law, and I'm older than her!"

"My father—may God show him the right way—can't help loving women."

The family had scrambled up the hill far enough. By now the road was no longer visible; it was concealed by clumps of trees scattered along an iron fence. Even so, the noise of a truck roaring by on the road below was clearly audible.

Now they all saw the tents pitched in the sunshine, and a number of water tanks that prominent people had installed near the shrine's dome.

"Look, Father," said the retarded child when he saw the tents. "We've arrived."

"You children," said the mother, "try to be polite. Your grandfather doesn't like impoliteness."

They were slowly getting closer to the tents. People seemed to be still asleep, not a sound to be heard anywhere. The tents managed to completely hide the shrine's dome.

Actually, as Lhadi had anticipated, the slut had not come, something that upset him, because he could imagine his aged father having to put up the tent and arrange things. "You see," Lhadi told his wife as soon as they arrived. "The slut didn't come up here with my father. She's getting even with him."

"It's what's good for him," Halima replied. "He clings to her closer than his own shadow."

"Never mind. Go and take care of the tent, then clean and arrange the dishes and prepare breakfast."

"The slut'll arrive this afternoon," Halima said. "That's her way. She avoids the first day at the shrine because there's a lot of hard work to be done."

"There isn't that much work," Lhadi replied. "She does it to my old father just to be spiteful."

"Don't say that," said Halima. "If she wanted, she could leave him and go somewhere else."

"Where would that be? He provides her with the only warm place she can find. Didn't she leave him three years ago? Only the Devil himself knows where she went. Why did she come back? Well, because the other men kept kicking her out."

"Don't talk that way."

"Why not? I didn't want my father to marry a whore, but what was I supposed to tell him? What can a son tell his father? You know that I can hardly look him in the eye. If he didn't want specifically her, I could . . ."

"I know what I want to say," Halima told him. "But it's better to stay silent. You wanted to find him a wife, didn't you?"

"Why not? I didn't want my old father to marry a whore. Everybody keeps talking about her, or actually, about me."

"Don't pay any attention."

She fell silent. "People talk about him as if he was a *Caid* or a *Pasha*," she went on with a scoff. "But he's just a poor farmer. Forget about it. Leave him to the slut and mind your own business."

By now the tents were starting to rouse. All kinds of din permeated the air. Lhadi opened the tent flap and looked out. "Get breakfast ready," he said turning to Halima. "When my father arrives, tell him I won't be long."

He made his way through alleys between the tents, heading for the big square where merchants had begun displaying candy and perfumes. All along the square was a long row of crepe sellers, all of them squatting cross-legged behind their pitch-black frying pans. He thought about buying a couple of kilograms of crepes, but decided against it. Instead, he walked over to the dome to seek a blessing from the holy man's shrine. Crossing the square, he walked through the rows of tents to get to the dome, all the while telling himself that this year was different from previous ones. When he was young, for example, he had felt that the holy man was even greater than God; that made him very scared. But now, as he walked toward the dome, he no longer felt the way he had as a boy. Everything had really changed, he told himself, and yet he was still scared of the holy man. What mattered was that he was related to the Prophet—God's blessing and peace be upon him. When his late mother had been sick, she had never trusted a doctor, *fqih*, or anybody else, but she did believe in Sidi Lkamel. In her final moments just before she died in agony, she had let out a feeble cry. "Ahhhh!" she had muttered. "Take me to my grandfather, Sidi Lkamel. Aaayeee!" But no one had managed to do that. Who knows? Maybe it was her grandfather who had decided to relieve her of all the pain and suffering she had endured for so many years. The people present at the time said, "Our grandfather Sidi Lkamel answered her plea quickly and sent the Angel of Death to take her." Back then, Lhadi had believed it all, because he had watched his mother dying peacefully without moving hand, foot, or lip. Actually, she died smiling gently, as she stared fixedly at them all. Then she closed her eyes, the smile still implanted on her lips, and turned into nothing. "Her grandfather rescued her," people said at the time. "He's generous."

"By now," people also commented, "the Angel of Death has certainly taken her soul."

After that, a cry went up, followed by weeping, wailing, and slapping of faces and thighs. Bodies collapsed in hysteria. A woman whom he could not remember now walked over to the cacti, cut off a thorny branch and started scratching her face with it, all the while crying and moaning, then she disappeared between the tents. Whenever Lhadi remembered that event, a tear would well up in his eyes.

Even though he felt tired, he kept on walking resolutely toward the shrine. He felt a very special sensation, one he could neither understand nor describe–a simultaneous feeling of power and weakness. Apart from these special moments, nothing mattered any more. He lingered for a while before crossing the shrine's threshold. Feeling totally relaxed and safe from any danger he may have felt in the past, he went in. Many, many people want to die in this holy man's aura, because of his close affinity with the Prophet. Almost everyone had the same wish, even people who idolized other holy men from the nearby tribes. Sidi Lkamel was specially esteemed, indeed. More than that, whenever people thought about him it was with a combined sense of awe and fear.

Two days passed. Presumably the slut had arrived by evening on the first day or else the following morning. When some pilgrims arrived from Bni Yessef, Lhadi rushed to ask them about his stepmother. They all thought she had arrived before them, and blamed their own lateness on a lack of funds. If so-and-so hadn't come to their rescue by giving them some money, they couldn't have made the pilgrimage to the shrine this year.

"So the slut has really done it," Halima thought to herself. "She is quite capable of doing it. She must have gone off somewhere else with some unmarried man."

"Doesn't that slut have any shame?" She asked Lhadi. "Especially at this special time?"

"We don't have to concern ourselves with the sins of others," said Lhadi. "Maybe she's sick."

"I don't trust that slut."

When Lhadi's father did the rounds visiting friends, he discovered that all the families he knew were there.

"Your father should get on the first truck leaving," Halima suggested. "And go bring her here."

"What if he can't find her?"

"It doesn't matter. He should try. People will talk about him. Have you ever heard of a man visiting the shrine without his wife?"

She told him that if he was unwilling to understand, she would go to see his father herself and make the suggestion.

The father agreed and fumbled in his bag for a few coins. He decided to take the first truck to Bni Yessef. But he did not find her there. The slut had finally done it.

A huge number of tents were spread out as far as the eye could see in the blazing sun. Merchants' shouts and the chants of the possessed, they all mingled with a heavy layer of dust that rose to the sky. From time to time gunshots could be heard, followed by celebrations of joy. Lhadi and his father stared at the ground, heads bent. They were both deep in thought and completely oblivious to their surroundings.

"So my son," asked the father. "What do you think the slut has done?"

Lhadi did not reply. He dearly wished that his father wasn't with him, so he could buy a cigarette, smoke it, and think seriously about the problem. Lifting his head, he looked into the distance where the river flowed between the trees. A few naked children were sliding down the mud, then crashing into the water with a big splash. As a child, Lhadi had done exactly the same thing. He could still recall the sight of women's naked bodies as they splashed each other with water, breasts dangling and hair stuck to their bronze bodies.

The father lifted his head and followed Lhadi's gaze. Standing up, he walked wearily over to a small fig-tree. Lhadi shook off his lethargy and joined his father.

"What shall we do with the slut if she decides to leave? Didn't you realize before now that she was a loose woman?"

"Yes, I knew, but I couldn't go on living by myself. That's why I married her. What bothers me now is how I'm going to face people. They'll all be gossiping about me, saying she's left me. Do you realize how enormous a disgrace this is?"

"I do. Especially since she's so much younger than you."

Lhadi thought about taking his clothes off and heading for the river, the way many men and women were already doing. He wanted to tell his father, but eventually he decided against it.

"Are you pining for her?" he asked when he saw tears shining in his father's eyes. "Aren't you a man?"

"It's not her I'm crying about; it's the scandal. You don't even understand what people are going to say."

"It doesn't matter now. We'll find a solution later. Don't bother yourself about it."

He grabbed hold of a small branch from a nearby tree and broke it off, causing a loud crack. He remembered that the children were still sliding into the water one after another, and that made his own desire to go for a swim even stronger. A woman caught his attention; she was lifting up her dress as she squatted under a short shady fig tree in the open air.

"We should head back to the tent," he told his father, lowering his head. "We can discuss the problem later."

His father did not seem to have heard him, but, once Lhadi headed back toward the tents, his old father followed behind. The dust was still high and the sun hot; there was the smell of gunpowder and other things, and the endless expanse of tents. Everything was fine, except that the slut was not there. Why had she chosen precisely this occasion to do it?

"What about visiting a *fqih*?" the father suggested as he walked alongside Lhadi.

"What for?"

"Or a psychic?"

"No point."

"Maybe she fell into a well or had an accident."

"Or perhaps she ran off with another man?"

However hard the old man tried to convince Lhadi that she had not done that, Lhadi was not convinced. He suggested that he had the solution, but this was not the right time. Scandal was avoidable, indeed more than that. He proposed to wait till the end of the pilgrimage season. Then he would take his father to the small city, and his father could stay with him till people in Bni Yessef had forgotten all about the scandal. He would only go back to take care of his land at harvest time, if he were still able to do so.

They kept walking through the layers of dust without saying a word. As they passed the shrine where many poor beggars were gathered in crowds, they almost lost the way to their tents . . . but the mentally handicapped boy grabbed on to his father's pants.

"Father," he said, "Mother's looking for you."

Lhadi did not reply but walked ahead of his father to the tent. When Halima saw him, she rushed over to him.

"The slut finally managed it," she said.

"What?"

"She did it. Your father shouldn't find out, or else he'll kill himself."

Lhadi looked behind him. His father was sitting at a distance from the tent, staring at the distant horizon.

"What do you mean?" Lhadi asked.

"Can you believe it; your father's married to a whore. They took them both away."

"Who?"

"She did it. The gendarmes found her under Aisha's boy."

Lhadi thought for a while, then walked away from Halima. It occurred to him that now was the time to suggest the solution to his father, even though the pilgrimage season was not yet over.

"People are bound to have heard," he told himself. "It's Sidi Lkamel's will."

The Tight Rope

We were sitting on rickety old chairs facing a big square. It was hot. The square was surrounded by shops and stables and looked dirty. Small alleys converged on it from every direction. We sat there drinking tea and listening to strident, dull music, music talking about cigarettes and alcohol, but not women. There were some animals as well, lolling around the square in the heat and looking for a cool spot under overhanging roofs or close to walls that shade had long since deserted. People sat close to their pack animals; most of them were eating bits of dry bread and olives without showing any hint of disgust. Some dirty Europeans were sitting next to us on rickety chairs too, staring vapidly at nothing in particular. A small group of wealthier Europeans crossed the square and started taking pictures of us and other people who were sitting close to their pack animals, eating.

Once in a while some men and children would emerge from the narrow alleys and gather in the square. The square would empty, then fill up again. It was incredibly hot, but that meant nothing to the children; they just kept on playing.

Then we spotted another group of children coming out of a small, narrow alley in single file. They were heading for the square, slowly and listlessly. We kept watching them intently because they seemed so regimented and in line. When we noticed that their hands were tied, we assumed it was a kind of game that downtrodden children played. Not only that, but they were all barefoot; in fact, one of them had no pants, and his tiny genitals showed unashamedly.

By now the small group was getting closer to the square, all regimented and in line, but the other group of children seemed completely uninterested. Now we observed that each child in the small group had a rope attached tightly to his hand; actually, it was a single rope that was tied to all their hands. The children kept walking across the square in a single motley row. Some of them were crying.

We now realized to our utter amazement that this was no game, but something much more serious. Some of the Europeans picked up their cameras and started taking pictures of the naked children, who kept on crying as they continued across the square, all tied together by a single rope with its end trailing behind them. Just then, we spotted some men who came rushing out of another small, narrow alley into the square—men with hats and uniforms. Later we discovered that they were the police. We did our best to construct a picture of what was going on.

Eventually the policemen started grabbing the children who were playing listlessly in the square in the hot sun. We watched the entire scene: policemen using a long rope to tie the children to one another and laughing out loud. As they arrested the children, we watched Europeans taking pictures. At this point, the policemen started to leave the square, pushing the two groups of weeping children ahead of them.

The sun was hot, the square was dirty. All over the place people were crammed together like pack animals, eating bread and olives. No one seemed to care. For them it was perfectly normal for the police to tie up dirty children and take them away.

"Why are they doing that?" the man next to me asked, as he sipped iced tea. "Is it some sort of game?"

"Yes," I replied, "it's a special game."

"They are ridding the city of dirty kids," said the other man next to me. "But they keep forgetting the dirty elderly people."

"Those policemen are certainly hard-hearted," the first man said.

"They're bastards," I replied.

With that he leapt to his feet and stood in front of me. "Are you insulting the police?" he said. "Get up and come with me to the station."

I stood up nonchalantly, without even paying for what I'd already drunk. I walked on ahead of him. We crossed the square, walking among all the men and pack animals. No one bothered about me. In spite of everything, I wasn't worrying about my fate. To the contrary, I walked ahead of him with supreme confidence.

Daily Concerns

An official government communiqué has stated that construction is booming.

That certainly explains why the rent for a simple room in a popular neighborhood is the equivalent of a month's salary for a low-level civil servant. No one has any idea where people who aren't civil servants manage to live. Maybe there are lots of holes-in-the-wall in the center of the city for people who can't afford to pay such rents.

All around the city, workers were perched on top of scaffolding. The building in front of the café was almost finished. It had been white-washed, and now people were waiting for the installation of doors downstairs for the shops and windowpanes.

"If God provides for you," the waiter told a customer, "no one can prevent you from making a living."

"I used to know the owner," he went on. "He was poor and needy like everyone else. Now look at him, just five years later. He bought that entire lot very cheap. Nobody can even begin to guess how much he's going to make off that new seven-storey building."

"Get me another drink," the customer asked. "As the old saying has it, 'Fate smiles on some and rains on others.'"

The customer, a low-level civil servant, noticed a colleague whom he knew very well; he was at exactly the same level. That colleague of his managed to change cars every other month and had two wives; somehow he could pay the rent for both homes. One of the wives made no attempt to hide what she did. The husband wasn't bothered;

44

the only thing he cared about was changing cars and frequenting bars. Even so, the money rained down on him.

"If God provides for you," he heard the waiter telling him again, "no one can prevent you from making a living."

"Exactly," the customer replied with a nod, and then shook his head at the row of shoeshine boys and the beggars who were crowding around him. Another waiter came over and sternly told the shoeshine boys and beggars to move; however, he did allow three shoeshine boys to take a turn around the café.

The customer watched as the man with two wives left his car and walked over to the café. But then he changed his mind and went to another café. The customer was thinking about his colleague with two wives, while the stern waiter, who by now had given up chasing beggars away, was having other thoughts as he sat down and stared at the stools all around the counter.

Meanwhile, throughout the city loads of construction workers were still perched on scaffolding.

"It's twelve o'clock," one of them working in the eastern part of the city said to another. "Let's get something to eat. Do you have any money? Go get some bread and butter. I don't have anything on me. Yesterday I had to give everything I had on me to cover the cost of my son's insurance and school books."

"You're crazy!" his fellow-worker replied. "Why on earth did you pay for the insurance? They'll expel him next year anyway. That's what they did to my only son last year."

He continued singing his favorite Hawziya song, while his fellow-worker was thinking about what he'd just said. In fact, that was not his only problem (I mean the man whose son had been kicked out of school). He had another problem, but it was one he never discussed with anyone. His daughter was spending her youth in prison. She'd been arrested while leaving a baby in an abandoned area. Even though she'd told the court that she was hungry, her father was unemployed, and she had no choice but to do what she did, she'd still been sentenced to twenty years without parole. Now her father was singing his Hawziya song, trying to forget it all. Meanwhile, the other worker perched on the scaffolding beside him was still thinking about today's lunch and other things as well, some of them possibly important.

"You really enjoy your drink!" the waiter told the customer.

At that moment the other waiter, who had been so stern with the shoeshine boys, was glowering at the customer. When their gazes met, the waiter reluctantly lowered his eyes. The customer now noticed a little girl and assumed she was the waiter's daughter coming to look for him.

"Fate smiles on some and rains on others," he repeated. "We agree. Get me another drink!"

The waiter served him, then went over to the corner of the bar.

"All right," he thought to himself. "You may be right. Let's assume that Fate does smile on some and rain on others. That means it's all your own fault, you idiot. You've been coming here for years, assuming that somehow luck would smile on you. Now start acting like the people fate has smiled on. Aren't you ashamed, you jackass? You've got three children, and yet you still get drunk every day."

Sitting by the bar, the waiter kept talking to himself. "So, thank God, I used to be a shoeshine boy, but now I own three buildings and a grocery store. But what about you, you jackass? What do you own?"

"I must have sex today," the customer told himself while he was still drinking. "Life's so beautiful, and there are lots of pretty young girls."

The stern waiter was up again, wrestling with a strong beggar. When people saw the waiter fall to the floor, they intervened and the fight came to an end.

"He's as strong as a mule," one customer said to another. "Why doesn't he get a job?"

The beggar heard what he said.

"Shut up, you jackass," he yelled, "or else I'll flatten you the way I did him." He was pointing at the waiter.

The man was afraid of making a fool of himself, so he said nothing. However, a plainclothes policeman who was not afraid of making a fool of himself walked right up to the beggar with a confident stride.

"How would you like to spend the night *there*?" he asked the beggar.

The beggar knew full well what he meant by '*there*,' and left the café.

"He always comes here," the nicer of the two waiters was telling a customer. "There are way too many of them. Thousands of them come by here every single day."

"If you traveled, you'd see worse," the customer replied laconically. "In the countryside, people have no idea what to do with themselves."

"They have land," the waiter suggested, "so why don't they work it? They're just lazy."

"You seem to have things straight," the customer said. "You must be smart. But don't forget: 'Fate smiles on some and rains on others.'"

What he didn't say out loud but thought to himself was: "That applies to you as well, you ass, mule, jackass," and so forth, on and on.

While the customer was talking to himself, most of the workers came down to have lunch, bread and butter, and maybe tea as well. At the same time people at fancy tables were thinking about one thing only: How could they get more money, build more villas, marry off their children to noble families with yet more real estate and stocks?

The father had taken his hat off, so his bald pate was shining in the blazing sun that filtered into the room through the wide windows. "Listen, my daughter," he told her. "That young man's no good for you. I suggest so-and-so, who's currently studying in France. This year he's going to get his PhD in chemistry."

"But he's not good-looking," the girl's mother said.

The girl stood up. She was a real woman indeed, slender and tall. Turning round, she headed angrily toward the lounge.

"I've told you a thousand times," the mother told her husband in exasperation. "Don't talk to her about it while we're eating."

"I'm sorry," the wealthy bald man replied. "I won't do it again."

The mother stood up, went to the lounge, and brought her daughter back, wiping away her tears. She didn't feel like eating any more.

On the other hand, the two workers coming down the scaffolding were famished. The loaf of bread and the small packet of butter they'd bought with it were obviously not enough.

"Thank God," one of them thought to himself.

Hundreds of cars of all makes were filling the streets with the noise of their engines and going in different directions. *Where do they all come from and how do their owners manage to make so much money? At the same time vagrants of all kinds are hell-bent on begging for alms, because in just a short while the streets will be empty.*

"It's lunchtime now." That's what one of the beggars told his female comrade, who was carrying a baby she'd rented from her blind neighbor and dragging along with her two scruffy little boys, who kept on kicking each other.

"You should stick around that café," he told her. "I'll stay here at this one. When I give you the signal, we'll switch places."

Snot was dripping on to the lips of one of the little boys and onto the woman's arms as well. He swallowed it because he was so hungry.

The nice waiter kept very busy, filling glasses for customers lined up by the counter; he was looking delighted.

Behind the line of customers a poor man blurted out, "And who confounded all mankind . . . ," but the stern waiter was ready. Grabbing him by the arm, he shoved him outside. "Damn it!" he said. "Let people drink in peace."

The waiter was frowning as he came back in. Sitting down again, he started looking at the customers, one after the other.

It all came in an official communiqué from the government.

The Locust

The little boy was sitting on the doorstep, watching the little girl in the green weeds and plants near the railroad tracks. The train hadn't come by for a whole week, night or day. The railroad workers had been on strike all week; it could well go on for several more days.

The girl was busy poking around in the weeds and plants, which towered over her tiny frame. While the little boy was watching the girl, he kept thinking about other things that mattered to him. He thought about joining her and helping, but instead he stayed glued to the spot. The girl headed for the railroad tracks and started walking on the rail, trying to keep her balance, but failed several times. The little boy laughed at her and told himself that he could manage to do it. But the thought just stayed there, stuck in his mind.

He noticed her stop her game and go back to searching among the weeds and plants. A stray dog was hanging about near her; its red tongue was hanging out, and ticks weighed down his drooping ears. She was afraid of dogs and would always cry for help. The boy was about to warn her about the dog close by, but changed his mind. The dog moved away, his ears still drooping under the weight of ticks. It trotted across the railroad tracks and disappeared down the slope.

The boy looked back at the girl. She seemed to be coming over with something in her hand; it was a small locust, unable to fly, a green locust.

"Aren't you afraid of locusts?" the boy asked.

"No," the girl answered. "Besides, it's a female. One female doesn't hurt another."

"How do you know it's a female?"

49

"Look how beautiful it is."

"That's true, it's beautiful. But is it female or male?"

The girl didn't answer. She moved away from him a bit and sat down on the ground. Placing the locust in front of her, she started slapping the ground with her hand, trying to get it to fly, but it didn't move. The girl began to shout and hit the ground near the locust, then pushed it with her hand, but still the locust didn't move.

"Take it out of the shade," the boy said, "and put it in the sun."

"Why?"

"It will warm up and try to fly. It's feeling cold."

The girl picked it up gently and put it in the sun. She kept slapping the ground, trying in vain to make it fly.

"No, let it be," the boy said. "Let it get warm first."

She left it alone. Going over to the boy, she sat down by his side, watching the locust. Finally it started to move. The girl thought it was going to fly and told the boy.

"No," he answered. "It won't fly until it's warm."

"It'll fly even before it gets warm," the girl said.

"That isn't true."

"Yes, it will," said the girl, "because it's a female."

"That's not true. It is neither female nor male."

"It's a female. It's green because it's a bride."

"And what's the groom like?" the boy asked, grabbing the girl's fragile arm.

"He's red."

"No . . . you don't understand anything. The groom's yellow, and so is the bride. This locust is green because it feeds on green plants."

The girl slipped out of the boy's grasp and walked into the sunshine where the locust was. It stopped moving. The girl started blowing on it and striking the ground to get it to fly, but still in vain.

The girl left it where it was and walked back to the railroad tracks. She started walking along a rail; for a while she managed to keep her balance, but finally she fell down, revealing her buttocks. The boy laughed as he watched her adjust the pleats of her short, faded skirt. The girl stopped that game and went back to the weeds.

Now the boy could not see her. When she'd been out of sight for some time, he went over and joined her. He found her crawling on her knees, watching a tiny worm.

"What are you looking for?" he asked.

"I'm looking for a male."

"For the worm or the locust?"

"For the locust."

"You won't find it. There are no locusts out now."

The girl stood up. "Look," she asked him, "do you know the 'bride and groom' game?"

"If you lie on your back," he said grabbing her hand.

"But you won't act like the locust."

"I know what to do."

Her mother came down to the first floor and called for her. The girl didn't hear her, nor did the boy. The mother looked along the railroad tracks. She went back inside the house to see if the girl was hiding in one of the rooms or in the kitchen, but she didn't find her. She went outside again and started calling for her loudly. This time the boy heard her, got off the girl's body, and scurried away. When the mother spotted him, she asked him where her daughter was. The boy ran toward the railroad tracks. The mother understood everything and found her daughter among the weeds.

"What are you doing?" she asked as she grabbed her violently.

"We were playing the 'bride and groom' game."

The mother started pinching her angrily. "When has your mother ever been a whore?" she asked.

The girl didn't understand anything. At first, she tolerated the pinches, but finally she began to wail, "It isn't me . . . him . . . h . . . h . . . aye . . . aye!"

The mother kept pinching her. "Tell me, you little tart," she kept repeating, "When has your mother ever been a whore?"

Meanwhile, the boy avoided the pinches. He was trying to keep his balance on the railroad track, which by now had been warmed by the sun.

THE STRONGEST

(1978)

Neighbors

She was strong," Mahsus told his friend. "Life positively glowed in her eyes."

"But she's dead," Latif replied. "Intuition and guesswork often let us down."

"She seemed stronger than death."

"Stronger than death! That's a rhetorical expression! No one can be stronger than death, not even the Devil himself."

"How do we know death exists?"

"However you look at it, it's a reality. Someone disappears from our lives; they can no longer talk to us, love us, or hate us."

Mahsus turned down the radio. Through the wall they could hear the sound of muffled voices: people coming to pay their respects, no doubt. Now she and her brother would realize for sure that they were not isolated from the world, but rather connected by a number of relationships. For some time they had both withdrawn into themselves, so much so that people started talking about a suspicious relationship. Some of them even thought they were married.

"She never responded to my '*bonjour*,'" said Mahsus. "At first, I thought she was deaf, but actually she was just very shy. Still there was a glint in her eyes. That was how she often responded."

"She often responded to me. I even thought she might knock on our door one evening when her brother was out at the bar doing what he always did—drink his two beers."

Latif took out a cigarette, but hesitated before lighting it. His gaze riveted on the wall as he listened to the soft music coming from the radio; he seemed somehow detached from the world. He could picture her, washing the pile of dirty dishes in the kitchen or arranging the books which were strewn all over the floor. He looked down at all the books and magazines on their floor. They did not possess a bookshelf to put them on, but instead, what they did have was limitless quantities of indifference and laziness. Here they were, two newly appointed civil servants sharing a room and saving whatever they could. In fact, so far they had not managed to save anything at all.

Latif lit his cigarette. Mahsus was lying on his stomach, paging through a magazine and listening to the noise coming from behind the wall by the door.

"She was so beautiful!" said Latif. "Do you realize that I've been in love with her but never even thought about it before?"

"Are you crazy?" asked Mahsus. "A living man in love with a woman who's dead?"

"I can't imagine her dead. Even now, I can still see her smiling, her eyes sparkling."

"All of us can imagine such things, but we can't be in love with the dead. I mean, physical love."

"You don't understand. Love isn't necessarily related to the body."

"Who smiles? Who is shy? Whose eyes shine? Are those the attributes of gods, or humans?" Mahsus closed the magazine, stood up, and looked out the window. He asked Latif for a cigarette, then went to the toilet. It was emitting a foul stench from the squat-hole; the very smell of it made him shudder. He could still hear people paying their respects.

"If your parents were still alive," a man was telling the girl's brother, "this would kill them. They loved her so much. They loved both of you so much."

Mahsus realized that the two of them had no living parents. It would be the young man's turn next, he thought. Was the whole family cursed by death? Buttoning up his pants, he went back to Latif.

"Latif, are you aware that their parents died a long time ago?"

"So what?"

"It's the young man's turn next."

"Since when have you started predicting the future? Can you tell me when you're going to die? Listen, I've an idea. Let's go and convey our condolences for his sister's death."

"But we don't even know him. We're not connected in any way."

"He's our neighbor."

Mahsus paced around the room for a while, thinking. "Okay," he said. "Let's go."

Just a few yards away they found the door open. The sound of voices grew louder. Mahsus led the way, with Latif following hesitantly behind. They went inside and found a few people offering condolences. Nobody noticed Mahsus and Latif, so they just stood there. . . .

"I don't know how to pay proper respects," Latif said. "You go first."

They spotted the young man. He was talking to an older man, who looked very tired. His seemed to be the voice Mahsus had heard from the toilet. When the young man spotted the two of them, he recognized them but hesitated for a second before coming over. Mahsus shook his hand and embraced him. "Our condolences," he said quietly. "We're your neighbors. Do you recognize us?"

"Yes, I do," the young man replied softly.

He shook hands with Latif, and they embraced too. Latif's eyes filled with tears, and he noticed the same smile and gleaming eyes. Shuddering, he couldn't think of what to say.

"We're sorry for your loss," he managed to say after an internal struggle. "Your sister was . . . I . . . I . . . love her."

"Thank you. She was kind. She deserves that and more."

The young man spotted someone else and walked over to him. Latif felt awkward. He was sweating. His body was ready to move on, but his legs refused to budge. He collapsed into the nearest chair.

Behind the Window

The police car was parked on the other side of the street, near the Italian Club. When K. spotted it, she panicked and came rushing over to tell me. I wasn't surprised; I had seen it through the blinds several hours earlier. I didn't want to tell her because she was pregnant; I was afraid it might affect her health and the baby's. But now she had found out for herself.

"Don't be scared," I told her, trying to stay calm myself. "They're just like dogs. They'll stay there till they give up, then they'll go away."

"I'm afraid that's not going to happen," she replied fearfully. "One of them is standing by the car. He keeps staring at the window."

"Don't worry," I said. "It's not that risky. . . . We're used to it by now."

In spite of all my efforts, I noticed K.'s expression change. She turned around, obviously not knowing what to do. She may have been looking for something, but I didn't ask.

"Just relax," I told her. "Do you need a chair? They've been stuck out there for hours. I didn't want to tell you. Once they're sure we aren't at home, they'll leave. It's not a problem."

"I don't trust them," she said. "Are they here because of yesterday's demonstration?"

"Yes," I replied. "But, even if they arrest some people, they still won't be able to stop the flood of demonstrations and strikes."

I could smell onions on K. "Go and finish your cooking," I said. "Today I want to enjoy a really good lunch."

"I won't be able to eat a thing till those vultures leave."

While K. went into the kitchen, I sat on the edge of the bed thinking. I started pacing slowly around the room, over to the window, then back to the bed.

The six people in the car were all wearing civilian clothes: faded hats and old coats, the kind you find in the flea market, sent over from America on big ships as a token of friendship, along, of course, with other ships full of tons of rotten grain which even animals refuse to eat. The fat one was standing outside the car, a dumb stare on his face as he looked up at the window. I watched as he went back to the car to get a cigarette from his friends inside; they may well have been discussing the best way to arrest me. I was convinced they would only be out to arrest me until such time as workers' and students' demonstrations tapered off. Whenever the political situation in the country got worse, they always used to go after people like me. They would arrest two or three hundred people who were already known to have bad reputations and had files on record at the police station. Actually, however, that wasn't the solution. The demonstrations were continuing without any consultations. Everyone was feeling guilty for not joining us. That is why resistance and demonstrations were still continuing in various cities and quarters. Even the large number of unmarked police cars parked everywhere in the streets could not stop them. The demonstrators were well aware of how to organize themselves.

Getting up from the bed, I went calmly into the kitchen. I found K. sitting there rigid at a small table. She was crying. When she saw me, she quickly wiped her eyes and tried her best to look calm. She was obviously afraid I was going to yell at her. She kept sneaking glances at me.

"Why are you crying?" I asked. "You know they'll take me away, and then bring me back again."

"I can't stand it. You're going to be a father sometime, but they'll squash you flat without even bothering about your children or showing any mercy."

"That's taking things too far. What happened to the revolutionary ideas you had before we got married?"

"But J., it's different now. We're going to have children. I haven't changed. I'm the same person you knew before. But something's worrying me, I don't know what."

"Not the gallows, at any rate."

"We'll go together."

"Get the meal ready," I said angrily. "I'm hungry. Don't be so scared."

Taking a deep breath she plunged her tiny hands in the water and started washing the dishes with soap powder. The foam was not quite white.

I went back to the other room overlooking the street, but I didn't glance out the window. I had always felt personally secure when confronting such a situation. Relaxing on the bed, I reached for the ashtray and pack of cigarettes and put them next to me. I started smoking and watched the curls of smoke as they vanished into the air.

"Why don't I listen to some music," I thought, "even though it may be for the last time?"

I turned on the phonograph, then heard K. rushing in from the kitchen.

"Are you crazy?" she asked breathlessly, "They'll hear you."

"None of your business. Don't be so scared. Go back to the kitchen."

"Listen J., one of them could be on the other side of the door. Right now."

"You're so stupid."

"Please, turn it down."

I did so, drawing deeply on the cigarette. For some reason or other I was smiling. In fact, I kept on smiling; I was feeling a particular and totally inexplicable kind of pleasure. I chuckled to myself. Jumping off the bed, I started pacing around the room again. I felt that the person chuckling inside me was somehow feeling sorry.

I went over to the window. The car was still there, but the man standing outside had disappeared. I decided I needed to do something, so I went back to the bed, lay down, and lit a second cigarette.

Ella Fitzgerald's warm voice filled the room. Now I felt overwhelmed by a kind of happiness that I'd never experienced before in my life. I was convinced they would leave when they got tired. Maybe they hadn't been given orders to raid my house. But who knows? They might just be waiting for the right opportunity. No one can possibly know what is going on inside those wooden-heads, who can only operate by resorting to secrecy and cunning. I imagined they were behaving exactly the same way with "comrades" in other locations as well.

Once K. had prepared the meal, we ate, but she didn't feel like eating. Every so often she went over to the window and looked at them, then at me. Even though I kept trying to convince her that it wasn't a problem, she wasn't convinced. Instead, she said nothing and simply looked puzzled and diffident.

"Listen K.," I told her. "Why don't you go and lie down for a bit? Personally, I'm going to get some sleep."

But she didn't follow my suggestion. She kept pacing between the window and bed, looking frightened. Marriage, I now realized, was a real obstacle. This K. here was different from the one I'd known before we had married. That one had been brave and fearless, but now I couldn't understand her at all. Was it me she was so afraid for?

Standing up, I pushed her into the other room. Closing the door, I warned her not to go into the front room again. I told her I needed to rest. I wasn't in the least bit worried about those dogs camping out there. K. disappeared. I had no idea what she was doing. I slept for over an hour. When I woke up, I didn't feel like getting out of bed, so I stayed there and turned on the phonograph again. Once more I listened to Ella Fitzgerald's voice, which I loved.

I heard a soft knock on the door. I went and opened it, guessing that K. wanted to tell me something. She seemed more relaxed than before.

"I don't think they're going to take you away," she said, calmly, "If they were planning to do that, they would have moved by now."

"That's what I told you before. Why were you so scared? Now are you convinced? Go and make some coffee."

"OK."

But before she went, she looked out the window.

"Are they still there?"

"Yes, but I'm not afraid."

"In such situations what's the point of being afraid? Go and make some coffee."

I took out a book and tried to read, but I couldn't concentrate. My mind was really somewhere far removed. I put the book away and asked for coffee. K. brought out a small tray, put it on the bed, and sat next to me. Then she got into bed with me. Her body felt cold, but gradually it warmed up. I poured the coffee and handed some to K., but she didn't want any. All she wanted, she said, was to lie down next to me and get warm. The room felt bitterly cold. Actually, it wasn't all that cold, but her particular sensitivities made her feel that it was. I sat up in bed and reached over to change the record on the phonograph. I lit a cigarette and started avidly sipping the coffee. By now K. had pulled the blanket over her distended belly and was staring at the ceiling. Just then, I had a strange thought: maybe the blanket might suffocate the baby; but I managed to put all such notions out of my mind.

"Listen J.," K. asked, "how long do you think they're going to stay there?"

I didn't try to answer, but kept listening to the music and sipping my coffee. When I'd finished, I stretched out next to her. I wanted to make love, but she was pregnant and touchy. Clearly she wasn't in the mood. I put my arm over her body; it felt very hot.

There was somebody knocking on the door, softly at first. K.'s senses were on the alert.

"It may be one of your neighbors," I said. "Don't open the door."

"I'm not going to. The neighbors may already understand everything."

"It doesn't matter. They do understand everything already."

The knocks grew louder. I turned the phonograph down. The sun was setting. The knocking became louder still, but after awhile it stopped. Whoever was knocking did not seem very persistent. K.

kept trying to appear calm and indifferent, but she was obviously upset. Eventually, I felt her body moving. At last, she got up and went over to the window. As she stood there, I looked at her wonderful, lithe body. She was really gorgeous.

"Are they still there?" I asked.

"They may well be on the other side of the door," she answered, clearly frightened. "There are fewer of them by the car."

"Come and lie down," I said. "Let's not worry about them."

K. came back and lay down next to me. She was shivering. The loud knocking started again. After a few seconds' pause, it started up again.

"Tomorrow you must leave," K. said. "Until the demonstrations are over."

I gave her a big hug. The knocking now became even louder. Even so, I still felt relaxed and unafraid. K. snuggled up against me and gave me a hug. I could hear her crying under the blanket. I hugged her again.

"Don't cry," I said as I felt the baby's movements inside her belly. "Don't be scared. They can't break the door down. Don't be afraid."

Even so, she was still crying and shivering. The baby inside her belly was shivering too. A few minutes later, we heard a car start and leave the street. By now the room was dark, but we couldn't turn on the light.

"They're leaving," K. said, "but they're bound to be back either in the middle of the night or else at dawn."

The Clinic

*T*he three men stopped in front of the uncovered cart being pulled by a donkey. On it was a sick man, and two women and a young boy were walking behind the three men. The tears the women were shedding mingled with the rain that was falling gently from the sky. They kept sobbing, while the boy shivered in the cold. The donkey kept trying to shake the rain off its drooping ears.

"Let's carry him on our shoulders," the first man said.

"How can we do that? He's in pain."

"We can try pulling the donkey through the swamp," the third man suggested.

"I know that stupid donkey," commented the first man. "He'll never go through the swamp, even if we kill him."

The three men paused for silent thought. The clinic still seemed a long way off, surrounded as it was by mud and filthy water. The door was closed. Just a single window was slightly open, big enough for a human head to fit through. It was the only clinic for about ten thousand people who lived in the villages and districts of the region. That's why getting there was considered such an endless trek.

"Try to help me," the first man said. "Spread his legs apart, and I'll put him on my back."

Now it started to pour. The wind was bending the trunks of a few short, tender trees so much that they nearly snapped off. Beneath the raincoat that covered him you could hear the sick man's feeble moans. Whenever he let out a groan, the boy started crying and clung tightly to his mother's dirty clothes.

"Is he going to die, Mama?" the boy asked.

The mother didn't answer. She reached for the raincoat and pulled it over the sick man's body. When she did that, some of the rainwater caught in the folds of the raincoat splashed off. The first man tried to catch his breath. He turned his back to the cart, and the other two put the sick man on his back. He could feel the weight, but still managed to straighten up and bear the extra weight. But he was soon out of breath again. Meanwhile, the two women busied themselves fixing the raincoat over the sick man's head.

The group now started crossing the swamp. The men hitched their clothes a little above the knee, but the women didn't raise them that high, which meant that their clothes got wet. Every time the men tried to hitch up their clothes a bit higher, more of their fat, hairy thighs showed. The sick man's body nearly slipped off the first man's back, but he reached up with his hands and pulled him back.

"I hope the nurses are there," the first man said.

"I wonder how they manage to get across the swamp to reach the clinic."

"They don't have to cross the swamp. They live there."

The rain was coming down harder, but nobody noticed. The sick man was the only one who responded to this natural phenomenon, with his non-stop and monotonous moaning.

"They'll be able to treat him, and he'll get better."

"If we want them to take good care of him," the second man said, fumbling around in his pocket, "we'll have to bribe them."

"Right."

They walked up a few steps to the clinic and gathered at the top. The man carrying the sick man was exhausted. He turned his back to the wall and tried to ease him down gently, but his strength gave out. The sick man fell to the hard ground like a sack. He gave a loud moan, then fell silent. The two women bent over him and tried to lean him against the wall.

The second man began to knock on the cold iron door with his fist. It took a while for anyone to respond.

A short female nurse looked out first, then came out to look at the sick man. "What's the matter with him?" she asked.

"We don't know."

"He's complaining of aches and fever," answered the third man.

"Carry him inside and follow me," the short nurse said. "The doctor only comes on Thursdays."

The sick man was carried inside. Once they reached a room with long benches, they tried sitting him up, but couldn't. The nurse disappeared into another room. She and a male nurse were the only people there. The male nurse was looking at her.

"Another dead one?" he asked, still lying on his bed.

"Maybe."

"When are we going to put an end to this way of life?"

"When we get married."

"You dream a lot. They've exiled us here to this district. I dream of one day returning to my own city."

"Then we'll get married."

"Marriage, that's all you think about."

"What's a woman like me supposed to think about?"

"Go and give that dog some pills before he dies."

He wasn't even looking at her, but kept on smoking contemplatively. He watched the rain falling and pelting on the windowpane.

The nurse went out of the room and looked at the sick man's face. She took his pulse and put her hand on his head, but she couldn't diagnose his illness. She pretended to be concerned, and returned from a back room with a box of syringes. "Don't worry," she said. "He'll be fine."

The group wrapped up the sick man in the raincoat and carried him outside. The donkey could be seen in the distance, moving his hoofs and shaking his head and ears. Once again the men and women hitched their clothes up above the knees and started wading through the muddy water. Meanwhile, the female nurse joined her fellow-nurse and snuggled up next to him in bed.

"I've some jewelry," she said. "I can sell it, and we can get married."

"Are you tired of abortions?"

"How long are we going to live like this?"

"Give me the ten dirhams you got from them."

"I only got five dirhams. I swear."

She pulled out a five-dirham bill and gave it to him. Just then they heard a loud cry, immediately followed by others. She got up, looked out the window, and saw a woman slapping her face and splashing it with water in the rain. She also saw two men who looked as though they'd lost consciousness, rolling in the swampy water.

"Oh my God!" she said, as she came back to the middle of the room. "He may have died."

The male nurse stood up, walked over to the window, and watched the drama taking place in the rain. He had a strange feeling and started walking slowly around the room. His eyes stared restlessly at the floor, then into the other nurse's eyes. But there was nothing he could say.

Illusions

She threw herself out the window; it was not very high off the ground. He heard her running away, crying. Poking his head out the window, he watched angrily as she disappeared into the frigid darkness. In two minutes or less, she would be going home and telling her mother everything. After bolting the door, he started pacing nervously around the room, thinking hard. The little boy had cried, and his sister, who was two years older than him, had tried to shut him up. They both looked like mechanical dolls.

He had stared at her and watched as she tore at her hair. "I'm so miserable, so utterly miserable!" she wailed as she headed straight for the window to throw herself out.

"Give me a cup of tea," he said to al-Hajj.

The chair creaked under him as if it were going to break at any moment. He flipped through the newspaper till he reached the culture page and began reading a poem written by one of his friends. All his friends had become poets except him. He had claimed to have larger ambitions. He was in no hurry to test his talents now; in ten years, perhaps, when his writing would be more mature than what his friends were producing now.

"Where do you get all these newspapers from, Si Abdelkrim?" the Hajj asked. "If I'd opened a bookstore here," he went on with a laugh, "I could have been rich years ago."

"Who would you sell the books to?"

"Just you."

Abdelkrim began sipping his hot tea. He was tracing the lines of the poems, half-line by half-line.

Like you, I have never seen one before. You are far more beautiful than the Paris commune. Oh, sorry, I mean, you are far more ridiculous than the revolution of Bouhmara.

The dirt square was full of dung and manure, with skinny chickens pecking at the ground.

Martine walked by carrying her tote bag, and greeted him with a smile. His response lacked enthusiasm.

"Don't you have class now?" she asked him.

"No, I'm off this afternoon."

"Come by tonight. André's brought some good wine. I'll prepare a paella. Do you like it?"

"I'll try to make it. I love paella."

Martine left.

"Thanks to high school education," said al-Hajj, "we now get to see people like her. Not long ago we only saw foreigners walking by here. If we had Arabized the education system, we'd never see such beautiful women."

"Go to Casablanca, and you'll get your fill."

"Oh, Casablanca! It's a dream, Si Abdelkrim. But they say there are a lot of gangs. Girls even rape men. What did that foreign woman say to you?"

"None of your business!"

"You're right, Si Abdelkrim."

He began to distract himself by staring at the chickens as they strutted around pecking at the dung and manure. There were only a few shops scattered around the square. Behind them was a poor neighborhood teeming with small children, and beyond that, clusters of huts where hired laborers and field workers lived. Those huts were so crowded that the owners had no choice but to throw people out.

Abdelkrim picked up the newspaper again and started flipping through the pages, but without any real interest. Raising his head, he watched a villager beating his donkey with a cane, but to no avail; the donkey did not respond, and refused to move.

At this time of day, if Abdelkrim is not teaching at the secondary school, he likes to sit and chitchat with al-Hajj or else read. Whatever the case, it's certainly better than sleeping, which is all some of his friends ever do. What can you do in a small village a hundred and twenty kilometers from the nearest town? One of his colleagues has chosen to drink, while others have decided to chase their female students. But he reads and sleeps with Martine whenever he has the chance or André is away. Even so, André is very fond of him. Every time they have a drink together, they discuss the events of '68 and remember how André managed to destroy so many street signs and Martine set fire to a big perfume store.

"Those good old days! Do you remember, Martine, when we vented all that anger? Those were happy days, indeed."

"How wonderful it was," Abdelkrim said, "to be able to vent so much pent up anger! Do you realize, André, that anger isn't a psychological state of mind; it's something we inherit from history? It's the summation of an entire past."

"That's true! And we managed to vent a portion of it."

Abdelkrim watched as the villager tightened his belt, then bent down and picked up his cane. He was about to hit the donkey again, but it raised its ears and started moving forward. The owner had to chase it. Abdelkrim stopped watching the man, put his fingers in his cup of tea, picked out the mint leaves, and began sucking them. They tasted delicious.

Sometimes he feels he has to do that; it's a habit that takes him back to his childhood. When his mother used to tell him to clean the teapot, he would make himself scarce and suck the mint leaves. How deliciously sweet the mint tasted! Even after he got married, he still kept up the habit; sometimes he just felt compelled to do it.

"You aren't a child any more," his wife would tell him. "Go and buy a pacifier, and we can dip it in honey or jam for you!"

He would pay no attention, and simply carried on sucking the leaves and spitting them on to the tray. Actually, he may have deliberately annoyed her because she kept on doing her utmost to prevent him enjoying this simple pleasure—the very essence of human happiness. As far as he was concerned, things that seemed so utterly trivial to some people were actually very important for the person involved.

He made it a habit to show respect for the simplest and most banal human behavior. In fact, that trait may have been the thin line that separated the two of them, because she did not share his attitude.

Her image remained with him. She had thrown herself out the window, then disappeared from view. Actually, she had not only disappeared from view, but also from his imagination. The two children appeared, jumping up and down and calling out to him in unison. He told himself that he could be just as cruel as he was kind and tried as best he could to resolve the clash inside his head. At least once in a man's life he should definitely show some courage by making a specific decision, however stupid it might seem. He put his cup down on the table, stood up, and walked over to al-Hajj and paid him.

"You're leaving already, Si Abdelkrim?" al-Hajj asked as he retuned the radio. "Are you going to see that foreign girl?"

"Does it matter to you? I'll give you a call when I'm in bed with her."

"Oh my-my!!" said al-Hajj tapping his chest. "How magnanimous you are! I've never been wrong about you! I'll leave you with her and call the neighbors. They'll see how a dirty old man like you manages to seduce a really beautiful woman."

"In that case they'll make me a statue. The *Caid* will respect me even more and do his best to help me win the coming election. I'll become a big feudal lord."

"Will you forget me?"

"How can I possibly forget my agent?"

They both laughed, and their hands met in a strong grip. A joyful tear rolled from al-Hajj's eye. As Abdelkrim left the café, he felt as though he were inhabiting some vast imaginary space with no houses, trees, roads, farmers, or army bases, just vast spaces. But the idea disturbed him; it felt terrifying. He could not live in such a space; it would make anyone feel tense and miserable. At a certain age he had been able to put up with many similar things, but he could not do it any more. Now the simplest things would annoy him. He could no longer tolerate anything, even if it stopped him sucking mint leaves.

"It's not so easy to get rid of these two children, is it?" he had asked. "They're so innocent."

"I know."

"I beg you to stay, if only for their sake."

"If only you were willing to make the smallest gesture in that direction!"

"I've done a lot."

"You haven't done a single thing. We have to separate."

"Why can't you put up with a few difficulties like anybody else?"

"I can't do it any more. At a certain point in the past, I might have done it, but not now."

By this time the village was empty. All that remained was the sun and a panting dog with its tongue dangling. Without even thinking, Abdelkrim headed for a door with faded green paint. After knocking, he looked behind him and watched students who were playing with a ball. (Maybe their teacher was away.) He knocked again. A scruffy little girl opened the door and peered through the gap between the wall and the door.

"Tell your father I want a bottle of any kind."

"Impossible. The gendarmes came by yesterday. They confiscated all the wine on orders from the *Caid*. Lucky they didn't take all of us away to jail!"

"Just tell him Si Abdelkrim wants some. I'm sure they didn't check the well. You know that perfectly well. Now don't tell lies, you little bitch!"

"They even checked the well."

"You liar. They don't even know you have a well in the house."

The girl closed the door in Abdelkrim's face. When she took a while coming back, he knocked again but to no avail. She did not open it again. He moved away, cursing her aloud. At this point he remembered some of his friends who regularly drank or chased their female students. In this small village the only regular recreation involved drinking and adultery. He picked up a few stones and began tossing them, but then it occurred to him that that was not the proper way for a teacher to behave. If anyone happened to see him, they would think he had lost his mind. He lowered his arm, and the last stone fell quietly to the ground. Even if the well was really dry or the gendarmes had actually checked it, there was still André and Martine. He smiled to himself. Even when times were bad, he could always find a way out.

"*What I like about you is your resolve and perseverance.*"

"*I'm not like that at all. I simply know what I'm doing.*"

"*That's why I don't want us to separate. Let's make an effort to make our children happy.*"

"*You should have thought of that before. It's too late now.*"

"What I like about you is your stubbornness," Martine said later in the evening.

"Either the well's dry, or else the gendarmes decided to search it."

"What are you talking about? I don't understand what you're saying."

"It's not important."

"Have a drink. You seem to need one. Are you thinking about your wife and children?"

"The same way you're thinking about André."

"It's not the same. For me, André knows everything."

Abdelkrim lay on his back. Martine came closer and started playing with his hair. At first he enjoyed it, but eventually he moved his head away. She stood up, went into the kitchen, and came back with two slices of meat. She started drinking one glass of wine after another. Now Abdelkrim could feel that he was not alone in this world; he could know a number of people and be convinced that they all loved him a lot. Even if that was an illusion, he was content with it. Besides, how can we distinguish between illusion and reality? He wanted to tell Martine that, but decided not to.

They heard the doorbell ring. Whoever it was, it couldn't be André.

(*"Forget about the illusions. We can overlook what is past and live again for our children."*

"*I never cling to illusions, but sometimes I can't distinguish between them and reality.*"

"*That's your problem.*"

"*I don't believe it's just my problem; it's everybody's. You'll figure that out as well, if you think about it carefully.*")

Abdelkrim heard loud voices at the door; one of them he recognized as Martine's. They seemed to be getting closer, with Martine's being the sharpest. At this point the gendarme officer appeared.

"Unbelievable," Martine kept saying.

"Come on," the officer told Abdelkrim. "Get up and bring the bottle with you. You're charged with drinking and adultery."

"Unbelievable, Abdelkrim!" Martine kept yelling. "This gendarme wants me for himself; he's tried a number of times. I've never seen anything like it. Unbelievable, unbelievable! What a strange country!"

The Tin Can and the
Epaulette Stars

When we reached the small park, we sat on a cold stone bench. I looked up at the trees that towered so high above me, seemingly to infinity. A few birds were perched on the thinner branches which hung down in gray and colored clusters.

Khalil spread out the newspaper between us on the bench and put the sardine can on it. Breaking the bread into pieces, he handed me some. I was not paying attention, so he gave me a nudge. Lowering my gaze from the trees, I stared at the scant fare laid out between us. The picture of fish on the can looked far more appetizing to me than its actual contents. I'd never bothered counting the number of fish in such a can; I'd just eaten them. Depending on how hungry I'd felt, I'd either been satisfied or not. This time, however, my small share was clearly not going to be enough; I couldn't even guess how Khalil would feel about the small number of sardines.

It was somewhere between twelve noon and one o'clock. We could tell because three young working-women were sitting opposite us on a bench, and two others on still another. There were other women around too, but they preferred to sit on the ground around a young man who had a transparent plastic bag full of French fries and sandwiches.

Khalil was still busy tearing the bread apart.

"How about moving over to the other bench near the girls?" I suggested. "Shall we offer to pool our food?"

"You must be joking. These sardines aren't enough to satisfy a girl who's not even hungry."

"Don't think I'm serious. I'm well aware that those sandwiches cost more than two sardine cans."

Khalil started using his long, dirty fingernails to take his share of sardines and insert them carefully between the pieces of bread he had in his hand. I then tipped out the ones that were left, without even bothering to count; I think there were three. My problem was simply hunger; I didn't care how many were left. One day it's Khalil who buys me lunch; the next day it's Jalil. Today one person buys me dinner, tomorrow someone else. When there's no Khalil or Jalil in this world, I'll still be clinging to the illusion that I can find someone or other. Khalil's just like me, living on the illusion of being able to find a Jalil: two people who've lost everything in life except hope.

I got to know Khalil in a bar. I still had some money left from the job I had had at the Ministry of Post and Communications before I was fired following a violent strike. But he'd never had a job in any ministry, plant, or factory. He was both clever and socially aware, but he'd failed the graduation exam many times. In the end he'd decided not to live with his family, which was very poor. His three sisters were professional prostitutes, and his father sold mint and pepper. The first time we met in the bar, he paid for me. I duly reciprocated. We had started talking about women, songs, and compulsory military service. I'd told him that I hadn't been called up because I was lucky. He told me that he'd paid some bribes and been discharged. We discussed the difficulty of getting a passport and talked about Europe and Ben Barka's murder. We insulted the regime, then ordered still more rounds of drinks until we could barely stand up. Later, I invited him back to my house, and he decided to live with me.

"How long are we going to be poor?" I asked.

"Listen," he replied. "We're alive. It isn't luxurious, but it's a life."

I stared again at the group of pale working girls devouring their sandwiches. Khalil looked at me, and I noticed he was smiling. I expected him to say something.

"They're just as miserable as we are," I said.

"But they're richer."

"I was rich once when I worked at the Postal Ministry."

But what kind of richness was that supposed to be?! The pay-check would go up in smoke on the very first day of the month, simply paying the rent and the store, and sending money for the family. The whores used to take their cut in the form of household items: it might be a towel, an ashtray, shoes, or something else. Khalil was well aware of it all. I'd already told him. Maybe one of his sisters came and took some of the items. Who knows?

The sunshine began to filter through the branches, but it wasn't particularly warm. Even so, I could feel sweat coursing down my spine. Khalil had nearly finished his food when he stopped and belched twice.

"Those gases are going to be the death of you. Your liver will disintegrate from too much booze."

"And too little food."

"How wonderful it'll be when we can eat our fill and drink till we drop."

"God willing. But mules will be giving birth and cocks laying eggs before that ever happens!"

"You're a born pessimist."

"No, I'm not, just a realist. If you want to eat till you're full and drink till you drop, you have to work for it."

By this time the young women had finished their lunch. I watched them as they sat there, laughing and playing with something. One of them had moved away from the rest and was standing in the shade with her hands on her hips and legs apart.

"Isn't she gorgeous?" I said to Khalil.

"She can't be bothered with people like us."

Khalil started collecting the bread crumbs and putting them into the empty can, then crumpled up the newspaper and threw the entire package on to some small plants that were not growing very well.

At this point a policeman and an unarmed Garde Mobile man entered the park, walking quietly but with an arrogant air; the policeman in particular looked all puffed up like a rooster. The girl standing by herself now felt uneasy and quickly rejoined the others;

with the police around, even the simplest of pleasures was forbidden. Even though the women were all behaving very modestly, the policeman still walked over and started chatting with them. At first the girls were shy, but soon the laughter began. The two policemen leapt at the opportunity, eagerly compensating for the cold-shoulder treatment they would usually get when out of uniform. I could imagine them having to use a third of their paycheck for rent, and another third for food; the rest would be sent to some poor family in a village far away in the countryside. But in uniform they looked powerful and prosperous. But what kind of prosperity?! Obviously, the same kind of situation as I'd found myself in when I worked at the Postal Ministry.

They were all talking at the same time; the laughter came in fits and starts. By now the policeman had abandoned his phony posture. I watched as his hands moved deftly to a spot under the breast of one of the girls. She backed away with a giggle; she almost tripped and fell backwards. Meanwhile, the Garde Mobile man was busy flirting with another girl.

"I bet you, they won't have any luck," said Khalil. "Women don't like the police."

"How do you know? They seem happy enough."

I took out my pack of cigarettes; it was almost empty. Khalil took one and lit it with a fancy lighter. I don't know where he got it, but he insisted on keeping it even when he had no money. But what I really wanted was girls; standing or sitting—I didn't care. Even though I had no luck with women in general, I always gave my imagination free rein. I heard Khalil give a deep sigh and understood what he really wanted, as well.

The two men kept on flirting with the girls. By this time things had now gone far beyond the initial innocent phase. After initially just brushing bodies, hands had by now moved on to other more sensitive spots. The playful laughter was continuing too, and that made us sigh even louder.

Just then we heard a car door slam outside the park. An officer rushed past us, followed by two policemen in their khaki uniforms.

The heavy bronze stars on the officer's epaulettes tilted forwards. The girls stopped laughing and looked scared. The policeman looked behind him. When he saw the officer, his facial expression completely changed. Both he and the Garde Mobile man saluted. They were both looking very nervous, as though they'd been caught red-handed committing some terrible crime.

"Where do you think you are?" the officer asked, scratching his nose. "In a brothel?"

"The way we found them, Sir," the policeman replied with a stutter, "it might just as well have been a brothel. This is a public park, not a brothel."

"Who are those men over there?"

"It was those two men and these girls. We were asking to see their IDs."

The officer seemed completely convinced by his story. The two policemen who had followed him came over and asked us for our IDs.

"What are you two doing?"

"Nothing."

The working women started to cry. "We were just eating lunch, sir. We don't even know those young men. It's not true. He's the one . . . tell the truth, Soumia . . . it was him. . . ."

The officer did not bother listening to any protests. They pushed us both towards the police car. The officer got in next to the driver. Through the small barred window I could see his epaulettes weighed down with bronze stars. As we left, the wails of those still-unknown girls were getting even louder.

THE HOLY TREE

(1980)

The Second Marriage

He was worn out. Beneath his wool *jallaba* he was feeling extremely hot. Some of his clothes felt damp, particularly his shirt; against his skin it felt alternately hot and cold. His feet were feeling tired, as well.

He decided to sit down and lean his back against a tree trunk. Taking a cigarette out of the pack and lighting it, he inhaled deeply. He let his eyes wander over the open space in front of him, with its smattering of trees and houses, some clustered together, others scattered, all in a completely disorganized fashion. Close in front of him he noticed some donkeys and mules; further away, sheep and cows with heads lowered, grazing. Some of them were lying down in the shade.

By now he'd been searching for half a day in three different districts. Eventually he was bound to find her, unless, of course, some unmarried layabout had decided to hide her in a well or haystack. This time, if he didn't find her, he'd buy a pitchfork and stick it in every haystack or pile of firewood, even if that should prove fatal.

"She only did it because she loves you," 'Abdi had said. "She wants you for herself. Women are all the same. Then there is the jealousy factor; women never like having fellow-wives."

"But I'm going to marry a third and fourth. A virile man like me shouldn't have to live with just one woman."

"Do you think you're the only virile man in Awlad Ghayat?"

"I don't care if other men are impotent. But, as far as I'm concerned, no one can stop me from getting married again."

"What that crazy girl did is a disgrace!" her mother said. "My first husband had four wives at seventy-five, and we were all quite happy with him. We can say exactly the same thing about women as men. After my first husband died, I myself married five more times. When you catch her, teach her how to respect her husband. I don't like having such a girl for a daughter. It seems as though the time when men alone could think of such things is long gone."

"I'll tie her up," Qarqouri said, "and leave her with no food or water for seven days and nights."

"Do with her as you please. Even if she's my daughter, she's still your wife."

He took a final drag on his cigarette. By now he was feeling more relaxed as he leaned against the tree trunk. He had to concentrate really hard in order to overcome the drowsiness that was weighing down his eyelids. He was well aware that he had to keep looking for her. She'd find out that he wasn't impotent. She already knew that, but this time she'd ignored it. Here she was, a mother of three children, running away from her husband simply because he'd taken as a second wife a young girl who was just two years older than his elder daughter!

It was still very hot. In front of him the animals were flagging in the scorching sunshine. Some of them kept lifting their heads and shaking off insects from their ears and eyes; others were clustered at a spot where there were a few short plants here and there.

The last district he was going to was about two kilometers away; it was there that the search for her would come to an end. If he didn't find her, he still wouldn't despair. She had somewhere to go, the home of a cousin in Casablanca who was married to a soldier. He shook off his *jallaba* between his outstretched legs, then stood under the tree and savored the shade. But he still insisted on walking those remaining kilometers.

"You whip her," her mother had said, "and I'll tie her up. She's blackened my reputation in Awlad Ghayat. She deserves to be stoned to death in public."

"How long-suffering we women were in our day," a neighbor had commented. "Now it's the TV era. Women are influenced by the actresses they see on the screen."

Her husband had poked her. "You, old woman!" he'd said. "When have you ever seen a TV? Here, get your donkey moving and shut up!"

The woman had shut up and hit the donkey with a cane. The saddlebag was almost falling off the donkey's back, so she adjusted it.

"No woman in Awlad Ghayat has ever behaved like your daughter," Qarqouri said.

"I know. It's all because of Crédit Agricole's wheat. If she'd been hungry, she would never have done this."

"What are you talking about? The Crédit Agricole office takes more from us than it provides. Your daughter's run away because I've spoiled her and provided too much for her. I spend all my time working the land, plowing and sowing, with no respite."

"Forgive me, my son. She's your wife, so do whatever you want with her."

The tents seemed nearer now, scattered over a plain fenced in with bushes and thorny plants. In the distance he could see a group of men clustered in the shade of a tree. He imagined they were either playing cards or *dama*, or else scooping from a bowl of cold *saykouk* as a way of countering the excessive heat. Dragging his tired feet, he walked toward them, assuming that they would have the latest news about her. If he found her, she would pay the price for the entire distance he had had to walk through all the different districts. His left foot stumbled into a small hole, and he fell to the ground. He stood up, shook the dust off his shoulders, and continued walking toward the men.

They noticed that he was a stranger, and one of them came over. They had a conversation that the other men couldn't hear; both of them kept raising their hands, opening and closing their mouths, and nodding their heads. Then Qarqouri walked off in a specific direction, while the other man returned to the group.

"He's looking for his wife," he told them with a smile. "He said he's walked from Awlad Ghayat."

"That far?!"

"What did you tell him?"

"I told him that a woman from Awlad Ghayat arrived here yesterday. I told him to go to Al-Daoudiya's house. That's where she's staying."

"That old *shaikha*?! Now she's failed with the women of this district, she's trying to make money off a married woman."

"That woman's too old. She's good for nothing!"

"Anyway, she's better than a she-ass."

"How do you know?"

(*"You whip her, and I'll tie her up."*) "I'm going to whip her and tie her up myself," Qarqouri told himself. "I don't need anyone's help. Any wife who deserts her husband deserves worse than that."

"She shouldn't have done that," one of his neighbors had said. "All men marry more than one woman, unless they can't afford it."

"That bitch ate her fill. Starve your dog, and it'll follow you."

Qarqouri now found himself in a ditch-filled square. Women were staring at him from behind the scarves draped over their eyes. "There's a strange man in the district," one of them commented.

"He might be a thief!"

"How do you know?" said another one. "He could be someone from the district who emigrated as a child. He's come back to look for his family."

Qarqouri sensed an unusual movement going on all around him. He could imagine women and children talking about him, and about her as well. He stood where he was, looking all around. The women pretended not to care. He walked over toward one of them, but she ran away. However, another woman came up to him.

"Why are you running away?" she asked her friend. "Does he have scabies? He's a virile-looking man"

She came closer. Qarqouri plucked up the courage to ask her where Al-Daoudiya's house was. Now the woman understood everything.

"Do you know her?"

"No"

"So why are you looking for her? Don't you realize what a bad reputation she has in this district?"

"No, I didn't know that. I'm looking for my wife. She's left me with three children and run away."

"Good grief! And she's chosen to live with a prostitute like Al-Daoudiya?"

She pointed out the house to him. He walked toward it, and she went back to tell the women the story. They all ran off. A woman with children running away from her husband's house? Clearly some powerful sorcerer had made her do it.

"Only a fool or a bewitched woman would ever think of doing such a thing," one of the women said.

"Or else a woman who's been struck by a *jinni* or demon."

"Magic can do worse things than that."

"It's a disgrace, sister. Even if my soul were infected by Shamharush himself, I would still never abandon my children and leave my husband!"

"God's mercy!"

"God's mercy and protection! No woman would do such a thing, no matter what her husband may have done."

"It's probably Al-Daoudiya who's bewitched her," another woman said. "She's planning to sell her to another man. All she has to do these days is to fill the brazier with incense and hang amulets in her house. She was eager enough to ensnare one of us."

"She's an evil woman. Instead of turning to God, she's persisted in her depravity."

"If only we could convince our own husbands to burn her house down!" a young woman said.

The children were listening in on the conversation. They were aware that Al-Daoudiya had a very bad reputation, but they didn't realize how bad. She was an old woman, a *shaikha* who used to sing, dance, and do other things as well. But no one knew for sure how she earned a living, except, that is, for a few men. The whole thing didn't bother the children so much as keep them amused. Deep down, even the women needed to have a woman like Al-Daoudiya in the district so she could serve as their one ongoing daily concern.

Everyone waited to see what would happen. Al-Daoudiya's end would come about at the hands of this stranger. Her sorcery would work against her. After all, magic can sometimes cause dire consequences for its practitioners. She had tried to destroy families, but now magic was going to destroy her life.

("You whip her, and I'll tie her up.")

Now Qarqouri was grabbing his wife by the hair. Once the women saw that, they started screaming, but then they covered their mouths with their hands so as to muffle their screams. Some of the children were scared, but others didn't seem to care. Qarqouri began yanking his wife's hair, pummeling her in the face and on the back of the neck, and kicking her. Some blows landed, but others missed. She was in agony. At times she let out a scream, but she kept trying to keep her pain to herself.

He started dragging her into the middle of the square. At this point Al-Daoudiya could be seen behind the line of women; she looked terrified as she stood there by herself near a shack. She rapidly went back to her own house. Meanwhile mouths were still chattering.

By this time, Qarqouri was tired of beating his wife, but he still kept pulling her hair, clinging to it so that she couldn't escape. He wasn't listening to what she was saying, but he did hear her say one thing.

"So you've married again! So what am I supposed to be good for?"

He hit her again till blood gushed from her mouth. She fell silent. She assumed that her eventual fate was going to be much worse, so she decided to give up without any further resistance. She also thought about the distance she would have to walk to get back to Awlad Ghayat. Qarqouri still wasn't satisfied, so he took off her shoes. She didn't try to stop him.

"You're going to walk barefoot on thorns all the way back to Awlad Ghayat. You'll see. Even if the *Caid* intervenes, he won't be able to rescue you from me."

"Poor woman!" said an old crone. "It's all Al-Daoudiya's fault. She tried to separate a wife from her husband."

"Hit her!" a child yelled. "She deserves worse than that."

"Shut up, you little bastard!" his mother said. "You don't understand things like this."

Drum Beats

*W*hen I saw it, I told myself it wasn't possible.

Why the drum beats? Why do I only hear them and nothing else? Maybe there is something. What could it possibly be?

The dark horizon stretches away in front of me. At times a glimmer like twilight carves a space between sky and sea, but for the most part, everything is pitch black. The drum beats come from everywhere and the darkness gives them a special significance. They seem to spread across the sand, forming dunes that I can't make out very well.

I wanted to smoke, but didn't have any cigarettes.

"It's your sister who wanted it," I heard him say. "I don't like women that much. She tempted me."

"I don't care. You should have done it in the forest or some other cursed space."

The drum beats inside my head intensified. Those words didn't emerge spontaneously from my mouth. I had no idea what to say. So much needed to be said: about the dark horizon, the gap between sky and sea, and those dunes and hollows, not to mention the lack of cigarettes. But I still didn't know which hand had stabbed my sister. Had it really been mine, or was there another powerful force that had managed to manipulate us both?

By now the drum beats had stopped, to be replaced by sounds of insects and splashing waves. A big fish had used a knife to kill a small one. But then, the sea is deep. Anything is possible, anytime, anywhere.

"Since when have you ever been bothered about your sister's honor?" she'd asked me. "If you were a real man, you'd be looking for a job. Aren't I the one who's providing for you?"

I spat in my sister's face and pushed her away. She was still looking around her and did not react.

"Get that mule out of here," I told her.

"No," she'd shouted at me. "You're the one I'm going to throw out of the house. Go sleep in the street."

"Since when did he ever pay the rent, you whore?" I yelled.

"Get out of here," she yelled back, "or I'm going to hit you with the bellows."

"Make sure you take good care of your sister," our father had told me before he died. "She's younger than you. Women know nothing about life."

"Only marry your sister to a real man," my mother had said before joining her husband.

But my sister had refused to get married, even though the man who had made her pregnant had been very insistent. That is when the drum beats had started banging inside my head, heralding the realization that a man has to be firm and stick to principles, even though they may be cruel and harmful. Now those drums were beating again as I realized that, in my case, a woman is indeed providing for a man.

"The neighbors are laughing at us," I told her. "One of these days they're going to complain to the police."

"They can all go to hell," she replied. "I've lots of contacts with police officers."

"I don't like having a prostitute for a sister."

"So can you provide for me instead, you lazy. . . . ?"

The sand under my body feels cold. Behind me the voices have almost completely disappeared. They're all sleeping, but I can't fall asleep now. It is still too early, and I've no idea how it's all going to end.

I see an image of her lying on the ground, bloodstained and screaming. The man is kicking the door open for all he's worth and rushing in. The floor is splattered with blood. All of a sudden the blood turns black. She's fallen to the floor screaming, but I don't think she's dead. She's like a slaughtered sheep that thrashes around and tries to fend off death with its hind legs. Blood is oozing from her open mouth. As I look around me, the entire room is splattered with blood. The walls are red at first, then they turn black. All the pictures on the walls have disappeared; everything has turned red, then black.

All around me drums were beating as though a terrible religious ritual was in progress. Is there, I wondered, a link between death and the drum beats? In my particular condition I wasn't even aware of what I was doing. I couldn't hear what either of them was saying. The only thing I heard was the beating of drums coming from afar. To complete the picture, black men in *jallabas* were crowding around me, gradually diminishing in size until they completely disappeared, leaving behind them only the sound of voices. As I flashed a knife in their faces, I spotted a man rushing for the door.

"The man's just a moocher," I heard one of them say.

"Could be," another one of them said, "but I wish I were in his shoes. He lives like a king. He gets two packs of cigarettes a day and pocket money."

"It's still a dog's life."

"Enough of that talk. If he was working, I wouldn't be able to enjoy his sister."

I pretended not to hear. It was all true, so what was the point of getting so worked up? But sometimes emotions can be too powerful to resist. It was at just such a moment that I grabbed the knife and thrust it into her body—I think it was into her stomach, or maybe her shoulder or neck.

Whenever those drum beats start pounding, you're totally deafened and can't control yourself. Now here they come again, pounding near the sea as they rise out of the roaring waves and endless darkness.

My body was shivering in the cold. I could just make out the shape of some rocks. Standing up, I walked toward them.

Out here there's almost no trace of humanity, just a few vagrants and men who have picked up some women. They take them to caves in those rocks and drink and sleep there. Once in awhile, the police come along to clean things up, but they usually go back without making any arrests. It's enough to slip them ten dirhams. Other times they'll take away one of the vagrants, but only to justify the raid.

I checked my pockets, just to make sure I had enough money to give them. When their drums start beating I just slip them the money, then I can relax. If you have money, you can do whatever you want.

Now the wind was blowing hard and it was terribly cold. I buttoned up my coat and held it tight around my throat. When I'd reached the rocks, the weather had been reasonably warm; you could have slept in a crevice between two rocks till dawn. I tried to be careful so as not to fall into one and break a limb. I could hear voices, men and women, and moved a little further away from them. Once they realized there was a human being close by beating drums, they sounded scared and kept whispering to each other. They seemed to prefer silencing their own drums for a while, so as not to mix their beats with mine. They also wanted to find out what kind of tune I was playing—was it just like theirs, or different? I chose a spot between two rocks. The wind was still blowing hard, but it didn't reach me. It felt less cold.

The specters of men and women started approaching me from afar. I could see cigarette-embers glowing like cats' eyes, so many that I couldn't guess their number. Then the glow of a cigarette started moving in my direction. I wasn't scared; actually, I felt quite safe.

"Are you on your own?" the tall man asked. "Come join us in things that are both sinful and lawful."

"What kind of law, what kind of sin?"

"Come and see for yourself. Your tune is just like ours. Link your drums to ours, and let's beat together."

I stood up and followed him slowly and watchfully. "There are rocks," the man added, "so be careful you don't stumble."

I joined the group, three men and three women, sitting in a circle around a plastic mat. One man had a bag on his back. Taking out a bottle of wine, he started pouring some into a single cup for all of us. Later, when matches were lit, I recognized them all. One of the women looked like my sister; she even had the same voice and smile.

I drank the wine quickly in order to erase the image. One of the men looked just like the man in our house. I felt a painfully sharp knot in my stomach, but didn't utter a word. Another man handed me a cigarette. As he lit the match, he brought it closer to my face so he could see who I was.

"Why are you so quiet?" one of the woman asked. "Do you have problems?"

I didn't reply.

"Beat your drums. We are in *terra incognita* here."

Again I didn't reply.

"If you don't want to beat your drum, then tear its skin with a knife."

With that I drew a knife and stabbed my sister. Maybe it was the stomach, or shoulder, or neck. Maybe I missed her entirely and hit the drum skin instead. In any case, its voice could no longer be heard.

The Final Meeting

In a café corner her world was beginning to take shape. A thick grey fog shrouded her eyelids, while he was floating in shadows as dark as night. They both seemed to have gotten tired of chewing words. Either that, or else they had both come to the conclusion that words could no longer convey meaning the way they normally do, so they had turned as cold as icebergs.

Silence spread listlessly across their eyes. Her lips looked colorless, dry, pale, and vapid, and even showed some wrinkles.

"You look very ordinary to me now. . . . I wasn't expecting it. I thought you'd always be something unusual, something valuable in my life, but now. . . ."

He was busy watching a customer who was invading their private space inside the café. He was tall and handsome.

"Men's outward appearances are always fake," she thought, as she stared at the fizzy juice in front of her. Picking up the glass, she drank it with relish. As the bubbles went up her nose, she felt a little awkward. Sensing that she had made an abnormal gesture that infringed norms of etiquette, she felt almost unconsciously upset.

Her boyfriend was indifferent to the fact that she was sitting there in front of him; he was deep in thought and sipping his coffee slowly.

He had taken off his clothes and stayed there naked. That's how she imagined him—naked, without a stitch on.

"Why are we always so fake? Why do we only meet outside? Before we met and got to know each other, you were something wonderful, a man I thought all girls would yearn for, but now you're nothing at all. There's dust in your eyes, and your lips are just like two pieces of rubber."

As she turned over such thoughts in her head, she lowered her thin left hand with its long fingers to the table. He put a hand on top of hers, perhaps involuntarily, and left it there long enough for her to feel the need to pull hers away. For her now, his hand felt as cold as his eyes, his lips, his tie, and his coffee. . . .

"You've changed a lot, lady angel."

"Daydreams don't last."

He took a sip of his coffee, a gesture loaded with palpable bitterness and sorrow. Her feminine intuition told her that he was far from happy.

"You look sad," she said in exasperation. "Are you?"

"No. You're the one who's sad."

"No, I'm not. It's you. I can see it in your eyes."

"Why should I be sad? Doesn't the entire world belong to me?"

She put her hands on the table again, and he repeated his previous gesture—putting his hand on top of hers. This time she didn't pull hers away, but remained as stiff as a marble statue in a museum. . . . Now she felt warmth, not coldness.

"But what a shame! It's too late now. A single moment's warmth can't make up for countless cold ones. Your eyes may gleam with affection now, but later they'll look crafty and deceitful."

She stared at his blue tie. It reminded her of a particular occasion. She tried vainly to remember when it had been, but her head was swimming in a chaos of confused thoughts. She kept begging the tie to remind her, but it refused to respond. Instead, it just lay there on his chest, hanging neatly from his pink shirt collar.

(*"He shows good taste in his clothes; no one can rival the way he looks. He may not be actually nasty inside, but he's still a bit boring."*)

"Do you remember the first time I followed you?" he asked affectionately.

"Why do you ask? You've done it many times."

"Because I like to remember our first meeting."

"You're a . . ."

She stopped talking, unable to muster enough courage to criticize him and discuss his personality.

He didn't give her any time. "A what?" he asked.

"I can't come up with the words."

"I want our final meeting to be completely frank."

"You know I'm frank."

He looked at his watch; its dial looked somehow strange and unfamiliar. He wanted to tell her that, but was afraid she would give him her normal response: "You only bother about trivial things." He had never felt trivial; instead he felt he was observant. Even so, his comments often aggravated her.

She had withdrawn her hands from under his. She felt that they'd spent as much time as possible at the café, but now they had run out of all the phrases they had prepared to use at this final meeting.

"We have to separate, and that's it."

She was the one who had taken the initiative. She had concluded that their love was absurd. He had tried to convince her otherwise, but all his efforts had come to nothing. Eventually, they had settled on this meeting which was supposed to be the final one.

When she moved her chair, he realized that she wanted to leave. He got ready to walk out with her.

They crossed the main street without saying a word. Both their heads were brimming with a host of unorganized thoughts. Her head was covered with long, soft black hair, while his hair was short and coarse.

"So," he told her as he adjusted his tie, "you're the one who's decided we should take this course."

"No, not me."

"Then who? Me?"

"Neither of us. Just pure chance. . . ."

"Nonsense."

The evening breeze was playing with her hair. As they walked close together, some of her tresses brushed his face, and he felt a painful shiver course through his body.

"During our love," he said, "we've stayed faithful to each other. So why part?"

He had wanted to say that to her, since the same idea kept echoing in the recesses of his mind. But he noticed that she kept up her resistance; even though it was all meaningless, she was still determined to see it through.

"You used to say our love was unusual," he said, "something above and beyond nature and human beings. Romantic dreams like those can easily seduce a young girl like you. You change your mind so often. You are both flippant and beautiful, and yet you don't understand the way things really are."

Her thoughts were running along similar lines. Neither of them could share genuine feelings with the other. So, even though both of them had decided that this would be their final meeting, they couldn't move beyond the obstacle that had always blocked their path during their relationship. It was clearly time for her to be frank with him. She felt she was about to say a final farewell, and so did he. That's why they slowed down. Eventually he stopped. She held his hand and kept staring at his cold eyes.

"All these deficiencies are of no importance to me . . . that you're flippant means nothing. . . . We each have our own shortcomings, but what's most harmful and important is . . ."

She wanted to tell him frankly what was most important.

"Do you think this is really going to be our final meeting?"

"Absolutely."

"I'm afraid you're going to regret it."

"No, never. The one thing I haven't discussed with you since we first met is your wife. . . . As long as you're married and a father, I don't think I'll regret it. You can be sure of that."

For a few moments they said nothing.

"She never got me to talk about my wife," he thought. "Women's feelings are difficult to fathom. If only she'd brought it up, we could have dealt with it calmly. But what can happen now when it's all coming to an end?"

"Let's try meeting once more," he begged, "so we can talk it over."

"I can't. My mind's made up, and that's it."

He tried to convince her, but in vain. She said goodbye with a certain determination. But for his part, he hadn't made his mind up yet. He found himself facing a problem that he had yet to resolve, not least because he knew he was still in love with her and was convinced that she was still in love with him as well.

Do Flowers Really Fade?

"ove closer. Tell me, where were you yesterday before your arrest?"

"Before my arrest? I was at home."

"But we picked you up from. . . . How's that possible?"

"I don't know, Sir. I was at home."

"Weren't you at the café as usual?"

"No."

"Tell me the truth."

"I wasn't at the café."

"And how about your friends? Can you guess where they were?"

"No. I don't know."

"Why?"

"Because I don't know."

"Don't be smart."

"I'm not being smart. I'm telling the truth."

"What about so-and-so?"

"I don't know."

"And so-and-so?"

"I don't know."

"And so-and-so?"

"I don't know."

"And so-and-so?"

"I don't know."

"Tell the truth, or I'll take you back down below. Where do they usually spend their time?"

"I don't know. Maybe at the café."

"Anywhere else?"

"I don't know."

"Fine. We've always seen you all at the café, arguing, your hands gesturing wildly and your mouths opening and shutting. What would you all be arguing about?"

"Nothing in particular. Sometimes we talk about women."

"Is that so? Talking about women doesn't involve the kind of intensity you were all displaying at the café."

"I swear, all we do is talk about women. We sit in the café so we can watch them."

"That doesn't mean anything. Isn't there some other way of watching women?"

"I don't think so."

"Why? There are other cafés and houses."

"Women don't go to cafés, because it is considered wrong. Houses are completely out. My friends and I don't have houses of our own. You know, Sir, it's not easy for an ordinary man like me. . . ."

"Enough of that. It's no concern of mine. Tell the truth, what do you usually argue about?"

"Nothing in particular, Sir. About women sometimes."

"Okay, so you talk about women. What about the books and magazines you had in front of you?"

"I love to read. I like reading. That's all."

"Why are you so fond of reading? Why don't you like movies, for example? What about your friends?"

"I don't like movies, Sir. I hate dark places; they make me scared."

"Do you know why we arrested you?"

"No, Sir."

"Okay, so relax and take a deep breath. Breathe slowly. We arrested you because you are involved in politics. Do you realize that?"

"No, Sir. I'm not involved in politics. I don't belong to any political group."

"And yet you're a revolutionary. You and your friends are revolutionaries. Do you deny that too?"

"There's no proof that I've engaged in revolutionary activities, Sir, or that I even have any political opinions. In any case, all political parties are banned in my country in one way or another, so how can you claim that I belong to one?"

"Why are you saying that? Now you're talking about politics. Do you realize that?"

"I'm sorry, Sir."

"Head up!"

"Here I am, Sir, head up."

"Tell the truth now. Do you belong to any secret organizations?"

"No, Sir. Are there any?"

"In your house we found a whole lot of books about socialism. Does that mean you're a communist?"

"No, Sir. I'm not a communist. It's never occurred to me to become one."

"So, what are you?"

"Nothing, Sir. I read a lot, then go to the café. But I never discuss what I've been reading with my friends. Believe me, Sir. We only talk about women."

"Don't you realize that that's punishable by law as well?"

"Pardon me, Sir; I don't know of anyone who's been arrested for talking about women."

"Stop talking such nonsense. That's forbidden too. How dare you talk about respectable women that way?"

"We don't talk about respectable women, Sir. We only discuss the ones who pass by in front of us. They tempt us by dressing the way they do and shooting glances at us."

"Do you realize that you're corrupting the morals of our society?"

"I've never harassed a woman in the street, Sir. Many men take women to their apartments or to the Corniche. But we don't do such things, Sir. We don't have . . ."

"You keep talking about a group. Who is this 'we'?"

"My friends, Sir."

"Aha! Revolutionaries, Communists! So are you going to tell me the truth or not? If not, I'll take you down . . ."

"Which truth, Sir?"

"Stop screwing around. Which political group do you belong to? What secret organization?"

"Nothing, Sir, nothing. There's no secret group. We're just a group of lost young men."

"Lost!? What do mean? Are you implying that the government's neglected you?"

"Oh no, Sir. I don't mean that at all. What I mean is that we can't figure out what to do. That's why we hang out at the café."

"Why do you go to the café?"

"Because there's nothing else to do."

"What are you trying to say? Explain yourself. Do you mean that the government is failing in its duty toward you and isn't finding you a job?"

"No, Sir. That's not what I mean . . ."

"So, what do you mean then?"

"Give me time, Sir. My thoughts are all confused inside my head. I can't give you a clear answer now."

"Okay then, take a break. You can go back downstairs again and smell the foul stench. That'll clear your brain for you."

He went back downstairs and collapsed like a worm. He felt cold, then warm. Staring into the darkness, he emptied his bowels and ate his own shit.

The Snake Pit

*T*he tractor stopped on the road running along the foot of the hillside. It was pulling a cart with three sturdy workers on it. The road stretched away toward the sea, traversing another hill that was covered with short trees. Hous Obaha stopped the engine and looked back at the three men.

"Get off," he told Tazeroualt. "And go tell him."

"I can't go into the café looking like this," he replied. "People who are as dirty as me don't frequent such places."

"Just knock on the window. When he comes out, tell him."

"I can't even walk across the café courtyard. Just look how clean it is. If I do, he's bound to curse me. In fact, he may well deal with me the way he did with the others. I don't want him to throw me into the snake pit. I have a wife and kids."

The Blue Shark was a café-restaurant at the top of the hill. It looked like an impregnable castle, surrounded on all sides by flowers and trees. Through the window you could see waiters in their tidy matching uniforms making their way between tables. They had epaulettes on their shoulders and shiny, golden numbers on their chests. On the opposite side the sea was visible, vast and expansive. On the cliff some long-necked backhoes were visible, working in slow and continuous motion.

"Why don't you go tell him?" Hous Obaha repeated.

"I can't."

Then Hous Obaha turned to someone else. "You go! Tell him we've thrown 'him' in the pit. He'll be happy to hear that. He may even give us a reward."

"I can't go. When he drinks, he gets wild."

"Are you that afraid of him?"

"Go tell him yourself! In just these few hours he'll have drunk a bottle of whiskey, for sure."

"He can't hurt me," Hous Obaha replied. "He's a coward. I've worked with him for more than ten years, so I know him well. If he didn't have authority on his side, I'd have killed him long ago. And he knows it. In any case, he can send anyone he wants to prison and throw anyone he feels like into the pit. What matters to me is that he keep out of my way and give me my pay every weekend."

With that, he jumped down from the tractor's seat. He was wearing a pair of black rubber boots that were plastered in black mud. He started climbing the steps toward the Blue Shark. On either side were displays of neatly cut flowers and shrubs. The three men watched him anxiously. He was really brave, the only man who could look 'Abiqa straight in the eye.

All the workers in the gardens and fields, both male and female, were scared of 'Abiqa. He was on good terms with all the authorities. He could kill or jail anyone who tried to oppose him or look him in the eye. Any worker he did not like would find himself transferred or fired within twenty-four hours. Even so, he was a coward, and he was particularly scared of Hous. But who knows, maybe one of these days he'd be preparing a "special kind of party" for him, too.

The men kept watching anxiously as Hous's hulking frame made its way up the steps, leaning forward and taking them two by two. By now he'd reached the courtyard in front of the Blue Shark. He stopped for a moment, then stretched his arms in the air. The sunshine was reflecting off the café's windows, so nothing inside was visible. When Hous Obaha reached the door, he paused for a moment. However, as it happened, 'Abiqa came out. The three men watched as the two of them walked across the courtyard, then stopped. Only their heads and shoulders were visible. 'Abiqa seemed to be showing little interest as he listened to Hous Obaha talking. Finally, he lifted his hand and pointed toward the sea. His arm stayed in that position for quite some time, then he slowly lowered it. Hous went on talking. The three other men kept trying to guess what they were talking about.

"If I were in Hous's place," Tazeroualt said, "that bastard would be kicking me or spitting in my face."

"He can do even worse things than that," said one of the others.

"I know," the other man replied. "Anyone who can throw a poor man into the snake pit is capable of doing absolutely anything."

People were always talking about the snake pit that 'Abiqa used to punish his enemies. That included everyone, whether they were from Suq Sebt, or Tlet Lawlad, or Jorf Lasfar. In addition, his father had a big open courtyard for whipping people. Every evening, he used to whip a peasant, his wife, or his son. Once in a while, the French military commandant or governor would enjoy strolling around the courtyard so they could watch the whipping in process. They used to laugh and show not the slightest sign of pity or concern. 'Abiqa used to invite them for dinner—grilled lamb, *shikhat*, and couscous. Once the dinner was over, another private party would begin. Those private parties gradually developed and expanded. Instead of the French, it was the *Caid* and the Super *Caid*, the Governor, and the District Attorney who would attend. However, barns and shacks were put up in the courtyard where calves, cattle, and men all lived together. His father never drank, but 'Abiqa was hardly ever sober. And, in spite of everything, his fortune kept growing.

Hous left 'Abiqa and began to rumble his way back to the tractor. He walked effortlessly down the steps two at a time, his rubber boots spraying stone chips all over the place.

He noticed the three men on the cart; they were staring at him, awestruck. He could picture them saying, "He's really brave." He didn't care what they thought of him. What really mattered was for 'Abiqa to pay him his salary every weekend and never stand in his way. Even the snake pit didn't scare him. He knew he'd be able to kill an entire tribe before 'Abiqa had a chance to throw him in the pit.

He jumped up on the tractor without saying a word. He tried to start it again, but the engine stalled at first. Once it started, he moved off along a winding road toward the sea. At the top of the hill, right in front of the Blue Shark, 'Abiqa watched as they left. Rubbing his hands and kicking the ground with his foot, he burst into laughter as he shook his fist in the air. Going back into the café from the restaurant side, he made for the bar and almost collided with one of the tables, but it just wobbled, rattled, then settled back into position. He didn't even bother with it. The waiter stared at him with a mixture of disgust, respect, and fear. He went over and joined two men who were perched on stools by the bar. He gestured to the bartender, who filled two glasses with whiskey.

"Next time" 'Abiqa said, "I'm going to win the parliamentary election."

"No one deserves it more than you," one of the two men replied.

"That mule only won by using fraud, bribery, and negative campaigning," the other one added.

"I did all that too," 'Abiqa answered. "Can you imagine? The peasants, those dogs who work for me, they campaigned against me!"

"Did you throw that particular dog into the snake pit?"

"Of course. Tonight they'll start biting him. Next time no one in the entire region will be able to campaign against me."

He raised the glass to his mouth, and the others did the same. The bar was almost empty. In the corner the barman was listening, but pretending not to care about the world around him. Nevertheless, he was well aware of the story of the snake pit; everybody used to talk about it, but in a very guarded way. They always talked about 'Abiqa and his father, but in fact they were afraid for themselves. Even the district governor himself was afraid of 'Abiqa. He didn't want problems. If the stench spread far enough, it would register disgust in Rabat.

'Abiqa emptied his glass and signaled again to the barman. "Drink up!" he said.

He took a deep breath. "I swear," he went on, "even if General Oufkir himself were to rise from his grave, he wouldn't be able to stand against me. This time I'm going to teach a hard lesson to those pigs who keep eating my leftovers, then campaign against me in the elections."

The others said nothing but kept nodding their heads. Even if he was wrong, they were doing their best to take his side and support him. After all, they were eating his leftovers, as well. One of them was the manager at a farm of his; every year he embezzled half the revenue. The other one was simply an admirer. Why not? The governor himself was afraid of him, and, even if General Oufkir did arise from his grave, he would not be able to stand against him.

Sunshine made its way across the café floor, then across the tables as well. Only two families were eating there. They seemed to have arrived late for lunch and were now ready to pay the bill.

'Abiqa's head started spinning, but it was unusual for him to feel dizzy when he had not drunk a lot. It was driving him crazy.

"Let's keep drinking," the man on his right said. "Just imagine you've won the elections."

"Don't you think it's the governor who pulled this dirty trick?" the other man said.

"Don't say that!" 'Abiqa replied. "He can't have done it. He's eaten all my sheep. If he did it, his stomach would surely explode from eating too much. In his sleep, my grandfather would be standing over his head; he would certainly cause him no end of grief. He knows that. That's why he can't possibly have done such a thing."

The two big families left; there were a lot of them. For a while the sun went behind some clouds, then re-emerged to cover the floor and tables, then spread toward the kitchen on the left. The barman raised his head and stretched up to glance out the window.

Outside in the square the gendarmes' jeep was seeking a suitable place to park. The driver found a spot right in front of the café door. The lieutenant looked out his window, opened the door quickly, and was followed by four gendarmes with rifles. They all rushed into the café. When 'Abiqa saw them, he felt more at ease. He knew the officer; he had eaten his sheep, as well.

"Well, you rogue, who are you looking for?" 'Abiqa asked, "Throw those bastards out and come have a drink. No one in the café is dangerous enough for all this bother."

"How can there be any dangerous men when 'Abiqa's around?" his farm manager asked.

"Call me 'Si Abdelkader,' you dog."

"Sorry. Si Abdelkader."

However, the officer's expression did not change; he still looked severe. When he gestured with his hand, the four gendarmes moved toward 'Abiqa, their rifles aimed straight at him.

'Abiqa was confused. At first, he did not believe it.

"What are you doing?" he asked. "Don't play with fire."

"I'm not playing or joking," said the officer. "It's an order. I've been told to arrest you."

"Like this, you dog!"

"It's your mother who's the bitch."

One of the gendarmes pounced on him, twisted his arms behind his back and handcuffed him. He frog-marched 'Abiqa over to the jeep and shoved him inside. 'Abiqa was frothing at the mouth and cursing, but it was all useless. The gendarmes' ears were sealed shut.

GYPSIES IN THE WOODS

(1982)

Worries

*W*hen you tell people about things that are worrying you, you have to believe that they understand. You're looking for some support, but in fact that's not going to happen. On the contrary, people may even stoke the embers of such worries.

The trees all around him in the public park are tall and green; the benches are placed close together. All the people in the park certainly have their own private worries, but who can they go to, to talk? Some of them sit by themselves, while others chat or read. He listens to the deafening roar of cars and motorcycles; he's feeling so on edge that he can't stand any more engine-noise.

He resorts to his usual refuge when he feels so tense: a cigarette, followed by another, then another, till his throat and pharynx both feel dry. The bitter taste reaches all the way to his epiglottis and tongue. A feeling of giddiness radiates outward to every fiber in his brain, and his limbs feel numb; he wants to be sick. He dreams of chirping birds of various shapes and sizes, with their multi-colored feathers both bright and dark.

Stretching his legs out in front of him, he starts thinking to himself again. He tries digging a hole in the ground with his heels, striking the earth with deft, measured movements to avoid anyone thinking he's gone mad. So then what? Raising his right leg, he brings it down hard on the ground, creating a tingling sensation that keeps the pain at bay. He twists his heel nervously in the dust. The ground is hard. Small rocks are embedded in it which are either completely covered or else protruding a little, in which case only the tops jut above the surface like baby-teeth. Chirping birds, rustling trees, and westward-bound rays of sunshine beaming amid the branches and leaves: all are things he imagines as he presses his heels into the ground.

For sure, everyone has his own worries, but he has no idea how much pressure they can put on people. "Sunlight is scattered through the garden like gold coins"; those are the words of the Arab poet. Chirping birds, verdant leaves and branches, migratory birds, Muslim ibn al-Walid, and other things, as well. But what about the illusions that we all have? Poets certainly have had nothing to say about the kinds of worries that he has.

I always look down on other people. They all have second personalities that they try to keep hidden. They only discuss their real problems with themselves. No man ever admits to his wife that he loves another woman, or vice versa. Everyone has his own problems, his own reality.

And what about you? Why do you feel you need to talk to someone? Don't be content simply to dig at the ground with your heel. You can scratch it with your nails, or else use a whip, an ax, or a crowbar. You can even hide inside it, along with all the worries you may have.

Needless to say, he himself would not be able to do any such thing. The park warden would inevitably stop him. All the people, whether they had worries or not—the kind of things that made them frequent the park today or on other days—they would all gather round. For that very reason, he would be their only concern at that particular moment; it would be an exquisite game, attractive even to people who were apparently uninterested. How wonderful to have something to worry about!

However, he insisted on not becoming a victim of the game. Either let's all be victims or, if not, then let's cancel the whole thing. Everyone's life can be a game, not just some people's.

"Let's take the kid to Sinbad Park," his wife had suggested.

"Does he really like it there?"

"Of course, he does. He loves trees, roses, greenery, night, everything."

"You can find those things anywhere."

"But in Sinbad Park they're different."

"How's that?"

"I don't know."

"As far as I'm concerned, all parks are alike. Don't cut the flowers! Don't walk on the grass! And so on."

He didn't say any more, but stood there watching his wife, who was looking into the mirror hanging by the TV set.

That's not all, either. It's also forbidden to be alone with a woman in the park. Policemen are everywhere. All parks are alike. He kept mumbling such things to himself.

"What are you saying?" asked the wife.

"Nothing."

"So, let's go to the park."

"You take him."

"Let's all go."

"Since they're all the same, that's not necessary."

"We should go."

He took a deep breath as he enjoyed a fleeting sense of elation. By now, the tension of the moment had dissolved. His heels felt heavy on the dirt. It was as if his body was no longer his, but part of some other hidden force. The sound of chirping birds was getting louder. He could picture swarms of butterflies hovering around his head and forming a garland or halo. He stood up and began tramping across the grass. Once he realized where he was going, he headed for the paved walkway. A few cars passed by on the road, and the sound of other engines could be heard behind the trees. He'd been alone for more than an hour, sitting, standing, then walking. . . .

"I'll go push the boy on the swing," the wife said. "He likes that."

"Push him on a swing or take him to the bumper cars. Do as you like."

She was gone for over an hour, but he didn't think of joining her. He preferred to stay on his own and chew over his worries.

To have some moments of solitude is both pleasurable and painful, but there has to be a limit. He walked toward the lake. People were staring distractedly at the water, either talking, walking, or flirting. He spotted his wife chasing after the boy, who was trying hard not to fall on the grass.

"Look, here's Dad," she shouted when she saw him.

"You go after him and let me play," the boy replied.

He went over to the two of them and started staring distractedly at the water, just like everybody else.

"Daddy," the boy asked as he grabbed him by the leg of his pants "why don't people swim in this water?"

Not allowed. The water belongs to the park. It's forbidden to pick flowers. It's forbidden to walk on the grass. It's forbidden to be alone with a woman. It's forbidden to swim.

The boy left his father and ran on to the grass. He started doing acrobatics, kicking an imaginary ball with his head and foot. He himself was hugged from behind by his wife, but he did not move a muscle. He frowned a little as he continued staring at the lake.

"What's the matter with you?" his wife asked. "Shall we go home?"

"As you wish."

"No, as you wish."

"As long as I've been with you, I've never had the option of wishing."

"Does that mean you don't love me?"

"What does love have to do with it?"

"I don't know. You look as though you're carrying the world's burdens on your shoulders."

"Could be."

The world's burdens or my own? I don't know. But everyone has his particular problems and worries. Even that pelican in the lake has to worry about food, so do the birds in the sky and the butterflies on flowers in the wild.

He turned toward her. Don't tell her your problems. No, tell her. What's the difference?

"Let's go home then," he said.

She put her arm in his and called the boy. People looked just like statues, fixed in place all around the lake, glued to the grass.

Even car engines couldn't be heard anymore. The entire world around him seemed paralyzed.

"Do you really love me?"

"You can see that for yourself."

"But these days you look perpetually worried."

"More than that, I'm feverish."

"Can you talk to me about your worries? I'm your wife."

"I know, but at this point I can't. When the time's right, I will."

As they left the park, the boy was running ahead. He passed by the bench he'd been sitting on an hour earlier and glanced over to look for the hole he'd dug with his heels. There was nothing, not a single trace. Once he'd passed the bench, he glanced back. His wife noticed.

"What's the matter?" she asked

"Oh! Nothing."

"No. There's something. Why do you keep glancing behind you as though you're being followed?"

"I don't know. I was sitting there. I was afraid I'd dropped something."

"You aren't behaving normally," she sighed.

"I'm sorry, I have my worries."

"Sometimes I feel I'm the cause of those worries."

"I hope that'll never be the case. Keep an eye on the boy."

Don't talk about your problems. No one understands you. Everyone's alike, even the people you think are closest to you. They stoke the embers and wait for a chance to humiliate you. He was mumbling to himself again.

"What's the matter?" his wife asked.

"Nothing. I'll tell you later, when we get home."

In the Woods

*W*e discovered that this time the gypsies had camped in the woods. They come once or twice a year, stay for a week or two, then leave for somewhere else. They have no specific place to go back to, the way birds often do. Some of them put up tents; others don't, preferring to sleep in their big old American cars. They hang their clothes in the windows and put their bedspreads on top. Sometimes they tie a line from one car to another or to a tree.

This time they camped in the woods.

"There are a lot of them this time," said Hamu. "But they are not as dirty as the ones we've seen before."

"Are there any pretty girls?" asked 'Adi.

"They're very beautiful, gorgeous," I said. "But how can we get hold of one of them?"

"It's easy," replied Hamu. "A bunch of *kif* will do it. They love it."

"They don't smoke weed. They drink wine."

"No, some of them like hashish. Even though they're dirty, they're still beautiful. You'll see."

"They're not as dirty as that ugly, barefoot sister of yours."

"Don't insult my sister."

"Oh yeah, your sister's as beautiful as the moon."

"At least she's not a gypsy."

"Gypsies smell foul," 'Adi said. "Even from a distance. It must be because they eat a lot of pork. People say pork makes you stink."

"Lots of people stink without eating pork. Walad Sharqawiya smells like a skunk, but he's never eaten pork in his life."

"Why should we care?" I asked. "We want to get one of their girls, and that's it. They're dusky and beautiful, with black, shiny hair. Ah, how I love those gypsy girls. How I wish I were a gypsy!"

"They're like Jews. They don't accept other people."

"People say they were once Arab Muslims like us. But God disowned them, so they don't believe in Him."

Al-Mukhtar's mother came over and hit him between his shoulders with a stick.

"You still don't want to give up these loser friends of yours, do you?" she said. "This time they'll take you back to those filthy unbelievers whom God has deprived of His mercy. Heaven knows where they come from."

He took the blow without flinching but cursed his mother under his breath. As he walked away from her and us, he was making a furrow in the ground like an excited animal. His mother picked up the stick that had fallen from her hand.

"You son of a bitch," she went on. "Last summer, they were about to cut your prick off. You got the clap from mucking around with their women."

We started laughing.

"See, they're all laughing at you. They push you into the abyss, but then they pull back."

She walked back slowly toward her house. She too was filthy and barefoot. No one really knew if God was in His heaven and had refused her His mercy too, the way she had spoken about gypsies. Was it true that every dirty person with bare feet has indeed been refused God's mercy? We were all barefoot as well. One of us was wearing a pair of women's shoes that he'd found in a trashcan. They were bright red, the kind that women who have not been refused God's mercy wear when they're getting ready to go out to a party.

She stopped alongside a dilapidated wall consisting of thin wood poles, nails, and shingles made out of tin cans. The wall made a cracking sound. She almost fell down along with it, but managed to pull herself together. She put her hands on her hips. Her dress rode up to reveal a skinny leg covered with bruises and scratches.

The stick was between her legs, almost stuck in the ground with its upper end tilted toward her stomach. She started cursing and swearing, calling us children of sissies and describing our fathers in very offensive terms. If our fathers had actually heard her, they would probably have killed her; either that or started a fight. After all, using such words to describe Arab and Muslim men is considered a blot on family honor. Unlike French, Germans, Americans, and Jews, Arab and Muslim men are very sensitive about particular things in life. The others are all impure, God save us! God gave them this world in order to provide us with the afterlife. In them He killed those very sensitivities that make us fight and kill.

That explains why 'Adi now stood up shaking all over. He said he was going to rape her right in front of her own son. We told him that that would be completely inappropriate for both us and him. It would be better for her son to do it, provided, of course, that he was a real man and not the kind of person his mother had been invoking to insult our fathers.

After mouthing something inaudible, she disappeared. Her son joined us.

"Don't pay attention to her," he said, pointing to his aching shoulders. "She's nuts."

"If she were my mother, I'd know how to keep her in line. But she was right; she gave you away. Last summer, you did spend time with the gypsies behind our backs."

"She was talking nonsense. That happened somewhere else."

"That's not important. We need to find some *kif* and head for the woods where the gypsies are camped."

"They say gypsies speak Spanish."

"Maybe they are Spanish. During the famine, Spaniards survived on goat's milk; if they had flour they sold *choro*. They're also poor, like Arabs and Muslims, because we all have close blood ties. Maybe they'll go to Heaven with us."

When children younger than us found out about the gypsy camp, they tried to stick close to us like an evil curse. But we knew how to get rid of them. For sure, that Lalla Nsa's boy would already be there in the woods ahead of us. He was way ahead of his age in doing certain things and always gave us a run for our money, whatever we decided to try.

We made our way through dirt alleys that were full of foul-smelling puddles; there was no sewage system. After a half-hour walk we reached the edge of the woods. Once across the paved road reserved for buses, we saw silhouettes of cars, men, cows, and goats. Actually, when we came closer, there were no cows or goats.

"They aren't as many as we thought," said Hamu.

"Maybe there are more of them in the woods."

"No, they never separate. They only travel and camp together."

"Maybe they're inside the tents."

He pointed to some tents tethered to tree trunks that were scattered here and there in the woods.

"We should make a point of being polite," said Al-Mukhtar. "We don't want them to be on their guard."

"Look," said 'Adi. "There's that f—— Lalla Nsa's boy, with two other kids."

The boy stopped at a distance and stared at us. He looked scared. He was bare-chested and only wearing a pair of pants with the legs cut short. I yelled a curse at him and threw a stone, but he managed to avoid it. It only just missed hitting one of the two other kids on the head.

"Let me go and rape him," Hamu suggested. "It's what the dirty son of a bitch deserves."

"Leave him alone," I said. "He won't come any closer."

"We have to separate," said Al-Mukhtar. "We don't want to arouse the gypsies' suspicions."

"True enough. They suspect everyone. They refuse to buy or sell things involving anyone else."

"That's not true. They sell people odd things. Sometimes they'll even buy food if their own supplies run out."

"We've got to separate," I said.

So we did. I flopped down near a tent in the shade of a verdant tree. The others all chose their own way to get closer to the gypsies. I pretended to be asleep and felt one of their dogs licking my bare feet. I was scared, but did not pull my leg away immediately. I did not want the dog to get excited and bite me on the leg or somewhere else. Close by, a frog leapt over the grass that was growing in profusion near the tree trunk. When the dog spotted that, it left me alone and started chasing the frog. When it caught the frog, it started ripping it apart with its paws, growling all the while. Eventually the frog's intestines spilled out, all coated in dirt. With that, the dog settled down and squatted next to what was left of the frog; it was staring at the legs and intestines, things that it couldn't rip up any more, however sharp the nails on its claws. An acorn from the tree landed on the dog's head, and it growled, then barked and finally withdrew to another spot behind the car.

Once in awhile, gypsies could be heard yelling, almost as though they were having an argument. I saw Lalla Nsa's son approaching again, but without the other two kids.

"You son of a bitch!" I said. "If you don't go home right now, I'm not even going to tell you what I'll do to you till I've actually done it."

He cringed. "But just take a look," he said. "Some gypsy girls have come outside. They're cooking something."

"Where?"

"Over there. Behind that tent."

Abdi joined me. "I've looked around," he said, "There are more of them than we thought. I found some of them playing cards. They smiled as I came up to them and talked to me, but I couldn't understand what they were saying. . . . I watched a gypsy, completely naked, pouring a bucket of cold water over himself. No one was paying any attention."

"They're not shy about doing that. To them it's perfectly normal. Are you sure it wasn't a naked woman?"

"Are you kidding? His body's as huge as a mule, and his moustache is as thick as a donkey's tail."

"Where have Al-Mukhtar and Hamu disappeared to?" I asked.

"I don't know. They've probably found something, or else they're relaxing under the trees, watching the gypsies like two dogs staring at food they can't have."

"Let's go and look for them. Al-Mukhtar has a rare knack for getting gypsy girls, the same way he used to catch flies at the mosque."

As we made our way through various groups of gypsies spread out over quite a large area, 'Adi walked in front of me. Pots and pans simmered on fires. By now, Lalla Nsa's son and the two other kids had all disappeared somewhere close by the tents and the old American cars. Some of the gypsies were staring at us and smiling, while others were totally unconcerned. A little gypsy boy came up and gave me half an orange, which had a very special taste, unbelievably sweet. I gave 'Adi a piece, and he downed it quickly. The little gypsy boy ran back to the tent, and his mother emerged. She was wearing multicolored clothes open at the chest, so you could easily see her breasts. Her jet-black hair covered nearly all of her face. Even so, her sparkling eyes and wonderful smile were easy to see. But she quickly slipped back into the tent.

"Oh, my God!" said 'Adi. "How can we get hold of a beautiful woman like that?!"

"Believe me: you'd never be able to get one, even if you cut off your fingers for her sake."

"She's really beautiful."

"Yes indeed, she's prettier than an angel. Come on, let's keep looking for Al-Mukhtar and Hamu."

We kept stepping over tent-ropes tied all over the place. I was asking myself: How I can attract a gypsy girl if I don't speak her language? What language can I use to talk to her? Al-Mukhtar knows how to speak with his hands, head, and eyes. He's as good at that as he is at hunting flies. But we could not find them anywhere. Lalla Nsa's son was probably looking for them, as well. Everything we had in mind, Lalla Nsa's son did too—strange, yet true. It's happened so many times: he manages to read our minds just by looking at us while we're talking about things. His eyes sparkle under his thick eyebrows, and he has a magician face.

"Lalla Nsa's son will be back soon," 'Adi said. "He'll be able to tell us where Al-Mukhtar and Hamu are hiding."

"He can certainly do that. I know him all too well. But assuming he's come here on his own, why did he take the other two kids with him? He's going to corrupt them. He's good, as good as a saluki hound."

The voices grew louder; so did the laughter. In the distance you could hear a gypsy baby crying. Strange! Even their babies cry like ours; the screams sound just like my little brother when my mother refused to give him some money to buy a balloon. He used to burst so many of them, it seemed deliberate. My mother would rush over to him. "You brat," she would say. "Did I wean you on balloons? Here!" Then she'd hit him with whatever came to hand; it might be a shoe (although there weren't many shoes at home), a comb, or a pair of bellows. He used to scream, whether or not he was hit. The noise he made was just like this little gypsy boy crying somewhere in the distance. But then, I've no idea how gypsies discipline their kids. Do they use bellows, combs, tongs, and shoes to beat them?

Suddenly 'Adi stopped, and started listening to a noise inside one of the tents. He looked at me as though he was about to tell me something important. But what could he say? He did not know their language. As he was listening, his gestures gave me the impression that he could interpret what was being said inside that tent. A gypsy head peered outside, and we got scared. The man's broad shoulders suggested that he could take on three people our size.

"Hurry up," a scared 'Adi said, as he walked on in front of me, "or that rogue's going to catch us."

"Listen, 'Adi," I said, "I've an idea. Al-Mukhtar and Hamu must have gone to the spring."

"Why would they do that?"

"The place has lots of hiding-spots, so you can't see them. They must have flirted with one or two gypsy girls and taken them off to smoke *kif*."

"You're right, that's a good idea. It's what Al-Mukhtar always does. He much prefers vacant, isolated places."

We left the tents and cars behind us and walked along a dirt path with trees, plants, and weeds on either side. Over the ages it had been leveled by human feet and animal hoofs. It led to the spring. We used to burn pieces of rubber there, coat plant stalks with the melted goo, then bury them in the soil close to the spring. That way we managed to catch tiny birds that would shiver fearfully in our hands. The area all around the spring was thick with trees, but they were different from oaks and not fruit-bearing.

"Look!" said 'Adi, "There's Lalla Nsa's son again."

He was standing behind a tree trunk. It looked as though he had left the other two kids somewhere else. He was watching us the way a rabbit does a hunter before running away, scared, yet defiant.

"No big deal!" I told 'Adi, "He may have found out where Al-Mukhtar and Hamu are."

I yelled to him, and he walked edgily toward us. Stopping a few feet away, he scratched his snot-encrusted nose. His eyes were gleaming under his thick eyebrows.

"They are over there," he said, pointing toward the spring.

"Who?"

"Al-Mukhtar, Hamu, and some gypsies."

"It's creepy how this damned boy manages to do these things!" I told 'Adi. "Didn't I tell you? Whatever we think about doing, he manages to do it first."

"Are there any girls with them?" I asked him.

"Yes. And I saw some gypsy men as well hanging around the spring."

We left him frozen in place. No doubt we would find he had gotten to the spring ahead of us, taking a shortcut we didn't know. He could do anything because he is Lalla Nsa's son; things occur to him that no one else, male or female, even contemplates.

We drew close to the spring where the trees were thick, short, and intertwined. We did not see any gypsies or anybody else, either.

"Maybe they've drugged the gypsy girls," I said to 'Adi.

"They must have had their way with them by now."

"We shouldn't surprise them. Let's spy on them."

I could picture the water rippling and the birds finding it hard to flap their wings amid the rubber-covered stems we had buried. We used to grab them, and their tiny bodies would pulse and quiver in our hands. The little birds would look right and left, perhaps emitting a squeak like a cry for help.

"Let's approach from the other side," 'Adi suggested. "It'll be better, and we won't be surprising them."

"It'd be better if we separated," I said.

He disappeared for a moment. I walked to the other side and saw the spring. There was no one there. The water was glinting in the sunshine that was poking its way through the boughs and branches. There was no sign of anyone. All I could see was an empty, rusty jam can and an old torn shoe, but no trace of any human beings. They had to be somewhere in the trees. In situations like this, Al-Mukhtar was always cautious. I heard the sound of small branches cracking, and walked in that direction. I spotted 'Adi walking stealthily through the trees and pushing the branches aside with his hand. I called his name, and he looked in my direction.

"You?"

"Yes, me! I didn't find anybody."

"Nor did I."

"We've got to keep looking for them. The earth can't have swallowed them up."

"Everything's possible. The area by the spring is haunted."

"Oh, shut up! May you be possessed by a jinni!"

We started walking all around the area by the spring, not really believing that they were there. Could our intuition be wrong? But then Lalla Nsa's son doesn't tell lies!

"We have to find them," 'Adi said.

We changed direction. Now the weeds were tall enough to cover half of a man, weeds and plants with saw-like leaves. Just then 'Adi stopped and starting listening.

"They're there, for sure. Can you hear them?"

I couldn't hear anything.

"Be careful. I heard something like laughter."

We moved a bit closer. Now my ears did pick up the sound of human voices. Then I spotted a young gypsy girl standing in the middle of the fern field, pushing her black hair back. She did not see us. She disappeared again.

"I wonder what they're doing there now," I said.

"Smoking weed."

"Shall we join them?"

"No. Not now."

"But I want to get high with them."

"Don't do that. Al-Mukhtar and Hamu know that we're here. When the moment's right, they'll call us."

I watched a small chameleon as it crawled slowly over my foot. I was scared because it stopped and began looking around vacantly. Picking up a stick, I prodded its back, but it still refused to budge.

"Ugh. *Tfoo*," said 'Adi, spitting. "Leave that filth alone."

"Look," he said craning his neck, "there's a gypsy."

I looked where he'd been pointing. The man was very tall with a handsome tanned face. He looked sullen, as he stood there listening.

"Was he smoking with them too?" 'Adi asked.

"Be careful not to let him see us."

We saw him take out a huge knife from his belt and walk cautiously toward them. He must have got so high that he was about to commit a crime.

"Hamu!" 'Adi yelled, terrified.

Heads rose from the fern field. The gypsy went berserk, pointing his knife firstly at us, then at them. He could not make up his mind which way to throw it. He started running, tripping over plants, falling many times, and grabbing whatever he could find around him or in front of him. We saw Al-Mukhtar and Hamu run away, while the three girls stayed riveted to the spot. We ran and ran through the woods.

At a certain point we stopped to catch our breath.

"If only he hadn't had a knife," Hamu said.

"What would you have done, you chicken?!" 'Adi asked. "Let's get out of here before he calls the other gypsies."

"That short girl was really gorgeous," said Al-Mukhtar.

"We'll be watching," I said, "when you catch you-know-what."

Why Is Dinner Late?

$\mathcal{A}$ stagnant light was filtering through the window. The heads of some of the guests were visible, but the roaring waves drowned their conversation. Halim was far enough away that he couldn't hear what they were talking about. He just stood there, barefoot in the dark, moonless night. Karim, who was also barefoot, caught up with him.

"I've had too much to drink," Halim panted.

"Me too," Karim replied.

Halim farted, then grabbed Karim by the hand. Feeling cold, they both walked toward the water.

"We'll catch cold as soon as we get to the water," Karim said.

"That won't happen," Halim replied. "We've drunk too much."

"You mean, alcohol protects you against colds?"

"Precisely," replied Halim.

"I didn't know that," Karim said. "That's really weird,"

"No it's not."

Halim let go of Karim's hand. They hadn't met before, only now at a friend's party. They'd had a drink, talked, got to like each other, and decided to take a walk till dinner was ready. Halim was walking in front of Karim. The latter let out a belch.

"Hey!" he yelled out to Halim.

"What?"

"Why are you walking so fast?"

"I am not rushing. I'm walking slowly."

"Let's go back. Look at the light in the window. Dinner's probably served."

For the fourth time Halim farted. He could feel the cold water lapping his bare feet. Leaning to his right, he looked behind him but couldn't make out Karim's features.

"Dinner's going to be late."

"Let's go for a walk. It's stifling inside the house."

"But they'll start eating."

"Is food all you think about?"

"No, but they'll be looking for us everywhere."

Karim felt something pricking the bottom of his foot, so he stopped. He removed whatever it was and flung it into the water. It was hard and spiny, but not sharp.

"Hey!" Karim yelled again in a drunken tone,

Halim didn't hear him. He was still walking and savoring the cool sand in the hot weather.

"Hey!" Karim yelled again. "You there!"

Again Halim didn't hear him; he couldn't possibly hear him. Karim unbuttoned his shirt and ran his fingers through the thick hair that covered his upper chest. He ran after Halim, but couldn't catch up. He fell on the sand and started listening to the roaring waves. Looking up, he could see people's heads moving in the lighted window; he could even make out some of the voices. Standing up again, he turned around.

"Hey," he yelled a third time. "Hey, you over there!"

But no one heard him. He started walking back toward the house, the light, the window.

"Where's Halim?" his friend who'd organized the party asked Karim.

"He's asleep in the barn," Karim answered.

"We don't have a barn," the man told Karim with a laugh. "You've had too much to drink."

"No, I haven't," Karim replied. "He's sleeping in the trees."

"Oh, right!" the man said, still laughing. "You haven't drunk too much. But there aren't any trees either."

"I don't know," was all Karim could say.

"Come and have dinner," the man told him. "I'll go and look for him."

The Pound Street Game

*R*ight at the start of Pound Street we paused for a moment. Fatiha was picking her nose, so I slapped her. She dropped her arm to her side and wiped her finger on her pants.

"There," she said, staring at the shop window. "That necklace."

"Which one? I can see lots of them."

"The silver one with the engraving."

"That's lovely."

"I should at least find out how much it is. Will you go in, or shall I?"

"You go in."

She hit me with her handbag and hesitated for a moment by the store's entrance. I moved away from the window, staring at nothing in particular. For me, many women, beautiful women, are very attractive. Looking over my shoulder, I could see Fatiha still standing by the entrance. Eventually she went inside.

I kicked the curb with my shoes, as though I were testing its strength against that of my shoes. Actually, I wasn't really doing either; I was just keeping myself amused.

When Fatiha emerged, she was playing with her handbag and rubbing it against her thigh.

"How much?" I asked, once she'd joined me.

"I don't know."

"Didn't you ask her?"

"No, I didn't. I just looked around the store for a few minutes."

"Is the old man with her?"

"No, she's alone."

Once again I kicked the curb with my shoes, while Fatiha kept twirling her handbag in the air and rubbing it against her thigh and knee.

"Yikes!" she yelled when she hit herself hard.

"Quiet!" I said. "You're just a baby."

She stopped twirling her bag and looked serious. "The woman's alone," she said.

"So you did ask the price?"

"No, I didn't. Come on; let's have another look at the window. Maybe the price is on the back."

We went back and looked in the shop window. Fatiha tried craning her neck, but still could not make out anything; nor could I.

"Shall we go inside and ask the price?" I asked Fatiha.

She went into the shop, and I followed. The saleswoman eyed me.

"Monsieur?" she asked.

"How much is that necklace?" I asked, pointing to the one in the window.

Turning round, she went over to the shelves to get some boxes and started looking through them. Fatiha quickly opened her handbag and dropped the necklace inside. The woman came back.

"That's the only one we have left," she said.

"Okay. How much is it?"

" . . . "

"In the medina it costs a third as much!"

"But here we have to pay taxes," the woman replied. "What's more, our craftsmanship is first-class. We get our stock from the south. Everything here is original."

"Okay, but lower the price."

"Impossible, monsieur."

Fatiha left first while I was still talking to the woman. Fatiha paused by the door.

"We'll come back another time," she said. "*Bonne chance, Madame.*"

"Everything we have here is original," she said once again.

I linked arms with Fatiha, and we walked quite a long way together. Eventually we went into "Cappuccino," and I ordered ice cream with Chantilly. Fatiha took out the necklace and put it in my hand. After I'd examined it for a while, I gave it back to her. Opening her handbag, she put it back in. My Chantilly tasted wonderful, and Fatiha was obviously enjoying hers, too.

The Cripple and the Whore

She was a kind-hearted woman, naturally shy and with a nice, modest smile. She was very kind to us. Even when we used to sneak up on her tin shack and cause mischief, she never minded. Our mothers were much meaner; in fact, most of them were spiteful and merciless. They used to shower us with their slaps, kicks, curses, and heaven knows what else, all in revenge for the treatment they themselves used to get on a regular basis from their husbands.

"Finish up what your father's left, you son of a pig. Just take a look at your mother's body! It's all skinny, just a mass of bones."

Every mother used to say things like that, even though she weighed a ton, had breasts that sagged like sacks, jowls bulging like drums, and buttocks like rolling hills. By contrast this woman was kind. She had no children of her own, which explains why it was she liked us.

"She's barren," Ghalia's son said. "She's been to visit all the holy men and *fqihs*, but to no avail."

"Maybe it's her husband who's sterile," Daria's son responded. "A woman like her must be able to have children, fat and fleshy ones at that."

"People say he's impotent," Ghalia's son said. "How can a virtual cripple like him possibly have sex with a woman? She's just submissive and unlucky."

All such things were a mystery to us. Every husband and wife was supposed to do whatever married people do, no matter how crippled, insane, ugly, or bald they might be. One woman was an exception, the bean seller's wife; she had cheated on her hillbilly husband with another man. I was the only boy who had not slept with her. I couldn't stand how filthy she looked; I found her utterly repulsive. She could always be found in the dung, animal droppings, and manure; she used them to feed the fire under a huge barrel. Every day she would put almost half a bag of black-eyed peas into it. She was on her knees all day, either blowing on the fire with her breath or fanning it with a piece of zinc or cardboard in her hand. Her soft buttocks would stick up in the air.

"He can't be impotent," Daria's son replied. "His legs are crippled, but the rest of his body is perfectly normal. Poisonous oil may have paralyzed a lot of people's feet, but it didn't cripple their legs, thighs or the rest of their body."

"How do you know he's not impotent?" Ghalia's son asked. "If he weren't, nothing like this would have happened."

"Such things can happen even if a woman loves her husband."

We could not understand—or at least, I couldn't—how such a thing could happen to a woman, whether she loved her husband or not. If it had happened in my absence, I would never have believed it, but in this particular case I'd seen everything for myself. I came to realize that, one way or another, everything impossible in life may actually happen.

The police jeep had stopped by the tin shack. We were running behind it and managed to catch up easily. The loose dirt on the coast-road was slowing it down, and it had almost stopped several times. We, too, stopped some way away in case they might suddenly decide to take us into custody.

"Her husband must be a *kif* dealer," one of us said.

"He certainly is, but I've never seen him smoking."

"Many *kif* dealers don't smoke it."

When they raised the flap at the back of the jeep, the husband was thrown to the ground like a bag of hay. He had trouble getting up because his crippled legs were completely useless. He didn't have handcuffs on or anything of that sort.

"So, it's nothing to do with him."

"They have stolen his shack."

"She isn't in the shack. She only comes back in the evening. They say she's been lucky enough to find a job as a washerwoman with the French."

"She knows all the officers, even the head of the naval base."

Leaning on the jeep, the man struggled to get to his feet. We kept watching the scene from afar. First one policeman got out, then a second. The first made a show of threatening us, so we scattered. The younger ones ran away and disappeared inside dark tin shacks. The second policeman kept kicking at the door of the shack, while the first one went over to join him and peered inside. He started kicking the door, too, but far more violently than the other one.

"Maybe the police have some robbers trapped inside. I bet it's Buserwal who's inside the shack."

"Look behind you. Buserwal's over there. If he could hear you, he'd slit your throat."

"If it isn't him, then it's got to be Walad Tamou."

The two policemen kept kicking the tin door with their boots and peering inside. This went on for more than ten minutes. The cripple was still leaning on the jeep, looking distracted. Although it was obviously a struggle, he managed to walk a short way with the help of a long stick. His coloring looked different, bluer than it should be—a blend of blue and yellow. His turban was unwound, with part of it dangling over his shoulder. As he tried to fix his turban, he was looking really flustered.

The two policemen kept on kicking the door and hurled some really foul curses at us. But, even if our mothers had heard what they were saying, they would not have been able to answer back.

"If the robbers don't come out soon, that policeman may well set the shack on fire."

"He can't do that."

"I bet you he can. It's very easy for someone with a mouth like a garbage disposal."

"If he heard you, he'd shoot you for sure. He could easily hit you. I'm sure he's practiced on rabbits."

The foul-mouthed policeman moved back. One of his feet sank into a hole, and he almost fell over. Charging at the door like a bull, he managed to get inside the shack. Now we were able to get closer. The second policeman was much nicer, but even so he still unbuckled his nightstick and took out his handcuffs. The cripple kept watching distractedly. He pointed his cane at us, but we realized that he couldn't hurt us. Had he been able, he certainly would have done so. It was only later that I realized he could have done us some real harm; after all, the instinct for evil is just as powerful as that for good. The second policeman disappeared inside the tin shack. Or rather, he didn't completely disappear; we could still see half his body. If we had moved even closer, we could have seen everything.

Now the sound of voices could be heard, more like wails, sobs, and cries for help; sounds steeped in human weakness and shame. The cripple was clearly shaken to the core. He almost gave the impression that he'd been cured of his ongoing condition, because he reacted in a way that no one with his problems could possibly have done. Later on I learned that a shock like this one can make even a cripple leap to his feet and lay a standing man out flat.

First, the woman was pushed out of the shack, then her crippled husband spat on her. The policeman didn't stop him from taking his revenge. In fact, he helped the cripple, using his nightstick to poke her in the buttocks and push her toward the jeep. She was carrying a brazier and *tajine*, while another woman who hadn't had enough time to put on her *jallaba* properly followed her, weeping and slapping her thighs. Two men walked behind them: one was wearing a hat, and the other seemed to be missing an eye. Both men's hands were tied. One of them kept shouting.

"I'll never do it again," he yelled shamelessly. "Who's going to look after my wife and children?"

All the young children and old folks around us started whistling. The husband collapsed on the dusty soil in a heap.

"Oh my God," he groaned. "How much that woman has changed! From angel to devil, and in no time at all. I couldn't believe what I was seeing; I kept trying to convince myself that she wasn't involved. I told myself that she couldn't possibly do anything so disgusting."

One of the two men, who was weeping, kept lagging behind, so the policeman hit him on the shoulder. He pushed all four of them toward the police jeep. The brazier and *tajine* almost fell off her head several times, and eventually they did. Sauce and meat were spilled all over the dusty soil. Our mouths started watering as we noticed the greasy sauce reflecting the sunshine. But the foul-mouthed policeman started trampling over everything. Giving her a slap, he shoved her into the jeep, then pushed the other three in after her. Once the two policemen had got in also, the jeep moved off.

Now everyone started coming together in clusters, then separating. Insults were thrown back and forth. The jeep had some trouble turning around, but then it came speeding back toward us. We all tripped over each other, but managed to save ourselves from the foul-mouthed policeman's crazy driving. Behind the vanishing jeep a dust-cloud arose. The roar of the engine drowned out the wails and moans coming from inside.

The cripple started laughing hysterically, banging the ground with his stick. Everyone was chasing the police jeep. Some people picked up stones and started throwing them in the air. Everyone kept talking about the woman and insulting her. She would be going to hell for sure, they said. All four of them would.

I wasn't with them and didn't throw any stones. I preferred to stay at the back, wondering to myself all the while if she was actually a nice, kind-hearted woman.

THE KING OF THE JINN

(1984)

Shamharush, King of the Jinn

On both sides of the road, trees stretched upwards into the sky. Even so, they still left room for a view of a few green mountain peaks that were shrouded in dark-gray clouds. As the thick cloud-cover moved slowly across the sky, it all suggested some terrifying, gruesome unknown. The greenness of the mountains kept moving upward till it blended completely with the dark clouds.

Two male passengers wrapped in their warm *jallaba*s stood up. Helped by the father and driver, they managed to get the disabled young man off the bus. They sat him down by the roadside like some kind of sack. Without saying a word, he simply looked all around him, resigning himself to his fate with a stony indifference. As the men climbed back on the bus, the mother of the crippled young man blessed them for helping.

"All in God's good cause!" one of the men replied, then covered his head with his *jallaba* hood.

He avoided looking at the mother; the only woman he ever looked at was his wife. At the same time, the driver's assistant clambered up the back of the bus and started handing down some of the baggage. The woman and her husband took turns grabbing it. The bus driver remained silent as he watched the scene; he was smoking a cigarette, his elbows leaning on the wheel. The people sitting on the driver's side looked out at the young man by the roadside, who was watching the driver's assistant.

When the bus pulled away, the woman sat down beside her son on the pile of bags.

"Are you hungry, Sulaiman?" she asked.

"No. Have we reached Sidi Shamharush?"

"I don't know, son," the mother replied. "Ask your father."

"Not yet," the husband answered, without looking at them. "We're in Asni. The driver told me we still have seven kilometers to go to reach Imlil. From there we'll go up to Sidi Shamharush."

"Is there any kind of transport to Imlil?" asked the wife. "I can't carry Sulaiman on my back the way I did when he was young. I'm old now, and he's a young man."

"Why are you acting so worried?" he replied. "I've been told that there are lots of trucks, taxis, and carts to take people from Asni to Imlil."

The husband walked into the middle of the empty road and looked off into the distance to see if any other means of transport was coming. Nothing. There was only silence and the sound of birds chirping on the tree branches.

When a cart emerged from a dirt track in the closely packed trees, the woman sprang to her feet.

"A cart!" said the husband. "Stay there."

"It isn't as cold as we were told it would be," the young man said.

"That's right," said the mother, "but Sidi Shamharush is surrounded by snow. We're not there yet."

She watched her husband silently as he walked toward the driver of the cart, which was being pulled by a donkey. The donkey seemed to be glued to the ground, so the driver set about dealing with the situation. The cart came to a stop in the grass beside the paved road. The husband now asked him to take them all to Imlil.

"I wish I could," replied the man, "but this isn't my cart. It belongs to the orchard's owner. I wish I had a cart of my own! Are you going to Sidi Shamharush?"

"Yes, we are."

"Don't waste your time here. Go over there to the left, behind that white building. Do you see it? There you'll find a stand with carts to take people to Imlil."

The man hit the donkey with his stick and made a noise to get it moving again. The cart started off along the paved road. Meanwhile, the husband waited till a speeding car had passed, then came back.

"Wait for me," he said. "I'll go get a cart. I won't be long. The carts are over there, behind that white building."

"Ah, if only you could walk, Sulaiman!" said his mother as she watched the skinny donkey move away. "We could walk those few kilometers and save the money we're going to have to pay the cart driver. But, with God's will and the blessing of Sidi Shamharush, the King of the Jinn, you'll be able to walk."

When the cart arrived, Sulaiman's eyes gleamed with joy. Soon he would be reaching Sidi Shamharush. After that, he'd be able to walk like everybody else. He could chase after the boys who kept yelling "Hey cripple!" at him. No one would be able to call him that anymore. He would not have to crawl; he, too, would be walking.

The cart-driver helped the husband. They grabbed the young man under his armpits, while his mother put her hands under his backside; his legs were splayed apart. His mother laid out a sheet in the cart, and they laid him on his back. The wood cracked. That made the donkey look back, as it twitched its ears and raised one of its hind legs.

"Are you in pain, son?" the boy's mother asked him.

He shook his head. He was staring up at the verdant peaks shrouded behind the dark clouds. Up there was Sidi Shamharush. How many cripples he had made walk up there!

Now the piles of baggage were put on the cart, and the husband and the wife climbed up. The cart started climbing the narrow road toward Imlil. They heard a Jeep horn and made way for it; it was full of European men and women.

"There are lots of Europeans up there, too," the cart driver said. "They come here to climb the mountains; they're everywhere. They use ropes to climb up to Sidi Shamharush, so he has laid a curse on many of them. They've fallen and died."

"So why do they keep coming back?" asked the husband.

"They love mountain climbing, but they aren't satisfied just with that. They do other bad things that displease Sidi Shamharush."

Alongside the road were some white buildings hidden behind the trees, and huts and barns as well. Herds of cattle and goats pranced around the open spaces; some of them craned their necks to reach the dangling tree-branches.

"Ouch!" cried the young man as he fell backwards. His mother rushed to help him sit up. One of the cart's wheels had fallen into a rut. The driver was used to such problems, so he paid no attention. He started hitting the donkey with his stick, and it stretched its head forward as it tried its utmost to pull the cart out of the hole. After the driver had hit it a number of times, it eventually succeeded, and the cart continued on its way.

"During the election campaign," the driver told the husband, "they promised to fix this road, but they haven't done it."

"They promised us many other things as well," the husband replied, "but they haven't done any of them."

"What can a dead man say to the people who are preparing him for burial? Not a single thing, of course! But God will repay both burier and buried!"

Another car passed them at full speed, pulling a trailer with a canvas cover.

"Are they Europeans, too?" asked the husband.

"Yes. You'll see for yourself. We're getting closer now."

"I've been told that people ride mules up to the King of the Jinn."

"Yes, that's true. But most Europeans use climbing ropes. I'll take you to a nice woman; you can rent a couple of mules from her. She's from my tribe. Poor woman! All her relatives are dead, and she lives alone with the six mules. Oh, sorry, five. One of the dirty Europeans rented one six months ago, and both disappeared."

"Even Europeans steal?"

"Tell me about it! But Sidi Shamharush won't forget."

"What's the matter, Sulaiman?" the mother asked. "We're getting closer, son. With God's will and Sidi Shamharush's blessings, you'll be cured."

Some houses and shops came into view on the left side. There were few people around. The cart went through an unpaved extension of the road that was full of stones and small, muddy puddles of stagnant water. The place was almost completely empty. There was a dirty square where some buses and donkey-carts were parked. The man hit the donkey with his stick and looked to the left, but there was no car or truck coming, just pedestrians. An old woman slipped into a puddle. A man rushed over to pull her out of the mud, but left without bothering to find out what she was going to do next.

The driver drove the cart to another square, one with short green plants on the side, and stopped. It was not all that far from the first square, which was covered in dung and animal remains. In the other unpaved square there were mounds of wet trash, as well.

"Come with me," the driver told the husband. "Get the young man and your wife down. We'll go see the woman to get you two mules. As I told you, she is a decent woman."

Without saying a word the husband jumped down from the cart. He followed the driver along the narrow street until they reached an empty space where there was a mud-brick house; trees and mules were also visible. The cart-owner went in through the open door and brought out an old woman with a greenish-black tattoo on her chin. She did not speak Arabic, but spoke a few words in Tamazight before going back inside. She left it to the driver to untether two mules and get forty dirhams from the husband.

"She's a nice woman," the driver said. "You can keep the mules as long as you wish, but you need to take good care of them. They sell hay up there."

"We'll only stay for two days."

"Visitors usually only stay one night. You'll see how your son will be cured, God willing. Sidi Shamharush never dashes the hopes of anyone who comes to him asking for his help."

The man urged the two mules into action. He slapped one of them on its rear with his hand while making a particular sound. With that, the two mules started moving obediently as though they were used to dealing with the driver. They kept going until they had crossed the clearing and were heading down the alley toward the square. They knew what their task was and would certainly perform just as well when they were going up to the mountaintop where the shrine of Sidi Shamharush, the King of the Jinn, was to be found.

The driver helped the father lift his son. The father grabbed him under his belly, and the mother put their baggage into one of the mules' saddlebags, then got up on the other mule.

"Don't worry about the young man," the driver said. "He won't fall off. The mules are very used to the road."

He now hit the mule under the belly, making the same clicking sound as he did so. The mule started moving, followed by the second, which the mother was riding. Two hours later they reached the top of the mountain, where there were rooms for rent everywhere. There was a white dome, as well.

Some Europeans were skiing, while others crowded into the only bar. A short man came running over to the two mules, followed by three others. Together they eased the young man down and brought him to a place right beside the door of one of the rooms.

"It's not very expensive," one of the men told the father. "You can stay here as long as you like. God willing, your son will be cured. Sidi Shamharush has a deal with our grandfather. If your intention is good, your son will certainly be cured. You must doubt neither our grandfather's ability nor the promise Sidi Shamharush gave him."

"Who could have any doubts, Sir?" the father said.

"Many people do, and our grandfather has managed to cause them all sorts of problems. Can you believe that the Minister of Islamic Affairs and the Minister of Tourism have tried many times to take this place over? Do you know what the result has been? Of course not! I'm not scared of anybody, so I'm quite willing to tell you. Any employee of these two ministries who has tried to accomplish that has been punished, suffering either an injury, fracture, or some other misfortune. Now that they've realized what they're dealing with, they won't be trying it again. So, let your intentions be genuine. Put your whole trust in the promise that the King made explicit to our grandfather."

"We have no doubts, Sir," said the husband, looking at his wife, who was trying to cover her son with a wool blanket. "That's why we have endured such a hard journey."

"Give a *baraka* tip to the servants of this holy place," the man went on. "You'll pay the rent when you decide to leave. Everything's here–hay for the mules, and a barn."

With that, he pointed to a site covered with pine trees, behind which were patches of white snow with black spots sprinkled throughout. The father nodded, then handed each of them a dirham.

"What's this supposed to be?" said the man waving the dirham. "Are you kidding? I'm afraid your intention isn't pure."

"Who would dare to jest in front of such a holy place?" the father commented.

"Then find some more dirhams. Ask your wife to prepare you some hot tea. It's very cold. Go and get warm, or you'll catch cold."

"Okay, Sir."

He gave the man some more dirhams, then joined his wife. The other three men were standing a little distance away. As they chatted in front of the dome, they seemed unconcerned about what was happening and quite willing to trust their friend.

"Sulaiman can crawl on his own inside the room now. When shall we take him to the dome?"

"I didn't talk to the man about it. Go in and make us some hot tea."

"All right. Come inside and get out of the cold."

In the morning, Sulaiman crawled his way to the dome of Sidi Shamharush, the King of the Jinn, with his mother walking beside him. Other cripples were there as well. From time to time his mother made him some tea and *ka'b al-ghazal* cookies, but his teeth were hurting and so he couldn't chew them. The mother learned from conversations with the other cripples' families that some of them who had visited the place many times were still not able to stand up. But in fact, Sidi Shamharush knew what he was doing.

In the evening, Sulaiman crawled back to the room with his father and mother, and they shared food with a woman whom the mother had met at the dome. A widow, she was living with her brother who had a crippled son. In fact, she was the one who had told the mother that they had been visiting the shrine for two years. Only the will of Sidi Shamharush determined that the boy would not stand on his feet this year.

"We can't stay more than two days," said the husband. "You know I can't pay more."

"Poor Sulaiman!" the mother said. "If his father were rich, he could sacrifice a bull to Sidi Shamharush."

"Sidi Shamharush doesn't need a bull. He's King of the Jinn. Do you realize that he owns all the sea-pearls and golden cities? He only walks on musk and amber."

"But sacrificing a bull in front of Sidi Shamharush's dome is the right and proper thing to do."

Sulaiman was listening to what they were saying and staring at his spindly legs. Looking through the crack in the door at the dark night outside, he imagined an army of jinn invading their tiny room; at their head was an old jinni with a tail and two horns. He would extend his long, bright-nailed hands toward Sulaiman's spindly legs. "Stand up!" he would say in a soft voice. The army of jinn would leave, and Sulaiman would stand up, push the door with his strong foot, and walk out into the dark.

"Drink your tea," his mother told him. "You need to get some sleep. We have only one day left, and we're going to spend it in the dome. God willing, my son Sulaiman, you'll be cured."

Next morning, one of the dome's servants knocked on the door. The mother went to open it, then came back and disappeared to talk to her husband. When the man saw the husband, he gave a lazy yawn.

"Are you going to stay," he asked, "or are you leaving?"

"We're only going to spend one more day here till my son can stand up."

"What matters is that, even if he doesn't stand up today, he'll stand up somewhere else. You need to know that the last bus for Asni is at 6:30 p.m. Maybe, if your son doesn't stand up here today, he'll stand up on the bus. That's often happened."

"But what if he doesn't stand up on the bus?"

"Come back next spring. There are periods when Sidi Shamharush is absent, but no one knows when."

"Thank you, Sir."

At 2:00 pm that day, the two mules were again proceeding downhill.

Snake Hunting

J'm just an old widow," she said, "childless, and with no one but God. If I don't defend myself, who will?"

"What worries me," another woman said, "is that one of these days a snake's going to kill you."

"When God really wills someone to die, even if it's from a snake bite, nobody can stop it. And I can kill a whole load of snakes in this region throughout the year, but they still never die out."

She was renowned for killing snakes. She had a special way of searching them out, under haystacks and rocks. She wore snakeskin bracelets and belts of different colors and sold snakeheads to itinerant merchants in exchange for sugar, tea, oil, or soap. She'd been told that the heads could be used for magic and sometimes even to cure children. But never in her life had it occurred to her to bewitch even the person closest to her, her now-deceased husband. Magic's taboo, and the magician's fate is known only to God. What she did know for sure was that every female witch came to a nasty end: broken legs, blindness, or diseased children and livestock.

The other woman had a basket full of clay on her head. "Sister," the woman said staring at her, "I'm amazed that God has endowed you with enough courage and strength to deal with snakes inside their nests."

"How can I be afraid?" she replied. "I've seen my grandfather as naked as God made man. He got on a horse in the middle of the night and chased a group of thieves who'd stolen our cattle. Neither the cold nor the thieves' rifles put him off. That night I watched him chasing after the thieves and firing into the air. He only came home once he'd managed to recover the cattle. My grandmother grabbed a cloth to cover him up so that we wouldn't see his private parts. How can a woman with a grandfather like that be afraid of snakes?!"

As the woman departed, the old widow stayed where she was, leaning over slightly. She had wrapped parts of her body in colorful snakeskins. She was scattering grain for the chickens and calling to two roosters who were standing far apart from the group. Sticking her fingers into the soil, she grabbed a clump and threw it at the two roosters. They immediately rejoined the group, their colors gleaming brightly in the sunlight.

She made sure to count her chickens every two hours; after all, a snake or some other animal might come by, or even a human being. Forty years ago, there had been foxes and wolves as well, but they had finally disappeared. They may have been killed by the same people who had built those widely scattered houses; they only used them at night to do things with women.

The number of chickens had not decreased, nor would it. She was determined to keep them all, since she never sold any chicken until it got really plump. Her chickens were always the plumpest and her eggs the biggest, and that made her proud. Other people's chickens laid eggs that were the size of pigeons' eggs or else shaped like goats' dung.

She waved a small dry branch in the air and walked toward her mud-and-hay shack. Just then she spotted 'Azouz coming toward her; he had just got off his cart. She smiled because she'd thought of something to tell him that would get him annoyed, even though he never lost his temper with her.

"How are you doing, little mouse?" she heard him ask just a few steps away from her. "Still hunting snakes?"

"Even men don't dare go after snakes. Don't you remember when you were eight and couldn't handle a single snake? You could barely kill it. What kind of manhood is that supposed to be? You became a joke for your wives and daughters."

"Unlike you, we never sucked poison from our mother's breasts."

"What kind of manhood is that? Your master's dead, the master of all men. That's why I refused to marry again after he died. No one else is worth his pinky."

"God have mercy on him! Why are you talking about the dead, you old mouse?"

"Your wife's no better off than me."

They both started laughing. She threw the small branch to the ground, then brushed the dust off her hands, and wiped them on her dress.

"Did you come from Ain Diab?" she asked.

"Yes, but I left the cart on the country road by the coast. I've carried two bags of forage sacks to the village on my back. I stayed clear of the main road. You know what the gendarmes can do if they catch me."

"I know."

"We needed a sack of sugar, too. We'll divide it between us. That's why I'm here."

"Leave me a kilogram or two. But I don't have any money."

"Ever since he's died, you've been one of us. When have we ever asked you for money? You can pay with a chicken. I'll see about it when I talk to the group."

He headed back to his cart. "If you need any seeds," he said, "I have them. Come over and get them, or else I can send them back with the little girl, Manana."

For a moment she had the feeling that she wasn't really alone. And yet, when she thought about the damned snakes that had kept threatening her chickens all down the years, she still felt lonely. If her chickens caught a disease—that would be God's will, there was nothing to do about it. Once she realized that she could still kill snakes, she was certain that God would never use hunger to kill her.

She had a special way of killing snakes. Whenever she heard the chickens' clucking, she would lie in wait. Once she located the snake's hiding place; she'd pounce, grab it by the tail, and start twirling it in the air till it became dizzy. She would then strike it repeatedly against a rock till it and the area around it were stained with blood. Once she sensed that the body wasn't resisting any more, she'd throw it away and watch it from a distance. Only rarely did it move any more; usually it died instantly because she would never discard the body till she was sure it was dead. Once in a while, a snake might escape and hide between stones in the wall, but the old widow would wait the whole day till it came out again.

No sooner had she gone inside the house than she heard a voice calling her, one that she instantly recognized. She came out into the courtyard again.

"Manana!" she said, "Come over here. Do you want an egg to boil?"

"My father's sent this bag," the girl said. "It's full of bird-seed."

"Come here."

The girl was barefoot and her head was wrapped in a torn scarf. She was half-carrying a *doum* bag full of birdseed that was dragging along the ground. She put the bag down and started scratching her buttocks and hair.

The old woman watched her. "You're filthy," she said. "I'm sure you didn't let your mother wash you. You'll get head-lice in your hair; that shortens people's lives. You need to have a long life so you can get married and give your mother grandchildren."

The old woman came over, picked up the bag of feed, and hung it on a wooden peg protruding from the wall. She went inside the house and came out with an egg which she offered the girl. "Don't break it!" she said.

"Do you still hunt snakes?" Manana asked.

"These days they've disappeared," she answered. "But if I stopped doing it, there wouldn't be a single living chicken."

"I'm afraid a snake's going to bite you one of these days."

"Don't be scared. I'm still strong enough to kill all the snakes in Oulad Jarar. Do you want me to boil the egg for you?"

"No. I'll do it at home."

"Boil it and eat it alone. Don't share it with anyone."

"Okay."

The girl disappeared behind the clump of trees that served as a fence around the old woman's house on the west side. Near the door was a clay brazier that the old woman had filled with dry coal hours earlier. She was waiting for the fire to catch, but, even though she had added a bit of kerosene, it was still useless. At first the flames had flared up, but it hadn't been enough to ignite the dry coal. Once in a while she heard crackling and sparkling sounds coming from the brazier and checked to see if the coals had ignited. She fanned it several times with a piece of zinc and blew on it. Eventually she put a fish and carrot *tajine* on top of it along with a few sardines. She still didn't know whom she'd be sharing it with today.

As she was sitting there on the hot sand, she heard the chickens clucking and scattering. Assuming that it was a snake, she got up and went over to wait for it. She peered into the weeds. Then she heard Manana's voice.

"Is it the snake?" she asked.

She turned to look at the girl. "You didn't go home?"

"No, I dropped the egg, and it broke."

"I warned you. Stay there so the snake won't bite you. I'll boil you another egg."

The chickens were obviously scared; they were running everywhere and jumping over short branches. The old woman looked for signs of the snake, but found nothing. It was just a frog crawling along slowly, with its head buried in its body.

"No snake," the old woman said, "just a frog,"

"Kill it the way you do snakes," the girl said.

"No, I don't kill frogs," the old woman replied. "Come on, you do it. Learn how to kill frogs before snakes."

The girl came over and watched the fat frog. "Quick, pounce on it," the old woman told her. "And grab it by the leg. Twirl it in the air till it's dizzy, then smash it against that rock."

Manana was scared, but she still managed to pounce and grab the frog's leg. She started twirling it in the air like a ragdoll. The woman kept cheering her on.

"Keep going! It's not dizzy enough yet."

Going over to the rock, Manana smashed the frog against it. Its innards were splattered all over the place, but the body was still twitching in its death throes. The old woman went over, looked at the dead body, and tugged at the girl's arm.

"That's how I deal with snakes," she said. "Now you need to wash your hands. I'll boil you an egg. Next time, I'll teach you how to kill a snake."

Antonio

He was sitting on the doorstep of the deserted club. As the sun moved to the west, it was still hot. His legs were spread-eagled, his pants hiked up to his knees. His sandals were completely worn through. Occasionally he would raise his head toward the north to a point where a picture of a female flamenco dancer still hung on the wall; it was etched on a metal sheet that was almost falling over. But as he stared at the picture, his expression showed a complete lack of interest.

I noticed two children playing near him; actually, they were not so much playing as fighting. The girl had beaten the boy by successfully pushing his head into the street sewer. He had started screaming and yelling for his mother. With that, the girl had let him go. She'd gone over to the doorstep of the building across the street and sat down.

Antonio watched the whole thing without displaying the slightest emotion. The street was empty. Once in a while a car or motorcycle passed by. The girl and the boy grabbed each other again; they started screaming, then pulled apart. Every time they started fighting, Antonio just stared at them with complete indifference.

I felt bad for the boy being beaten by the girl, but realized that he would certainly get his revenge when they both grew up—the way men usually do with women. But then, he might still turn out to be the loser. Antonio had certainly been a loser years ago. That's just a guess, of course. But, given that such things are beyond human comprehension, everyone has the right to speculate about victories and defeats.

Once again, the girl managed to stick the boy's head into the sewage drain. I listened to his moans as he croaked out his insults and cries for help. His tiny legs were thrashing in the air, but the girl was merciless and kept pushing his puny body into the drain. I was worried she was going to kill him. I was about to yell at her, but just then I noticed her fall back into the street on her backside. Her spindly, fennel-like thighs were exposed. The boy had managed to kick her and get half his body out of the drain.

Antonio still watched indifferently, but he kept talking to himself. The sun was in his eyes, so he couldn't look westward; the slanting rays were glancing off his thin frame, and by now he was soaking with sweat. The hair on his pale legs was glistening. Oblivious to everything around him, he started scratching his legs hard with his long, black, dirty fingernails. He grabbed his hat with his other hand, took it off, and placed it upside down next to him on the doorstep. But even if he had put it down by his feet right in front of him, no one would have dropped a measly coin in it. After all, the street was completely empty. His bald pate was gleaming in the sunshine, and the dry wind kept ruffling the hair on his temples. He started rubbing his head with his hands.

Now I spotted another man carrying a bag and scavenging in the garbage. The garbage truck had not come round yet, and, in any case, garbage-men will sometimes ignore certain streets where the inhabitants don't give them enough tips. The man scavenged for quite awhile, but all he dug out was half a doll; he put it in his bag. He crossed the street to where Antonio was sitting.

"Scram!" he said.

As Antonio stared wearily at the scavenger, the man repeated his threat. Antonio shook his head.

"Go on," the man said again. "Get out, you lousy Spaniard. You'll get sunstroke and die."

"No," replied Antonio. "Leave me alone. I'm not going to die of sunstroke."

"Get up!"

"No."

"I told you, you're going to die."

"No."

The man shook his head. He left Antonio, crossed the street again, and started scavenging in the other garbage can. Antonio started cleaning between his toes; I can only imagine the stench. "Ugh!" I thought to myself. "That's absolutely disgusting."

He wiped his fingers on his faded pants, which were held up by a belt—even though the pants had no loops for it. At this point the girl and boy were moving closer to each other and talking. A temporary truce, at least.

The girl's mother looked out the window and waved her fat, white arm. "Soumia," she yelled. "What are you doing in this heat? Why don't you leave that boy alone and stay inside? When your father comes home from work, I'm going to tell him everything. It's time you were married. We need to find a man to take you in hand."

The mother disappeared. The girl wasn't bothered by her mother's remarks. Meanwhile, Antonio kept rubbing his hand over his bald head, almost as though he could feel the sun's effect on his scalp. He picked up the hat and put it on his head. Looking down at the curb, which was missing some of its paving-stones, he noticed a small hole a short distance from where he was sitting, with a plastic bag and a small stone in it.

Now the boy's mother looked out the window. She was wearing a scarf. She began shaking out a sheepskin, utterly unconcerned as to whether there might be someone under the window. She noticed her son, who was now clutching the girl.

"You son of a bitch!" she yelled. "Isn't it about time you gave up that little viper? But no, more's the pity. You won't leave her alone until you've caused a huge scandal in the neighborhood. Most people give birth to human beings, but I've produced a devil."

She kept on shaking the sheepskin, then disappeared from the window. The street was still empty. The two children were still edging closer to each other, then moving back. The girl was clearly trying to employ her feminine wiles to get him back inside the drain so she could close the iron gate on him and relax. That's just a guess.

As long as things are beyond human comprehension, people have a perfect right to assess a human's ability to tolerate spending time in sewers.

All that said, the boy seemed to have steeled himself this time so he would not have to get stuck inside the drain again. He would not have to scream; the girl would not fall in the road on her backside and show her naked, fennel-shaped legs; her mother would not yell at him; and his own mother would not call the girl a viper. Of course, that's all guesswork.

Sometimes, Antonio stared up at the window across the street, shifting his gaze from the picture of the Flamenco dancer to his pair of sandals, to the curb, then back to the window. Soumia's younger sister might be up there behind the window. Once he had given her a tiny turtle. I presume that he's never had any children; Soumia's sister is the only one he really cares about. She loves him too. But in fact, she wasn't there. She may have gone to Sidi Abdarrahman beach with her elder sister.

Antonio stared up at the window; but he was dazzled by the bright sunshine and shielded his forehead with his heavily veined hand, which looked just like a hat-brim.

The girl picked up a pointed stick with irregular knots on it. As I stood there watching, she talked to the boy. Maybe he agreed with her idea, maybe not, but, when she started walking away, he followed her—implying that he eventually agreed. She walked slowly toward Antonio. Lying on her stomach on the curb, she started digging in the dirt as though she were searching for a worm. The little boy stood a few meters back, in the hot sunshine, watching her. Then he moved closer and sat on the ground. Now it was his mother's turn to look out the window.

"You're sitting in the dirt, you son of a bitch," she yelled. "Your mother's hands are already worn out from so much washing." And with that she disappeared again.

From time to time Antonio looked at the girl as she was digging. Crawling on her stomach, she came closer and closer to Antonio till she was poking at his toes with the stick. He pulled his feet away as though he'd been bitten by a mosquito. The girl laughed and did it again. The boy kept watching her with a forlorn expression, but eventually he decided to join in the fun and egg her on. Antonio kept pulling his feet away wearily, but she kept on doing it.

"Go away," he muttered.

As he opened his mouth, saliva glistened on his lips in the bright sunshine. The girl was scared. She stood up quickly and moved away.

"Is the turtle you gave to my sister male or female?" she asked Antonio.

At first he did not bother to answer, but started scratching his legs again. His pants were pulled up as far as his knees.

"It's a female."

"You need to bring my sister a male one," she went on. "And a bag full of lettuce as well."

Antonio kept staring up at the window, then at the sky, trying all the while to avoid looking straight at the sun. Once again the girl lay down on her stomach in front of him, and so did the boy. She started poking him with the stick again.

"I am talking to you," she said. "But you won't answer,"

"Don't wear yourself out," the boy said. "He'll never talk,"

"I'm going to keep trying. He isn't mute."

Her mother looked out of the window. "What are you doing to that poor man, you little slut?" she yelled. "If you get your clothes dirty, I swear you won't eat a thing today. Stand up, Monsieur Antonio. That little devil will poke your eye out with her stick."

The girl and boy ran away and took refuge in the doorway of a building. The street was still empty. The mother disappeared from the window.

Now a Garde Mobile patrol car appeared, cruising slowly down the street. "We'd better go up to the roof," the girl said, "or else they'll take us to the station."

They disappeared and shut the door behind them. When the patrol car came closer, one of the men jumped out of the back. He did not come from that particular town; perhaps an officer relative of his had put in a good word, so they'd hired him as a *mokhazni*. He grabbed Antonio by the shirt and yanked him to his feet. A group of beggars and homeless men could be seen staring cautiously out of the back of the van. The officer glared at the *mokhazni*.

"You ass!" he yelled. "Who told you to get out? Are you trying to arrest a European? Are you out of your mind? Do you want to cause us problems?"

The man immediately loosened his grip. Antonio went back and sat on the club's doorstep, calmly observing the patrol car. For a moment his aged heart had been pounding, but now it had calmed down.

"Next time," the officer continued, "don't get out unless I tell you."

"Yes, Sir," replied the *mokhazni*.

"Get in."

"Yes, Sir," yelled the *mokhazni*.

"Load of donkeys!"

"Yes, Sir." yelled the *mokhazni*.

The patrol-van went on its way. The men inside all wished they could be Europeans, too, so they wouldn't get arrested. Antonio watched as the van drove away slowly down the street.

The scavenger had left the same street awhile ago, still searching through the trash bins.

An Ongoing Summer

Brigitte was cooking something in the kitchen. I could tell that François was saying something to me, but I couldn't hear it. I was on the balcony looking at the minaret of the mosque across the street. It was decorated with red and blue lights, apparently for a religious celebration of some kind. At the time, I wasn't feeling particularly religious. I was just looking; I've no idea why, exactly. When I heard François calling me, I left the balcony and went inside.

"What do you want?" I asked.

"Didn't you hear me?"

"I was looking at the minaret."

"Don't be funny."

"Go pray. Maybe God will help you."

"Do you want to pray?"

"For what?"

"For hell."

"Why did you call me in?" I asked angrily. "Let me get some fresh air on the balcony."

The stench of wine on his breath was disgusting, not least because it was cheap wine and I had not yet had any myself. When I'm drunk, I don't bother how the wine smells; I don't even notice. But when I'm not drunk, I can't stand it. I even tell myself that drunkards must feel downtrodden and dirty. They certainly shouldn't take to drink as a way of solving problems that can only be properly settled when one is completely sober.

"You're drunk," I told François. "I can't bear jokes."

"François," I heard Brigitte yell from the kitchen. "Leave Hamdoun alone!"

"Are you jealous of your husband?" François asked in a hoarse voice.

"What are you saying, you filth?" I yelled.

"Sit down," François said. "I'll tell you a secret. Can you guess?"

"Maybe."

"Okay then, guess."

"You're drunk, and you're going to annoy me."

"You're wrong. Look. Unblock your ears so I can tell you. Are they open? Like this. Very good. Brigitte, my wife, is in love with you."

"I told you you were going to upset me—and Brigitte, as well."

"No matter," he replied, his breath still reeking of cheap wine. "We're both always frank; we never keep things secret from each other. She told me."

"That she loves me."

"Yes. You can ask her for yourself"

He called his wife. "Brigitte," he said. "Come here and tell him yourself. My dear, we're being totally frank with each other."

"Stop this nonsense," said Brigitte from the kitchen. "Leave Hamdoun alone. Let him get some fresh air."

That suggestion was addressed more to me than to him. I stood up, walked over to the balcony and looked again at the night and the lights on the minaret. I enjoyed being scorched by the breeze, with its scents of plants and roses from the street and the public park near the house. This year, it was still hot at the end of October, and summer was extending well into November. It was very pleasant to sit on the balcony or in the park in the evening; that's precisely what I'd been doing for the past two months. I would often buy a bottle of wine, sit on the balcony, count the stars, and imagine things faraway that might not even exist beyond those infinite horizons.

My imagination often teases me by focusing on just one thing: I create a picture of other lands and suns stretching away ad infinitum. I give my imagination free rein till the wine gets the better of me. Then I turn up the radio because I like to yell. Even when I hear someone knocking on the door, I don't bother getting up to see who it is. That never worries me. I'm much more interested in relaxing and being intoxicated by both night and wine. Even if I was sure there was a woman on the other side of the door, it would make no difference.

Brigitte was at least twelve years older than François, whereas I was just two years older. Even so, he still looked older than me. Being with him was not all that enjoyable; nothing he told me was of much interest. I found it all a bit childish. Sometimes when he expressed an opinion, he looked at Brigitte to make sure he was right. In fact, he had no personality at all. He didn't really love her, but she made it clear that life without him would be impossible. She loved him, or so she claimed: the kind of love that no one else in the whole world can gauge. For me, personally, I placed a good deal of value on it. In particular, I was well aware of what it meant for a woman to love a man twelve years younger than herself.

The night air was stimulating. Streetlights, evenly spaced along the street and in squares and rectangular spaces further away, provoked an endless feeling of tension inside me. I was listening to the dialogue going on behind my back, but could not make out what Brigitte was saying. As she left the kitchen, her voice grew gradually louder. As she came over to the balcony, I was still listening but did not turn round. Instead, I bent over and placed my head between my hands. I decided to ignore her, but felt a hand on a sensitive part of my body.

"Hamdoun," I heard her say.

"Yes."

She put her arms around my waist, and I felt a fire flare up inside me.

"He's drunk," she said. "Come see what a state he's in."

"He said you love me."

"It doesn't matter. Come and see. He's flat out on the carpet. He's started snoring."

"What do you mean by that?"

"I don't know. I mean, he loves it when people tease him."

"I said he's drunk. Come and see."

"I know he's drunk."

"But he didn't have any dinner."

"Maybe he wasn't hungry."

Brigitte walked past me on the balcony. Now for the first time, she had my full attention. François was really drunk. Splayed out on the carpet with his eyes closed, he lay there flat on his back with his arms by his side. He looked like a squirmy worm with long arms and crooked legs that poked out of his trousers to reveal a thick mat of blonde hair. The few veins that showed seemed almost to be moving; I could even imagine the blood coursing through them like water gushing from a pipe. I kicked him again and again, till it hurt.

"Wake up, François. Hey, let's go to one of your favorite places."

"He doesn't hear you," Brigitte said. "He can't."

"He isn't drunk," I said. "Maybe he needs some sleep."

"You're talking as if you don't know him. Haven't you two gotten drunk together many times?"

"But I've never seen him like this before."

"So now you have. I think it's your fault."

I looked up at Brigitte to see if she was really trying to insult me, but her eyes were warm and she looked very sensual. I realized that she did not really mean what she'd said, but was just trying to provoke me. I did not know exactly what she wanted. She tossed her slippers clear of the carpet where François was lying, and started circling around him barefoot. Her feet were tiny and her legs were certainly plump enough. At any rate, I told myself, she's a woman, and I'm a man; sorry, he's a man.

I shoved François again and tried to wake him. He was not asleep. Brigitte picked up the empty bottle and glass from the small table and went into the kitchen. I was about to follow her, but changed my mind. Instead, I kept prodding François with my foot. Then I tried using my hand, but to no avail. I heard him mumble something and asked him what he was trying to say. He just kept on mumbling. I picked up the word "Brigitte," but could not make out anything else.

I began to wonder if I behaved like this when I was drunk and if this is bound to happen to anyone who gets drunk. In the end, I couldn't decide; the entire question was complex and shrouded in a kind of fog. How could I make an unfounded judgment without crystal clear evidence?

I sat down on the carpet near the spread-eagled corpse, which was still emitting pig-like noises. I thought of saying to François: "Wake up, you pig!" But then I asked myself what was the point. If I used the word "pig," would that be enough to rescue him from this utterly regrettable situation?

I felt like asking Brigitte to get me a drink, if there was anything left in the bottle. Actually, I envied François his state of utter oblivion. How wonderful to be able to pass out and totally cancel one's reality!

Brigitte emerged from the kitchen.

"Why are you lying on the floor?" she asked with a cough. "Are you drunk, too?"

I didn't answer, but stayed on the carpet. My head was close to the backside of the corpse in front of me. Just then he let out a disgusting smell.

"You disgusting pig," I said raising my head.

"What's up?" Brigitte asked.

"Nothing."

"Who's the pig, you or him?"

"You," I said.

"Me?"

"Yes."

"You wretch! Shut up. Why don't you just get drunk like him and shut up?"

"Give me a drink. Is there anything left in the bottle?"

"Yes. There's poison. Do you want some?"

"Do you want to kill me?" I asked, as I sat there with the foul smell wafting all around me.

"Yes, both of you," she replied with a laugh.

"Don't you love me?"

"I love him, not you."

"He said you love me."

She didn't answer, but from the kitchen I heard her say "pig." I did not know which one of us she meant. I wanted to ask her, but found that I could not. There was only one thing to do. I stood up listlessly and went into the kitchen barefoot. She was bent over, searching in one of the kitchen drawers. I could not resist patting her on the backside. I expected to hear her say "pig" again, but she simply laughed.

"Stop it," she said. "Oh, Hamdoun. He'll wake up."

"He doesn't care about you."

"That's none of your business."

"He's impotent."

"That's none of your business either. He's your friend. Get yourself a girlie magazine and amuse yourself."

"I'm looking at a live magazine, one made of flesh and blood."

"No way! Relax on the couch or go out on the balcony and look at the minaret. Today's a Muslim festival."

"That's none of my business."

Metamorphosis

On the right were green trees occasionally flecked with color; behind them, the whiteness of buildings. Seated by the wall opposite me, Sulaiman kept looking out from the café; he was staring at the picture of the Virgin Mary holding her baby. He would ponder the way old folk, children, and simpletons behaved in front of the picture. Generous people would place a portion of the earnings from their daily labors into a slot beneath the picture at the bottom of the wall. Everyone could reach it, even children.

Sulaiman was sitting in the streaks of sunlight that made lines on the sidewalk; he had a blue suitcase under his feet. For him, home turf was dozens of kilometers away, so he felt a kind of inner peace as he sat there close to the almost empty café. Apart from him, everyone else was at work at that particular moment, but he was jobless and had no desire to sully his hands by working. Instead he enjoyed watching simple folk, dozens of people putting portions of their daily toil into the slot in the wall under the picture. He didn't own even a tenth of the amounts that they were placing into that slot—and all with no expectation of a return. If he'd had that much, everything would have been very different. And that was the entire issue here, plain and simple.

The music was coming from the back, deep inside the café,

"Do you like music?"

"Yes, I do."

"Can you make out what the tune is?"

"Sure, it's 'Georgia on My Mind.'"

He pushed the chair in front of him, and it yielded obediently. He looked again beyond the building and noticed a mountain, bare, devoid of greenery or snow. Within just a few years, he told himself, the entire top of that mountain would be covered with new buildings. The view of the town from the top would be a distant memory, a vista that once had been but was no longer there. In brief, it would be the story of something that had at the very least existed inside the mind—a prospect. . . .

The suitcase felt heavy; carrying it had worn him out. "Georgia on My Mind" was still wafting gently out of the café, a soothing presence at the core of an irksome silence.

"What are you doing here?"

"Nothing . . . just relaxing."

"You've obviously traveled a lot?"

"Could be. I don't recall anything from the past. . . ."

"Surely that's not too hard, is it?"

"I don't think you can . . . no one can remember everything he's been through. Why don't you listen to 'Georgia on My Mind' and leave me alone?"

"You seem to love music a lot."

"Could be. . . ."

"Okay then. Everything seems to reside in the realm of the possible, so I'll leave you alone. . . ."

People in their hundreds kept passing by on the fringes of the natural scene that presented itself in front of Sulaiman. There were also green trees, a variety of colors (and birds as well, although he couldn't see them but only heard them chirping). No one could change the way they were—that was the secret that would remain a mystery. In front of the left-hand wing of a large office-block there were clusters of cars. Hundreds of people passed by, crossing over to the other side of the road.

He stayed where he was, staring in dead silence, pushing the chair, and resenting the portions of daily toil that were being thrown away through that slot in the wall.

"Do you like music?"

"Of course, I do."

"Then listen to 'Georgia on My Mind.'"

"Okay, okay . . . let me relax."

Through the trees and buildings randomly spaced across the view, many shapes, images, and forests were visible. Distances and dimensions, too, were being violently and subjectively transformed.

All that, as well! I'm tired. That alone can justify my desire for relaxation, even for a little while. Even within the cycle of the universe itself, I believe that relaxation is necessary.

From far away Sulaiman could hear his father's voice. He looked carefully at the changing color of his fingers.

It's extremely exhausting to travel. After so much moving around, people really need to relax a bit.

"Listen, Sulaiman! Who killed your father?"

"No one. . . ."

"That's impossible."

"My father went to sleep quietly, and that's how he passed away—quietly. That same morning I'd seen him, as quiet as love or death."

"But there's evidence that he was murdered, rather than dying of natural causes."

"I don't believe there's any difference between death and murder."

"Fine. Stop beating around the bush. Who tore your father's slippers?"

"That's how I found them."

"And what about your mother's?"

"They were torn, too."

"And what about yours?"

"I don't wear slippers, I wear shoes."

"But who threw your father's *bedaia* out the window?"

"That's none of my business. That evening his *bedaia* was properly hung up. Next morning . . . well, you know the story: Hadda brought in the *bedaia*. 'Sulaiman,' she said. 'Here's your father's *bedaia*. It fell out your window.' I grabbed it and said that it was my father's. No one knows who threw it out the window. Hadda knows everything. That's all there is to it."

Sulaiman blew his smoke into the air. The music was still coming from the café; it had a special smell to it, like juniper trees during night rainfall. He could still smell the music, as he blew his cigarette smoke into the face of those shapes. Their daily portions were still dropping regularly into that slot in the wall right in front of him, and their supplications and prayers still rose skyward, even though not immediately answered.

"Everything in the name of Santa Maria . . ." That in itself was important. Hundreds of people kept crossing, and he—the only traveler—was feeling pretty relaxed by now. He'd come to the conclusion that he was the only one in this town, the only person, who—confronted with this catastrophe—felt that he was genuinely qualified for anything.

One morning, Sulaiman had looked at his sister's cold face, then turned toward the front window to feel the breeze blowing into the room. That was before he had said the sharp words that needed to be said. Before his father's death, his sister had been just a girl who knew nothing about life, but now people were saying that she was clever and certainly above average. By now, she appreciated the true significance of the full moon's appearance once a month and the fact that women menstruated on certain days. Whether or not you could talk about such things, these were the kinds of experiences that had matured her quickly.

"Our father's dead," she said.

"Yes, I know. Don't remind me. My heart can't bear any more. His death is a tough blow for my weak heart."

"I know that, Sulaiman. The thing I need to discuss with you is the fact that our father's death has put an end to a number of considerations."

"I don't understand. Do you mean that everything changes after death?"

"Yes. Private matters are different. What I mean is that you need to change. You should make an effort to do it yourself."

But what kind of change, I wonder.

Change only comes in one form: living according to the realities of life and death. There's also an essential link to circumstance. My father has died, that much is true. That's why I believe that the entire matter is clear and understandable. A person existed who could provide for me before he died because he had a small, yet sufficient, amount of money. Now I have to provide for myself. . . .

("Georgia on My Mind" is still filling the air, smelling like juniper trees on a rainy night. People claim that those trees suffocate while absorbing chlorophyll. That may be true, but the music doesn't choke even though it has the same scent; in fact, it perks up.)

His sister's face looked round and white; he could recall the shape exactly. . . . What mattered was that it had a particularly serious expression. Her lips had a seductive feminine quality.

By his foot under the table he could hear the suitcase leather creaking. A group of children had been playing with a ball, and it had rolled toward him. He kicked it away gently, then stared greedily at the slender figure of Santa Maria. She looked hungry and in quest of the absolute, so her eyes seemed almost suspended, and her body appeared to be ascending rapidly toward the house and the anxiety framed in the whiteness of the buildings. The exposed heights shrouded everything else that was visible and repelled the glances of the curious and meddlesome, just as a ball thrown hard against a wall will come back with the same speed.

The birds that Sulaiman could not see were still chirping in the nearby greenery. He had the feeling that the world did not belong to anyone; every nerve in his body told him that he'd traveled far and wide in quest of change, but now he'd stopped in a small white town. His home turf was not far from here, and yet the return, that impossibility, was something he couldn't contemplate any more. For change to come, strange and inexplicable things had to happen; in principle, change involved the occurrence of pointless things. It would all be simply hypothetical. That's the way I look at it, pure and simple; whereas other people see it differently. Maybe the point is itself the point, and not the pointlessness of the whole thing, as I happen to believe.

Just then many tiny tracks, like the ones made by goats' hoofs, appeared in Sulaiman's mind. Metamorphosis is the search for the meaning of existence. . . . Not only is it that, but also an abundance of relaxation, love, and other essentials.

"Personally, I'm trying to change. . . . Doesn't everybody feel that way sometimes, sister?"

"Yes. That's precisely what I asked of you in the very beginning. Go and look for a job. To be frank, our father's dead, and our mother can't do anything."

"I know she can't do anything. That's why I've been trying so hard to get a job."

"As far as I can see, your education should make that possible . . ."

"I know what you mean, but all the books I've read can't buy me food today . . ."

"Don't be like that. There are lots of people who don't have your qualifications . . ."

"That's true, but as of today I still haven't been able to locate the job you want me to get . . ."

"One has to change. Just look at so-and-so, for example . . ."

"You've become far more adult and mature than necessary."

The sun, which was at its zenith, was spinning rapidly around itself and breaking up into fragmented rainbow hues that penetrated the realms of the visible. The sunshine was like a needle pricking the body of music as it burst into the air. In front of the large office block, just a few feet away, cars started dispersing in different directions, and the sound of horns grew louder.

As Sulaiman reached down for his blue suitcase, fatigue was still pressing on his chest. The sun was no longer rotating at its zenith. He made his way through the city's many alleyways. Its broad and narrow streets continued to tempt him to wander around, and so he kept walking and walking and walking. Inside his head, linked circles intertwined as he puffed nervously on his cigarette, taking deep breaths.

Sulaiman put down his leather suitcase at the foot of the bed and thought about his hand for a moment; it was aching because he had been carrying the suitcase for so long. He noticed that his fingers were gradually cramping; they already felt numb, and the veins looked frozen. As he stared at his hand, the blood inside his head was boiling. His fingers were the same color as his suitcase; and the bedposts were blue as well, a bright blue that reflected the yellowish electric light in the room. His shoes felt heavy as he dragged himself over to his suitcase. It opened with a clicking sound that he always enjoyed. He gave the clasp another push, but it didn't make the same sound. That annoyed him, so he clenched his fist and used the air to punch the image of all the wretched souls on earth who were relentlessly procreating. Throwing himself on the bed still dressed, he tried his best to rid himself of the fatigue of the long trip. He made an effort to pull up the covers, but didn't succeed. Staring up at the ceiling, he saw a halo created by the light around the peeling white paint. After focusing his attention on this dead, frozen image, he looked over at the window, whose wooden casing was covered by a curtain. He felt a sudden desire to get up, pull the curtain back, and look out at the face of the night beyond the room. This certainly was night itself, unchanging and unchangeable. Sulaiman got up and unlaced his black shoes, then tied them again. He now remembered that he had not closed the curtain, so he went over to the window and looked out at the night. He tried to convince himself that this night was not actually that eternal night, but then he felt he was deceiving himself. As he gazed out at the black emptiness, it did not seem any different from the other blackness that he already knew; indeed it might not be any different from the one he would come to know. With that, he grabbed the curtain, whose texture was as soft as a cat's fur. He wondered if he was the only guest in the hotel. What should he do now, when he felt so tired?

He had spent some time looking for a hotel in the small white town, but failed to find one with four walls, a bed, and a curtain with a soft fabric whose name he did not know. But now he had found this room and could relax a bit. His legs felt tired, his shoulders were tight, and his bruised fingers were very painful. He used his left hand to rub the bruises gently. When he'd been younger, he'd wondered what the bruises on his father's fingers meant, but now that all seemed trivial. How trivial we can all be at times! I used to think of them as bulges on old trees, but now here they are sprouting randomly on my fingers, even though I don't do manual labor. I used to read a lot. . . ."

Once he'd had his fill of the night and assured himself that it was the very night that had been stuck in his consciousness since childhood, he pulled the curtain across again and dragged his weary feet toward the bed. He heard some words in Spanish on the other side of the door, which stood there steadfast in the face of a whole world, but he couldn't understand what they meant.

"I don't understand Spanish," he thought to himself. "And yet I'm alive. I eat, drink, and sleep. Then I ask for a room in a hotel like this one without knowing a single word. So why should I bother memorizing the dictionaries of the entire world?"

The wooden door looked like an iron wall confronting people who had no connection with it. Here he was, alone in a room, surrounded by four walls, and behind a door, believing he had rid himself of the many worries that would inevitably confront him as soon as he left the room and met the landlady and new lodgers. His relationship with such unwanted people might be either temporary or long-lasting. He remembered, too, that during his trip he hadn't made any effort to contact anyone. He was a prisoner in his own private world. In this voluntary exile he'd discovered the individual truth that transcends all others: namely, that relationships with other people only succeed in tiring us. That's why he'd found solace in his individual truth and could now observe things from the tower of his own truth. Everything he was seeing now, everything he'd seen before, was merely surface appearances. So it is that, whenever we establish a certain relationship, we're only connecting with the surface of things.

"I myself am just a surface phenomenon," he told himself. "Occasionally my personal truth is lost, and I find myself linked to external appearances. It is extremely difficult to escape from such a fusion."

Sulaiman walked over to his blue suitcase, took the small, shiny key, and opened it. What else could he do? Sometimes the deed itself precedes our decision to do it, and yet we still question it. Once, when Sulaiman was still in his own country, he'd had a quarrel with someone he did not know and had hit the person without even thinking about it. Yet in the end he'd been held responsible for his actions and had paid a fine in court. So now here he was, opening the suitcase without knowing why. His hand reached for his clothes, which were mostly dirty, and began to fumble through them nervously. Finally, he found some shaving cream and immediately felt his stubbled face, but put it back and closed the suitcase again. He went over to the window to look outside and tried to make out the sky's face, but it was hidden behind a pitch darkness in the infinite beyond. Even so, he kept looking and looking. A fresh evening breeze toyed with his face and blew the curtain hanging from the wooden window-frame. Clutching the frame tightly, he breathed in the gentle breeze. His facial features contracted, then relaxed. As he let himself feel the softness of the evening breeze, he had the sensation of entering a different psychological phase. His nerves had been on edge all day, but now his weary head was gradually beginning to feel lighter. Looking over at the bed, he noticed the commode. A nice round ashtray kept inviting him to fill it with cigarette butts.

His sister's face remained buried in the ashtray. By now, her face had lost its passion, and its round shape had turned to something else. It wasn't spherical, round, or oval any longer. Instead, it had turned gray with traces of smallpox. Even all the genealogists in the world would not be able to tell that she was actually his sister by the same father and mother. Everything was now gray and disfigured.

Sulaiman wasn't a heavy smoker. He took a cigarette out of his pocket and searched for the lighter in another pocket. Lighting the cigarette mechanically, he started blowing the smoke out of his nose into the room. He was taking rapid, deep puffs; the smoke cloud in front of him looked like a weird animal he'd never seen before and might never see again. He walked over to the ashtray and buried the fag-end of the cheap black tobacco cigarette in it. Now he rushed out of the room as though he was having an attack of nerves, but then he remembered that he hadn't closed the door or taken the key. After putting the light off and turning the key slowly in the lock, he grabbed the doorknob and pushed the door to make sure it was properly closed. He went down the stone stairs calmly, reached the door, and hung the room-key on the black board with the room-numbers—twenty of them. There were three keys on the board. With that, he left the hotel.

He looked as if he were drugged. Fumbling in his pocket, he found a few pesetas and told himself he could get a drink at the nearest place. As he went into a bar, his elbow knocked a short fat man who was obviously drunk; he was trying to put his hat on as he left the place. Sulaiman's glare confronted a pair of stupid eyes, looking completely blank. Walking over to the counter where bar-stools were arranged like so many guards, he sat down on one of them. The effeminate-looking barman came over.

"Señor?" he asked provocatively.

"Something cold," Sulaiman responded listlessly.

The barman went away. In the mirror, Sulaiman's face assumed a different guise. Before, it had looked round, but now it was turning rectangular. The mirror was foggy because of the atmosphere inside the bar, but even so, the image of his disfigured face scared him. Even in his own lonely world he felt alienated. He turned and looked at one of the other customers, his face, eyes, nose, and lips.

"I must give him a smile," he thought.

His own cold smile was met by an equally listless smile back; the other man had drunk a lot and was plastered. Even so, the other man's smile was warm and humane; it seemed to come from some other world, one whose reality was unfamiliar to Sulaiman. The stranger now put his arm under Sulaiman's arm, and some coarse phrases gurgled in his throat. Behind them the café was silent and the night had completely shrouded everything outside.

So what, precisely, did this man want? A short while ago when they were exchanging smiles, Sulaiman had talked briefly and concisely about his life.

"Are you Greek?" the man had asked.

"No, Moroccan."

"You must be a student."

"No. . . ."

"Worker?"

"No. . . ."

"So who are you then?"

"Nothing. . . ."

Sulaiman had refused to be more precise. He had scratched his nose, which had been trying to avoid a truly disgusting smell. This chance meeting made him happy.

"Are you from here?" he asked the other man, trying to change the subject.

"Yes."

"You work here?"

"Here and there, as circumstances demand."

"What do you do?"

"Everything. . . . You said you weren't a student or laborer. Do you want to work with us?"

"Sure."

"We had an Algerian working for us before you. I think you have the same temperament. But that's not important."

The stranger put his arms around Sulaiman's shoulder and gave him a warm hug. The stench of sardines and bread was escaping from his intestines as he led Sulaiman out of the café. Now here they were, walking along the street that led to the east side of the city. The man told Sulaiman that he'd explain everything to him.

"I'll lose my way back to the hotel. All my things are still there."

"I know the hotel."

His arm was still under Sulaiman's. He still looked drunk, because actually Sulaiman was dragging him along like a dead body discovered in a riverbed. The man tripped and fell slowly into a round hole on the sidewalk. Sulaiman pulled him out.

"You can stop now," the stranger said.

So Sulaiman stopped.

"Why? Are you tired?"

"Yes. I need to catch my breath."

"Take it easy."

The stranger gave Sulaiman's sad, stubbled face a fixed stare. Just a few minutes earlier, they had been complete strangers, but now here they were, friends.

"Are we done?" Sulaiman asked his new friend.

"Yes. . . ."

"Where to?"

"Take slow, deep breaths. You'll come up, won't you? Do you like the evening?"

"I don't know."

"Then there is no need to wait here."

"Okay then," Sulaiman said unhurriedly. "Let's go up."

By now the wine had penetrated deep into the other man's braincells and had dispersed throughout the various wires and fibers inside his head. He was feeling an excessive, feverish heat.

"Listen" he asked as he belched up a sickening smell. "Can you really work with us?"

"Yes, possibly. It all depends on the type of job."

"Okay, take your time. Can you help me up the stairs? It's the second floor."

Sulaiman heaved the stranger up the stairs, one step at a time. After awhile they were standing like two demons in the middle of a small, filthy room with a window looking out on a remote, nocturnal expanse. Sulaiman gazed out into the nothingness.

"Is this where you live?" he asked.

"Yes. . . ."

"Alone?"

"Alone or with my friend. It depends. Look. . . ."

Sulaiman looked slowly at the stranger's hands. They were holding a gold-like box that shone in the dim light coming from somewhere on the side.

"Is that gold?" he asked gleefully.

"It isn't important. It's from over there. We'll explain everything to you."

Now the wine smell was coming out of his bluish nose.

He put the box away again inside his suit pocket, then staggered over to the only bed in the room, laid his head on the dirty pillow, and glanced at the leg of the chair in the corner.

"Listen," he said, "get some rest now. My friend will be coming, he doesn't have a key. If you hear someone knocking, open the door for him."

"Okay."

The stranger fell asleep, leaving Sulaiman to get whatever sleep he could on the chair opposite the bed. He woke up with a jolt, not believing what his eyes were telling him, and lit a cigarette. Walking over to the bed, he tried waking the stranger (who was snoring like a pig), but in vain. He went over to the window and looked out at the night sky and the dim lights visible in the distance through the heavy fog and humid air. He was feeling hungry and was fed up with sitting in the chair; as far as he was concerned, it was all too tiring. He tried again to wake up the stranger, but without success. He moved away from the bed and looked at his dusty shoes. Feeling lonely, he opened the door, and went downstairs without closing it. The pig-like sound of the man's noisy snoring followed him down.

He really needed to get some sleep, because the day before had been extremely exhausting, so he decided to walk back to the hotel so he could get a good night's sleep. He would leave it till tomorrow to get his senses back so he could discuss the work issue with the strange man with the bluish nose.

The day before, his vision had not been able to make anything out, whether high up or low down. The foggy gloom and distant electric lights only revealed a world resembling that of the night. Today, however, he had had those dreams or nightmares about yesterday's strange man. He paced around the hotel room. Now its outlines were much clearer: there was the whiteness, for sure, but also darkness and light blue sky. Outside the window was a profound, heavenly visage. Yes indeed, everything was different from yesterday.

Dragging himself to the window, he let his upper body feel the morning air. He felt the cut under his chin that a razor had made a while ago when he was shaving; it felt deep and bloody, but actually it was just a light scratch and certainly not worth the attention Sulaiman was paying to it.

"That man will get me a job," he thought to himself.

"That's true. . . ."

"Yesterday he was certainly drunk enough."

"That was an amazing gold box he had!"

"He was a decent human being."

"I'm just dreaming," he added. "Just dreaming. . . ."

He licked his lower lip with his red tongue, which was divided into two by a small trench in the middle. He left it dangling for a while. When he retracted it, it was feeling a bit cool. His jaws were aching as though he'd been chewing on a piece of rubber for four hours. Never mind, he thought. But then, never mind what? Nothing. He didn't know. Beneath the window were plants of different heights and a garden alongside the hotel with white-painted chairs in a corner. Amid the greenery they looked like tiny rabbits nibbling the grass. He thought about going downstairs and having his breakfast there; he hadn't had enough to eat the day before.

"There's not enough money, but what am I supposed to do?"

"Seize the moment, and worry later about what to do next."

"That makes sense."

For the hundredth time that morning he felt the cut on his chin and told himself that here, he was simply a passer-by. It had never even occurred to him to stop and settle down. He went down to the small garden and basked in the warm sunshine. His clothes didn't look very attractive; actually, they were dirty. Despite that, he realized that one can substitute one set of clothes for another. The real and essential change is the one that is not at anyone else's disposal. As he told himself that, he started avidly chewing a piece of bread that lay crucified in front of him; under a layer of cheese, it looked somewhat inviting. Once he'd finished, he needed a smoke. Fumbling in his pocket for a cigarette, he failed to find one. Changing his mind, he started drinking his café au lait with unusual relish.

Two other people came down to the garden, talking loudly, and sat at a table far away from where he was sitting. He pulled off a leaf that had been dangling over his head, rubbed it, and smelled its scent. He was still feeling lonely and alienated. It worried him that his appearance might attract the attention of the other two people in the garden. But they did not seem interested; perhaps they were used to such things, or else they had more important things to worry about. He took another leaf, rubbed it, and smelled its pungent scent.

All of a sudden, the image of the strange man loomed before him, and he soon recalled the way he would need to go: from here . . . to there . . . then this street . . . then that one . . . and after that, the building, and the second floor. The scent of the leaves was filling his nostrils. He lifted the coffee cup to his mouth, but it was empty; he'd already drunk it all. Staring at his knee, he noticed black streaks on his pants, black oily streaks. Standing up, he turned around and looked at the center of the sun's disk, just like a Greek God. But his defiant posture collapsed in sudden defeat, so he turned around once more before sneaking out to the street through the small door. He took deep breaths, absorbing things that by now were completely awake. Scratching his nose, he watched two children at play. Before the scene ended, he leaped up the stairs like a squirrel and lit a cigarette.

It was eleven o'clock in the morning when he reached the door. Sulaiman pushed the doorbell and heard it ring in the other room. The door was immediately opened by an old lady of medium height.

"Yes, Sir?" she asked.

"Is the señor here?" Sulaiman asked in confusion.

"Yes, he is."

Whereupon she disappeared, leaving the door ajar.

Sulaiman felt he was in some kind of dream. Who was this strange woman? Could she be the strange man's girlfriend?

Sulaiman was now staring at the strange man. "I'm sorry about yesterday," he said. "I left because you fell asleep early."

"Excuse me Sir," the man asked in surprise. "What are you talking about?"

"Yesterday. . . ."

"Yesterday? I don't understand. . . ."

"Of course, you don't. You fell asleep and left me on my own."

"Maybe you're mistaken," the man replied, sounding even more surprised. "What do you mean, exactly?"

"I'm your friend from yesterday. Didn't you promise to get me a job?"

"Sir, I don't understand. Maybe it was my neighbor; he's alone and single."

With that, the strange man tried closing the door in Sulaiman's face, but Sulaiman pushed it back open.

"Why are you behaving this way with a friend?"

"Sir," the man replied. "You're not a friend of mine. I don't know you. I've never seen you before. I'm sorry if there's been some kind of misunderstanding."

This time he closed the door hard in Sulaiman's face. Sulaiman retreated downstairs to the ground floor and then to the street. The two children were still playing. By now the scene was complete in his mind. Actually, he had gone the wrong way to the street, the room, and the man himself. After trampling over dozens of cigarette butts with his dusty shoes, he started smoking. He decided to try his luck in a different direction. He'd come here the day before, and now here he was, leaving the way he'd come. His head was in a jumble; in his mind was a concept he called change. The dirt clung stubbornly to his shoes, and he was feeling painfully tired. Even so, he refused to give in because he was convinced first of all that winds blew in different directions and then that he would be willing to walk in one of those directions, whatever the cost might be.

"You live on illusions," his sister had told him.

"Do you really believe that?"

"I know you very well and understand your temperament."

"You don't know anything."

"At least I know a bit about your temperament. Take your suitcase and go look for a job somewhere. You're bound to find someone who'll help you. There are lots of nice people around who'll never give up on their principles."

THE WHITE ANGEL

(1988)

A Newspaper Report

We were enjoying a cold beer at "Juana di Arco." It was half past eleven. My English friend, who always looked tired, still had far more energy than me. He asked me whether there was a bus to Asilah. I told him that taxis were available. Looking out the window, he raised the glass to his lips. The street was deserted, except for some teenage girls who were laughing their way to the beach, with towels on their shoulders or under their arms.

He didn't seem to be bothered about either the world in general or the girls. But they got me excited; perhaps I was younger than he, or maybe there are lots of gorgeous blondes in his own country.

"Did you say something?" he asked abruptly as though he had been pricked by a needle. "Are you talking to me?"

"Those girls are beautiful," I said. "That's what I was saying."

"Who?" he asked.

"Those girls," I replied.

"Yes, they are," he commented. "Your country's changed a lot. Finish your beer. Do you feel like having another one?"

"No thanks," I said.

"Drink as much as you want. Do you want to eat something, or shall we wait till we get to Asilah?"

"Whatever you like," I said.

"No, whatever you like, not me. I've already had enough to eat this morning. Tell me, do you think the people there will help us?"

"I know them well," I replied. "They're as courageous as they are nice."

A sock-peddler came by, and dangled a pair of socks in front of me.

"New stock from Gibraltar," he said. "Pure wool."

"No, they're not," said the waiter. "They're from the Canaries. Didn't you go to Las Palmas a week ago? Listen, 'Abdu, you have to be honest if you want to get customers."

"Let me earn my living my own way, Hmidu," the peddler replied.

"Then find somewhere else to earn your living. Tangier is a big city. I've an idea. Why don't you go to Fes, Meknes, or some other inland city?"

"That's where goods smuggled through Ceuta and Melilla arrive," the peddler complained. "God save me from this lousy job! Give me some *tapas*. I haven't had any breakfast and, at this rate, I won't be getting any lunch, either. This season there aren't many tourists. I haven't sold a single thing since early morning."

The waiter handed him a plate of *kofta* and poured two small platefuls of tomatoes and potatoes onto it.

"What's this mess supposed to be?" asked the peddler.

"What do you want, you naked idiot?" replied the waiter. "A ring if you please, my lord, sir? Eat, you pig! Go on, fill your stomach. Whatever doesn't kill you makes you stronger."

The peddler started eating ravenously; he was really hungry. He was about to wipe his hands on the socks he'd put on the counter, but instead he grabbed a piece of paper in front of him. Once he had cleaned his fingers, he carried on eating.

"Shall we go?" asked my English friend.

"Just as you wish."

Putting his bag on his right shoulder, he paid the bill. I picked up the leather suitcase from the corner where we had been standing. Passing by the Rembrandt Hotel, we went downhill toward the Asilah taxi station, hoping to head for Dar Chaoui as soon as possible. He was hoping to be able to tape some interviews with the people who were fighting with Franco against the Rojos. He said he worked for a magazine in Manchester. I wasn't too sure about that. All those European types could be journalists, artists, or nothing at all. What was certain was that they were better off than me. I'd been trying very hard to get a passport to travel anywhere in Europe or the Arab gulf.

"Why are you rushing?" I asked my English friend. "Dar Chaoui isn't far. It's just a few minutes from Asilah."

"I'm sure you'd like to have a swim," he said. "But I need you to translate for me."

"I don't like the sea very much."

"OK. I know what you want."

"What?" I asked.

"Another beer," he replied.

I told him it was a good idea; after all, such opportunities don't get repeated very often. We went into the nearest café, and he ordered a tonic. I could tell he didn't want what I did, so I decided not to impose. That's why shortly afterward we found ourselves in Dar Chaoui, where a young man from the mountains was waiting for us. He was wearing a short *jallaba* and a colorful sun hat, and he spoke English. Apparently they'd met a short time before.

Now my task is over, I thought. "Are you from Asilah?" I asked the man.

"No."

"Where are you from? Tangier or inland?"

"Neither. I'm from Ksar Sghir. I went to high school in Tangier, but I didn't pass the exams.

"There are lots of people like us. Personally I've decided to live and move from one city to another. I've lived in London and Stockholm. I spent six months in jail in Sweden. Here I can live in total peace. Do you know Tom well?"

"No, we met quite by chance in Tangier."

"He's a courageous man. We meet two or three times a year. If you're trustworthy, you'll find out what kind of man he is."

"Does he always come here to interview people?" I asked.

"Interview people? What interviews? Oh, I see."

He fell silent and took out a packet of cigarettes from his *jallaba* pocket. We were walking along a dusty road full of potholes and solid white stones. All around us, birds were chirping in the wide-open spaces. A few small trees and thorny cacti were scattered here and there, exposed to the scorching heat. The man from the mountains took the suitcase I was holding.

"You have to wait here," said Tom. "They might be on their guard with you around."

"Why would they be?" I asked.

"When they talk about sensitive issues like war, they're very wary of people they don't know, especially Moroccans like themselves. This man is one of them."

"As you wish."

With that, he threw me the packet of cigarettes.

I jumped over a small dry ditch where crickets were jumping, and stretched out in the shade of a fig tree. I watched the two of them climb the hill till they disappeared. The sky was very clear. From time to time, some birds flew by, but that was the only sound to be heard. I let myself be lulled by a light easterly breeze and dozed off under the tree. I don't know how long I slept, but eventually I woke up when I heard a noise over my head.

"Did you have a good sleep?" Tom asked. "You must be hungry by now."

"I thought you must have eaten all the figs in that tree," the other man said with a laugh.

"I don't like figs."

The young man only walked part of the way with us, then went back and disappeared between some houses. Once we reached the paved road, I sat down on the milestone. Tom remained standing for awhile, but when he got tired, he too sat down on the ground. The young man had assured us that the Asilah bus would be coming soon. In fact, fifteen minutes later, the bus did indeed arrive. Some barefoot men and women from the mountain regions got off; the heads of their babies dangled from their mothers' backs like ripe fruit.

"How did the interview go?" I asked Tom once we were on the bus.

"Fine."

"All those old people must feel proud of killing a large number of Rojos."

"Indeed."

"They must be proud, too, of the number of women they've raped in churches."

"Indeed."

"Not to mention the number of children they've killed and cut to pieces."

"Oh, absolutely. I've recorded it all."

The suitcase was nestling between my knees. I started picturing the stories, real or imaginary, that were stored inside the recorder. Those old fighters sometimes lie and claim credit for other people's actions.

About ten minutes later, the bus stopped on the road to Asilah. No one got off, but the bus's front and back doors opened and gendarmes climbed aboard. I could sense that Tom was really scared. The two gendarmes opened the suitcase I had between my legs. There was no recorder; it was packed full of hashish.

"So, you want to get rich from hashish," one of the gendarmes chided me as he put the handcuffs on. "You do that while we have to die here in the heat."

"I swear, I . . ."

"I don't care."

I felt a hard kick in my back as I was propelled off the bus. As I fell to the ground, my mouth filled with dust.

A Tale of a Drunk

According to Ibn Mas'ud, if a man dies drunk, bury him in his grave, and then dig him up. If you don't find him turned away from the *Qiblah*, then kill me!

A.

When the policeman handed me back my ID, I slipped 100 dirhams into his hand. It was dark and foggy, and the dim streetlight made no difference. Just a moment earlier, while I was still drunk, I'd felt a few raindrops splattering my hair, but it had had no effect at all—nothing did. I wanted to bed a woman, something I hadn't done for ages. Maybe I had, but, if so, I'd forgotten. Sometimes when I drink too much, I can't remember what I did the night before. However, tonight I'm certainly going to remember everything. I may even be able to recall other things I've long since forgotten.

The first policeman was standing by his jeep, while the second one was staring at us through rain-splattered glasses.

"Do you realize," the first one informed me, "that if you're taken to court, you'll be immediately fired from your job? First you crash your way into a brothel, then you get drunk like this! I don't need to be any more explicit, do I? You're a teacher; you know all about it. The sentence will be harsh. How can an educator possibly behave this way? Your salary's low, I realize, but the 100 dirhams is even less."

"That's all I have on me," I said.

"Check your pockets."

Mariam was craning her neck, trying to see what was happening. The young girl was shivering by her side.

190

"She's my niece," Mariam kept saying. "She's not one of them. Please, Sir, I beg you."

She did not have the courage to jump out of the jeep, and I didn't dare run away.

"Shut up, you bitch!" barked the policeman. "We'll get things straight at the police station. Let me talk to the teacher. Tomorrow he'll find out he's caught syphilis. I know your type."

"I swear, Sir."

"Shut up, you bitch."

The policemen turned toward me. "You can leave now," he said. "But I can't guarantee you won't run into other police patrols. Where do you live?"

I mumbled.

"Scram!"

Mariam kept talking to the policeman, trying to act sober, but all in vain. It was obvious that she was drunk. She was trying to look out of the police jeep, but the policeman kept prodding her. Meanwhile, the policeman in glasses was still acting polite; he was like a good student, never interfering with what his colleague was doing.

"Don't touch her," the woman said. "She's my niece. How about me?"

"It's her I want. She isn't your niece. You're a liar. Whenever I find a beautiful girl with you, you're always inventing lies like this. You're just jealous."

Earlier she had staggered between the wall and the old closet, brandishing the empty bottle in my face. The little girl had looked scared and helpless, the way any normal girl would in such an unusual situation. She was standing over in a corner shivering.

"Are you completely drunk?" I had asked. "Put down the bottle and pour another drink. That would be best."

"Who do you think you are, giving me orders? No one on earth can tell Mariam what to do."

"Just don't do anything crazy."

But she did. She threw the bottle right in my face. The little girl jumped up and screamed. She covered her pale little face with her hands, then peeped at me through her fingers in wide-eyed panic. But Mariam was still not satisfied. Now she hurled the ashtray against the wall. It shattered, and the pieces fell all over the blanket on the bare floor. When she tried scratching my face with her nails, I poked mine into her side. There was a scream of pain, followed by banging on the door.

"Police! Open the door."

Now the police car was setting off in the rain down Mont Ampignani Street. For my part, I walked in the opposite direction. I didn't feel drunk and still had a few dirhams left; actually it was more than 100 dirhams. It was still early in the month.

B.

According to Al-Zahri, may God be pleased with him, the Caliph 'Uthman ibn 'Affan (. . .) once narrated as follows: A long time ago, a man (. . .) met a black woman. She ordered her maidservant to let him into the house, then closed the door behind her. Inside, the black woman had both wine and a young boy. "Don't leave me," she told the man, "until you have drunk a glass of wine and either made love to me or else killed this boy. If you don't, I'll let out a yell and tell everyone that you broke into my house. Who would ever believe you?" "I will not commit adultery," the man replied, "nor will I kill a soul." However, as God knows, he did drink the wine, and only left after he had made love to the woman and killed the boy.

C.

Poor man! He tried to avoid sin, but couldn't help himself.

A. Again

The band was making a nasty noise. My head felt heavy from all the stuff I'd been drinking. The girl beside me sensed that I'd grown tired of this world. Picking up her glass from the *comptoir*, she went over to hug another client from behind. I watched the whole thing as though it were merely a dream. In front of me everything was a blur, men and women alike. The music still sounded awful, especially since it kept repeating a boring Arabic melody. I reached for the glass, but it felt heavy; it started shaking and fell to the floor by my side. The glass was empty. I felt like vomiting, but I was hungry. I pictured myself eating my own vomit, then spat loudly over the stool in the space between my legs.

One of the customers glared at me. Don't spit on me. I didn't. Yes, you did. No, I didn't. You're a liar. Your father's the liar. The bottle is smashed on the *comptoir*, and the hand holding the sharp bottleneck shakes. Blood flows, then the ambulance arrives.

But nothing like that happened. The girl kissed him on his forehead while her hand proceeded to pick the pocket of his beautiful jacket.

"Don't pay any attention to him. These days there are lots of country hicks in Casablanca."

"They're just like vermin. You run into them wherever you go."

This time she was kissing him on the mouth while she fished into his pocket.

"I've no idea why they frequent bars. They're impolite. But it's these hookers, divorcees from the countryside. They're the ones who keep attracting them. Where are the real Bidaouis, both men and women?"

"Exactly."

Caressing his neck, she ordered herself a beer. By now he could definitely feel something down below, something warm that would cool down in a while, something that reached all the way to his toes. You could picture him falling to his knees and kneeling in front of her. The muscular black barman banged the glass on the counter and gave me a bitter, painful smile.

"You there!" he said "Do you think this is a hotel? If you want to go to bed, get out of here. Either have another drink or let someone else have your place. What are you doing here? Do you think I'm some kind of virgin or mermaid dropped from the sky? We've been here since morning so we can get something to feed 'the kids.'"

"Did you hear that?" I heard the woman telling the customer. "I like the way Hmidu deals with those country folk."

When I gave up the seat at the bar, my head was spinning; I didn't think my legs would hold me up any more. As I headed for the door, I heard someone behind me say, "Good riddance." Needless to say, I didn't look back. I stood on the empty street for ages, waiting for a taxi, but it was hopeless. A few private cars were parked along the street. . . . I needed to urinate, so I walked over to the tree on the sidewalk; its overhanging branches and leaves created a large shady area. Just then, I heard a voice behind me, "Alms, O Muslim."

There, she was peering over my shoulder. "Go away!" I said.

It was a filthy old woman who had left her face unveiled as far as the chin. Her *jallaba* was either black or blue, I couldn't tell which in the dark.

"Alms, my son!" she said again.

"Can't you see what I'm doing? Shame on you!"

"Sorry, son. I can wait. Take your time."

Behind me I heard a door slam. It was another police car. A young policeman got out and grabbed me by the neck and the old woman by the arm.

"You, get in the jeep. And you, show me your ID."

I gave him my ID.

"Are you kidding?" he said, pushing his cap back on his head. "I need the other sort of paper. Don't you understand? Do you think you can fool us?"

I tried to understand. I fumbled in my pockets, but only ten dirhams were left, the cost of a taxi ride. I gave him the money. He pointed his flashlight at it.

"Are you trying to make fun of us?" he sneered. "We're tired of you drunkards. Aren't you ashamed? On top of it all, you're committing adultery with this woman who's as old as your grandmother."

"I swear . . ."

"Get in the jeep. I don't want to hear it."

B. Again

Ibn Abi Dunya once said: "Once I saw a drunk on the streets of Baghdad peeing, then cleaning himself with his clothes. He was asking God to number him among the purified."

C. Again

You know what happened to the drunk who peed on the streets of Casablanca.

A. One last time

For more information, please refer to the following:
1. The things that happen in Casablanca day and night.
2. The collection of tales and stories from the Prophetic narratives and others, especially the chapter entitled "The tale concerning the censure of wine-drinking."

Monarch of the Square

He sat on the doorstep next to the Tanagra Movie Theater. The combination of hunger and roaming the city's alleys had made him feel totally exhausted. He'd searched through a few trash piles, but unfortunately had not come up with any food. All he could find were empty fish and condensed milk cans that people regularly threw in the trash after finishing with them. The city's garbage trucks would be collecting trash at dawn. Later, workers would spray the streets and alleys with their black hoses.

The square in front of him was empty, although once in a while a car would pass by. Nice American-made cars were parked on the street where he was sitting. He knew almost all the owners because he was very familiar with the square. They were all feudal landowners, bazaar operators, or drug dealers. How he wished he could have grown up the same way they did, for they now had fantastic cars and women as gorgeous as rare pearls, the kind who would emerge from the bars located on the square or behind it. They were both Moroccan and European, and made a point of swaying their hips as they walked.

He'd tried to get a job, but in vain. The head shoeshine-boy, who was also a police informant, had refused to intervene on his behalf so he could get a permit and become a shoeshine-boy himself. In the meantime, he'd brought a number of villagers from the Qal'at Sraghna region and helped them get work-permits. He knew them all. Some of them sympathized with his plight and gave him some food, but others kicked him in the stomach or backside.

He really was unlucky. Even so, he still dreamed of one day becoming monarch of this square. He'd have his own bazaar, a wonderful car, and a crowd of sashaying women, especially European ones. He'd eat and drink well and always be plastered. He'd play pinball with French sailors or American soldiers the way the *Caid*'s son, Umm Hani's son, or other people's sons always did. When he'd become monarch of the square, he'd do all those things.

It was about one o'clock in the morning. Loud music emerged from the bars and swept across the square. He wasn't feeling particularly drowsy because he'd slept all afternoon, although it hadn't been very restful; he'd made himself a bed of cardboard under a staircase. He might well have gone back and used the same bed again, but the doorman of the building had cleaned the place up and thrown his bed in the trash. He'd lost count of the number of times he'd used trash to hide from the police. He certainly didn't want them to take him away to the police station. He'd be assaulted by people older than himself; and he was always scared of falling into the clutches of a particular Corsican policeman. Those police were ruthless and violent. The Moroccan policemen who used to accompany the French police would always give him a kick, then let him go.

"Go home, you little bastard," they'd yell.

They didn't realize that he had no home or relatives. His mother had died in a camelhair tent in a city suburb. She'd told him that he had an uncle in a village near Sidi Kacem, but he'd never had enough money to go there and look for him. One day, when he would become a shoeshine or monarch of the square, he'd certainly go there. By that time, his uncle would certainly have passed away. But who knows? Maybe God would grant him a long life. Without his knowing about it, he might even be one of those feudal lords, just like the ones who staggered around the square every night. Anything is possible.

A skinny dog trotted past and was about to urinate on his foot, but he gave it a kick. The dog crossed the street to the other sidewalk and cocked its leg by the tire of a wonderful car under one of the streetlights. They stared at each other, but the dog looked utterly exhausted. Lowering its head to the ground, it stretched out its paws and either went to sleep or died. Again, anything is possible: sleep or death.

He too was exhausted and hungry, but that could easily be solved. When people got drunk, they'd leave their sandwiches unfinished. He'd be able to grab some scraps for himself as long as the waiter didn't get there first. He shifted his gaze from the dog to the square, to a point near the Kasbah Bar with its black marble tile work. He watched as three men and two policemen got out of their jeep. One of the three men was a tall American soldier.

He was curious, so he stood up and went over to see what was happening. A Moroccan man was interpreting what the American was saying for the two Moroccan policemen. The American was totally drunk. The boy just stood there watching them. He gathered that the American had not paid for his drinks and the woman who managed the bar had called the police. There was a prolonged discussion involving the policemen, the American soldier, and the interpreter, while the other person present remained silent. Eventually, the American pointed at him and said something that he didn't understand. The interpreter turned toward him.

"The American says that this boy's the one who stole his wallet," he told the two policemen.

The boy was stunned and frightened. The two policemen looked at him steadily

"Get in the jeep, son," one of them told him. "We'll let you go later. I'm sure you didn't steal his wallet. What can we do about these disgusting American soldiers? How can you understand such things?"

Hyena-Struck[1]

The hyena-struck woman speaks:

I sipped my coffee and took a drag on my cigarette. I was sitting by myself in the coffee shop. Young girls were hanging around with men their father's age. Other boys and girls were there too, who seemed unfamiliar with such places. Just a few years ago I'd been like them. It was in a place just like this that I'd first met my husband. On the street outside the shop-window, cars were all crammed together. Pedestrians walking by were either talking, gesticulating, window shopping, flirting, or looking at particular parts of other people's bodies. I used to like doing that too; I'd always look at the man's face or feet. Whatever their age, men would always look at my eyes first, then at my hair, my breasts, and my hips. Legs apparently were not important.

I only woke up two hours ago. Nightlife wears me out, especially when it's every single day. Sometimes, I'm obliged to have sex after an exhausting night at "Nafoura" or some other place. Isn't that bound to be totally exhausting for a woman like me whose life is such a mess?

---

1. TRANSLATORS' NOTE: As is explained later in this story, Moroccan lore has it that hyenas have the power to drag people away to their lair and "devour" them merely by pissing on them. Hyena piss is thus thought to render anyone unfortunate enough to smell it incapable of making sensible decisions. The adjective "madbu'" (literally "hyena-ed") thus comes to mean "stupid, silly, dumb." Hence the attempt via the title and the contents of this story to reflect both the literal sense of the word in its various forms and the implications of its folkloric background.

As I took another sip of my coffee, a slight shiver passed through my body and especially my head. My eyes became more open to the world. I may have felt alone, but not for long. God is the only one to remain alone. The girls were still chatting in the coffee shop, flaunting their hair, hands, and lips in that special way they have. At a particular age, they all look alike. Was I like them too? But give them five or six years, and they'll fade. The old men their father's age were faking laughter and offering them American cigarettes, which they lit for them. Outside, cars were racing by and causing traffic jams; motorcycles were everywhere.

This city decides to rush out of the genie's bottle all at the same time. The chaos on the street has no sense or meaning. When people finally get home, then things acquire meaning, and it's possible to impose a sense of morality. The girl sitting with the old man her father's age indulges in innocent chat, while the old man who's sitting with a girl his daughter's age is acting duly respectful.

Outside the window the street-lights had been turned on. Night was falling. Now we were in another world, completely different from daytime, the taste of which I'd often missed these past few years. I sipped my coffee again and lit another cigarette. A fat old man with a double chin gave me a lewd look. His lower lip dangled in a grotesque way. He lit a cigarette and pointed the lighter at me. I took a deep breath, convinced that he was the type of skinflint who frequents places like this to get himself a cheap woman. They'd never venture into nightclubs because they're too expensive. They're malicious as well; they're not like men who are prepared to pay a lot without worrying about what's in their pockets. In order to protect their precious reputations, they only show up at night to satisfy their primal urges. For my part, I only trust the generous ones; they're much more decent and open-minded. They may be having domestic problems, but they only talk about such things under certain circumstances.

Out on the street the lamps hanging down from the street-lights form circles of light on the pavement. The street is crowded with people using their elbows to push and shove. There are more eyes to be seen as well, but I can no longer make out heads, arms, or legs.

At times like these, I always used to be in control of the situation. I knew how to lie to my mother, and she knew how to lie to my father. She would be going out to do this or that with her friends. The next day I would be going to do this or that with my friends. My father would either believe us or not. When I got married, he still believed that I would never lie, but when I left my husband, he had the proof that I did lie.

The girls are all laughing the way I did in the past. Even to a woman, they're sexy. I've had that experience many times with girls under the influence of drugs or alcohol. They may be acting that way without taking anything; but on the other hand it might be having an effect on them. It may feel good, but it's forbidden. I'd tried it, too, when I was their age.

(I felt exhausted. I had no money to pay the bus fare. The trees in the street protected me from the early summer sun. I'd no idea what I was doing in this place. Why did I quit high school? I don't know. Lots of cars were honking their horns at me, and loads of motorcycles stopped beside me as they did with other women, disrupting the traffic as they did so. Insults were exchanged, but that didn't bother me. But I was scared. Leaning my back against a tree, I took a little break. I had a long way to go before I reached home.

The woman tooted her car's horn and stopped. At least it was a woman; she wouldn't hurt me. She opened the car door, and I walked over.

"Can I give you a ride?" she asked.

"Thank you, ma'am. Do you know me?"

"I know you because you're a woman."

"Many men have been tooting their horns at me, but I'm scared of them."

"You're right to be scared. They're all dogs. Next time they toot at you, tell them to go and play the drums as well. Before I take you home, let's have a drink somewhere."

I was feeling really thirsty. She was a kind woman who seemed to know about men better than me. Later on I discovered what she meant. Why shouldn't I drink something I'd never tasted before in my life? So that's exactly what I did. It was very delicious, even though it's forbidden.)

The girls are still laughing. Lamps are still hanging on the street, and cigarettes still dangle between the girls' lips or fingers. In a little while maybe something else will be hanging and something else dangling. Everything's possible.

"You should pay more attention to your studies," my mother told me. "These days I get the impression you're spending all your time smelling your armpits."

"People who don't smell their armpits smell something else."

"I don't understand you, but you must complete your studies."

"I'll try. But my father treats me as if I'm stupid."

"You mean, treats both of us."

"I don't know."

"Concentrate on your studies. Stupid people never think about the future."

"These days all the girls at school with me are acting stupid."

"Forget about them. Just take care of yourself."

I took a final sip of coffee, called the waiter, and paid him. The girls were still laughing at the men old enough to be their fathers who'd managed to turn them into complete imbeciles. The men were like real hyenas, sitting there smoking, sipping their coffee, and pissing under the tables where they were sitting. It all made me remember my mother's advice. At this point I had no desire to act stupid, even if I had done so in the past. Grabbing my bag, I left the coffee-shop. It was still crowded. Light was spreading further and further from the street-lamps. Amid the crowd I smelled a foul stench—hyena piss. I recognized it at once because I'd smelled it before—the kind of odor that, however you tried to avoid it, still followed you around. At first I tried covering my nose but, when I felt myself suffocating, I did what everybody else was doing—sniffed it with pride. Pushing my chest out, I teased my hair and started looking into men's eyes.

"No matter how bad the stench," I told myself, "it's my destiny to smell it."

With that I breathed in the air all around me.

The hyena-struck man speaks:

Actually, I wasn't in love with her, but there was something about her that attracted me at first. I knew that to a certain extent she was no different from the girls who would frequent places like this. But still, I eventually managed to convince myself that she wasn't like the others. It was just that she was impelled by some secret motivation—as I was to discover later on. As the saying has it, anyone who grows up behaving in a particular way will still behave that way when they're old. In other words, anyone used to doing something finds it hard to stop.

"You picked her up on the street," my mother told me. "So it's your own fault."

"She wasn't like that. In any case, she's changed."

"What do you know about café girls?"

"She used to spend time in the coffee-shop doing her homework with her friends."

"I don't care. Do whatever you like."

"She's a nice girl," my father said. "But you've introduced her to bad habits."

"She's in love with your boss," my sister told me. "I found his picture in her purse."

I'd been surprised when she took out a photograph. Everything was possible, she told me; even bringing earth and sky together. But I wasn't really in love with her, only attracted to her in some vague way, so I asked her about the photograph. She told me she'd never set eyes on either the boss or the photograph in her life. I pretended to be angry and told her to make some coffee to calm our nerves. For a moment she hesitated, then went into the kitchen. So I wasn't in love with her, but still there was something attracting me to her. We drank our coffee and calmed down. I forgot all about my boss's photograph and everything else.

"When are we going to get married?" she asked. "How long are we going to stay like this?"

"We need to learn more about each other."

"We've known each other long enough."

"Sleeping together in that student room isn't enough. Sex isn't enough for a man to know a woman. There are other things we don't know about each other yet that we need to find out."

"You're expecting too much. You have a strange way of looking at things."

We talked about other things like that. Should we get married or not?

Well, we did get married and stopped going to cafés and night-clubs.

"You should put an end to the kind of life you've been leading" was my sister's advice.

"But it's wonderful."

"Everything's wonderful, but it comes at a price."

"I don't like the way other people live," Ghita said. "Eating, drinking, and wearing clothes, they're all so utterly trivial."

That's true, I said; the way we live is different from other people. Everything wonderful does have its price; even going to a café's restrooms has its price.

(Feeling a twinge, I rushed to the restroom. When I'd finished, I left the water running in the toilet, closed the door, and walked over to the mirror. There were two girls there, Ghita and another girl whom she didn't know.

"Excuse me," I said. "May I look at myself in the mirror? Maybe I'm cute without even knowing it."

"You're really cute. You must be an only child?"

The other girl didn't say anything. She was combing her hair without paying any attention to our conversation. She went out, leaving the two of us standing in front of the mirror. We talked about other things, but I don't remember what.

"Shall we have a drink together?" suggested Ghita.

"Why not?" I replied.

She bent over, picked up some books and papers from under the sink, looked at her face in the mirror one more time, and adjusted some curls in her hair.

I had a coffee, and she ordered a soft drink.)

"We agreed about most things at first," I told my mother. "But then each of us started neglecting the thread that was binding us to each other."

"If either person drops the thread," she replied, "then make sure you keep your own thread to yourself. I keep talking about 'your thread' because it really does belong to you. You can drop it, as well, if you want, and let it fall in the street or anywhere you like without even thinking about it."

"You were the only one holding the thread from both ends," my sister said. "Actually, you had the illusion that she was holding the other end with you. There's nothing wrong with that. Everyone has the right to live an illusion he believes in."

"That's none of your business," I replied angrily. "I've never even talked about the number of threads that you're holding all alone."

"What are you talking about? Listen, Mom. Your son's insulting me."

"Your brother didn't say anything bad," Mother told her. "Actually, at one time your own mother may also have had a number of threads going. That doesn't matter. What does matter is that your brother dragged that girl in off the street."

"The street's not a brothel," I said. "Brothels are inside houses."

Actually, I had the same feelings as Ghita. The life she was leading had taken a totally different direction from the one we'd imagined together.

It's difficult to move easily from one planning phase to another. For his part, Aziz dearly wanted to be able to modify certain ideas that had been rooted in his mind for some time without any prior planning. Carts will never move easily along a road, unless it's been flattened and paved.

Ghita too was well aware that I felt the way she did. She'd chosen a world where one can live alone and not have to share it with anyone else. She may have been right about that, but it didn't stop her living a worthless existence.

After I'd drunk the coffee and she'd eaten the ice-cream, she still looked ravenous, although she did her best to hide it. We went outside and walked under the trees. We didn't bother looking in the shop-windows, but kept on talking. Each of us was trying to outdo the other so we'd be closer together; eventually that happened without either of us winning. I really couldn't tell who'd won and who'd lost.

"Do you drink wine?" I asked her.

"No, I don't," she replied.

"Why not? Doesn't anyone in your family drink?"

"All of them do except me."

Later on I found out that she drank more than I did, and smoked hashish, as well. But none of that mattered. What did matter was the enduring moment, not the ephemeral one—sincerity before loyalty. It was also important to do what you had to do and avoid what others didn't want to avoid because they couldn't.

Having moved past one set of trees we reached another and sat under them. We were scared that the Garde Mobile might come by and ask us for money or take us to the seventh district police station, the charge being that we weren't married. When I voiced my concern to Ghita, she said that her father was a *Caid* there. I believed her. I then stared defiantly at one of the guards, but he was completely uninterested. In fact, her father was neither *Caid*, nor caliph, nor minister, nor king. He was a kind man with no claims to any kind of authority, a really kind man. Fire leaves only ashes behind; occasionally a small ember will lurk in the ashes and burn everything up. In any case, Ghita might well be an ember in a heap of ashes or a pile of hay. The ashes may kill her, and the hay feed her.

"You're the one who chose her," Mother said. "Now you have to assume your responsibilities."

"In our family," my sister added, "we can accept anything except adultery. Our religion refuses to allow a husband to accept that. Husbands can do as they please, but a woman is required to respect her husband and his family."

"She's only been doing what she can do," I said. "Anyone who can do something, whether it's good or bad, will do it. An Arab from the East—I don't remember where I heard it—said: 'The only people who can't be tyrannical are the weak.'"

"Leave Eastern and Western Arabs out of it," my sister replied. "Actually, it was a poet who said it. Let's get back to Ghita. Shall I say it, Mother?"

"Don't you dare. You have a vicious tongue, straight out of the trash-can."

"She's actually a nice girl," my father had said later on. "If you'd known how to deal with her, none of this would have happened."

I didn't say anything, not wanting to explain how I should have taken care of her or she of me. Of course, once my sister had accused her of adultery, what happened went way beyond that—something only married people can appreciate. Personal things can happen. It's as though you're very stupid; a hyena has pissed all over you, dragged you back to its lair, and devoured you. That's the story we were always told when we were young. Children used to tell each other lots of stories about hyenas in the woods. According to those tales, the hyena doesn't hurt you in any direct way. Instead, it pisses right in front of you. Once you've smelled the piss, you follow it willingly.

Later on, I discovered that even in cities you could be made a fool of, at any time and any age. Thus, what happened between Ghita and me, the kind of thing that may happen at any time between husbands and wives, was all caused by hyena piss. Once it's pissed on you, you're no longer in control. You simply act without being aware of what you're doing. You love, hate, get married, fight, and cheat. The hyena's in charge.

My father asked me if I knew how to take care of her. How was I supposed to know? It's all the hyena's fault. That's what took me to the coffee-shop in the first place. It grabbed me by the arm, led me over to the mirror, and told me to talk to Ghita. I'm sure it was the hyena who told her to keep lying to me and led her by the arm to other places in town. It may even have told her not to take care of her child.

The hyena speaks:

Simple things do happen. What's clear is that everyone carries his own hyena within himself. If not that, then I might say instead that actually everyone is a hyena, a grown, widely experienced hyena that pisses all over smaller, naïve hyenas and drags them off to its lair—in other words, deep inside itself, where for a while it can do whatever it wants with them. Once in a while, persons so affected, be they male or female, may wake up from their psychological stupor and manage to shake off the hyena's evil spell. People also claim that there's a particular potion that negates the effects of hyena piss. That's why everyone should arm himself with a small amount of that antidote. That does not mean, of course, that the effects of hyena piss on human beings in general will not continue as long as the human species reproduces and procreates.

The strange thing that I've noticed is that children here in Morocco are born hyena-struck, so what's the story with their parents? Maybe it's because there are lots of forests and mountains that help preserve the hyena species; or perhaps Moroccan hyenas had already married and reproduced with other hyenas that Phoenicians, Romans, Visigoths, Portuguese, Spaniards, and, most recently, French, all brought with them.

Aha, that's it! So now you need to re-read what the hyena-struck man and woman have to say above. That very process will provide the antidote you all need.

A Night in Casablanca

*I*t was a dark night. The rain was coming down hard, so you could hardly glimpse the sea. Cars were speeding by, weaving erratically because their drivers were drunk. There had been a lot of accidents at this spot. The police always showed up late and conducted their routine procedures, questioning the nosey types who always crowded around such accidents.

"Was the driver drunk?" they'd ask.

The ambulance might arrive late too. The crowd would disperse. Some of the nosey folks might get either a slap on the face or a kick on the shins and be put inside the police jeep. They'd be dropped off later in the middle of the road once they'd paid a fine.

The roar of the sea could be clearly heard. The thunderclaps were even louder, and rain pounded on the tops of cars parked near hotels and bars.

Music came roaring out of the Oklahoma nightclub. Close by was a bar with people staggering in and out. They'd be making a lot of noise; often there would be fights involving fists or razors. When someone was stabbed, people who were not involved would gather around, but the victim would be left bleeding on the curb. Later on, they would have nothing to say to the police, who would make their usual kind of statement: "That's what happens to prostitutes. They suck men's blood, and theirs flows all over the sidewalk."

Now the sea was still roaring in the dark, but the rain was tapering off. Su'ad burst out of the Oklahoma's narrow entryway, as the bolt slammed shut behind her. She was trying to button up her coat as she approached a small area encircled by big clay flower-vases.

Now out came Sa'id too, talking to the elegant doorman, whom he knew very well.

"You're drunk tonight," the doorman said. "Can you drive?"

"I'm not drunk. That whore drank the whole bottle. Of course, she'll have to pay for it."

"Are you going to have some more fun tonight? Be sensible, Sa'id."

"I'll do what I do every night," he replied with a laugh as he slipped the doorman ten dirhams. "I'm King Shahriyar!"

"We're friends," he said, taking the tip. "You don't need to do that."

"Ouf!" said Sa'id, looking over at Su'ad, who was still waiting in the small circle, looking utterly exhausted. He went over to her, put his arm around her shoulder, and pulled her toward him.

"The car's close by," he said.

"What?!"

"The car's close by."

"Where to?"

"Anywhere you like. Other places are still open. Tonight's our night."

Once inside the car she had a struggle getting the makings for a *kif*-cigarette out of her purse. She started rolling it between her fingers.

"Sa'id, let's swing by one of my friends. Poor woman, she may not have had anything to smoke tonight."

"Why can't she get some? Dealers are everywhere along the Corniche."

"If she doesn't get some, she'll die or kill herself. She's a very close friend. She has lots of problems with her stepfather. Her boyfriend's the father of her beautiful little daughter, but he's from a big family and won't acknowledge her."

"I know those large families," he said. "But you still love them."

"Me? I don't love them, but I do like to live."

As she spoke drowsily, he was driving through empty streets that separated colorfully lit villas from each other. She lit the *kif*-cigarette.

"Do you want a drag?" she asked, her eyes half closed.

He inhaled, then handed it back.

"What are you saying? Where's my friend?"

"I don't know. Maybe she's somewhere in this world."

"Where are we?"

"Among those people . . ."

"Which people?"

"The ones you love."

"I don't love anyone. I used to love Al-Mu'ti, but I left him. He wasn't rich and used to take all the money I made at night. He smoked a lot of *kif* too. When we didn't have it, he'd go crazy and threaten to kill me. We went to the same high school and were both expelled. His father tried to kill his mother several times. I don't know his father, but Al-Mu'ti told me about him. He's certainly like his father. If I'd married him, he would've tried to kill me. I don't want to die. I love life too much."

Inside the slowly moving car the music was loud. The windows were closed because it was so cold and rainy outside. The car was like a closed can. The *kif* smoke was stifling, but Sai'd still didn't want to roll down the windows. A speeding motorcycle cut in front of him. He shivered and wiped the front windshield with his hand.

"I wish I had a big motorcycle like that one," Su'ad said.

"And when you got high, you'd be crashing through all the trees, wouldn't you?"

"Oh! Don't exaggerate. Everyone who rides motorcycles like that gets high."

He drove through the villas neighborhood. In the light of the street-lamps and the gently falling rain, the city seemed tranquil. Small puddles gleamed in the light. From time to time a patrol car cruised by with its lights off. It kept skirting the curb as it continued its hunt for homeless human dogs.

By now Su'ad was warming up inside her overcoat. She leaned her head back; once she'd closed her eyes, she had a hard time opening them again. She was talking nonsense, but Sa'id understood that she wanted something to eat. He felt hungry, too, even though on nights like this he'd rarely eat; sometimes he'd go to bed in his clothes and shoes.

"Are you hungry?"

"Yes," she replied.

"Let's get some *harira*."

"*Harira*'s sour, and the chick-peas and lentils are as hard as rocks."

"*Kif* makes you hungry."

"Very true! I once managed to eat a whole *kas'a* of couscous by myself."

"Don't exaggerate!"

"I swear on my honor."

"Do you have any honor, you . . . ?"

"You can shut your mouth! I'm more honorable than the daughters of those villa-owners. I know them well; I've smoked *kif* with a lot of them."

"Okay. Forget it. You're sure you don't want some *harira*?"

"No, I'd rather have a hamburger with *kofta*, eggs, and salsa. At Tangaoui's, near Cincinnati Ice-Cream, it's cheaper than *harira*."

"But it's always crowded there, and drunkards keep fighting over girls in the middle of the night. Police patrols usually come by and ask for IDs. Do you have an ID?"

"Do you think I'm from another planet? I'm Moroccan too, and I've a mother and father just like everyone else. Do you despise me just because you got to know me so easily? If I didn't like you, I'd never have talked to you. I can smell men a mile away. Don't think that I was attracted by your clothes or tie. There is something else about you; maybe you don't realize it yourself. People who know themselves really well are rare enough."

With that, she closed her eyes completely, but didn't fall asleep. She was listening to music and seeing different colors, little twittering birds, and other things as well, all jumbled up. They included a beach with small palm-trees, naked people swimming and sunbathing, and women with beautiful flowers in their hair, glistening in the sunshine.

Sa'id looked over at her. She had a dreamy, innocent expression on her face like that of a little girl. He lit a cigarette. After a while he managed to find somewhere to park. Su'ad opened her eyes and asked him to light a cigarette for her. By now it was only drizzling, but when Sa'id stared up at the sky, it still looked pitch black. In a few minutes it would be pouring for sure, and the next day and the next. The earth needs rain, he told himself. Everyone's been complaining about the drought, including his father who owned lands in Mdakra. They had not dug any canals there yet because the digging had stopped at the property-line of a local notable who was related to a senior government official.

Deep in his heart he wanted it to rain, but not for him. He already owned a house and had a car for himself and another for his wife. He had a bank account, too, something not easily acquired by people of his age.

Su'ad got out of the car after him and closed the door indifferently, trying at the same time to pull up her coat collar.

"Slam the door hard," Sa'id told her. "It's not cold, and it's stopped raining."

She opened the door again, slammed it, and checked to make sure it was locked. They walked toward Tangaoui's restaurant. Stevie Wonder's voice wafted softly out into the early morning sky. The place was small but very colorful. Some girls were perched on stools in front of the stone counter, but there were more men in the place than women. The staff, in clean uniforms, moved around the room with an acrobatic agility. One of the cooks kept flipping burgers while dancing to Stevie Wonder's song. A girl looked up from the counter where she'd been resting her head. She was beautiful, but a lack of sleep and too much drinking made her look exhausted. She seemed to be alone. She spoke to the waiter who was dancing, but it was the other one, who was not dancing, that came over.

"A glass of cold water," she said.

"You've drunk a lot of cold water. What's wrong with you? Did you smoke too much weed?"

"Mind your own business, or I'll go upstairs and complain to Tangaoui."

"Go up if you want. He doesn't like your type!"

"Bring me a glass of cold water and mind your own business."

He brought her a glass of cold water and put some ice in it. She drank it down, then went back to her previous perch.

"If you want to find a bed," he said, "go somewhere else."

She paid no attention. Sa'id and Su'ad ordered two sandwiches and waited in line behind the crowd. Some people were wolfing their food down as they stood there. Sa'id took the wrapped sandwiches, and they both went outside to eat them in the car. A few isolated raindrops, lost in the air, were falling here and there. Su'ad opened her sandwich and began to eat ravenously.

"Didn't you have any lunch today?" Sai'd asked as he chewed his own sandwich. "Why are you eating it like that?"

She didn't reply, but kept on eating the same way. A piece of tomato fell on her coat. She picked it up quickly and put it back in her mouth. Just then he sensed a shadow to his left and turned to look. The policeman was knocking on the window. Sa'id rolled it down.

"Your ID," the policeman demanded after greeting him.

The policeman peered inside the car and looked at the back seats. He stared closely at Su'ad's face but didn't ask for her ID.

"Who's she?"

"A friend."

"Go home and get some sleep. It's late. Unless you want to spend the night at the station."

With that, the policeman gave him his document back and left.

"*Tfou!*" Su'ad said, "They are just like flies."

"Shut up or get out of my car. He was nice, but you're insulting him. If you weren't with me, you would be spending the night at the station."

"What did I do? Did I kill Bouhmara or something?"

"And what are you doing so late at night? They're conducting a cleanup. There are a lot of thieves around these days and too many crimes."

"I'm just a . . . the real thieves are sleeping quietly in their homes."

"Don't talk about things that are none of your business."

"If you weren't with me now, I'd think you were one of them."

He lit her cigarette. When she threw the cigarette butt out of the car, she tapped his right leg with a laugh. Even though the butt was round, it only rolled a short way on the wet sidewalk.

"I always love to smoke after I've eaten," she said. "The cigarette has a special taste to it. Tell me where we're going? Don't tell me the hotel. I'm scared of the police. Do you have an apartment?"

"No."

"I know an empty place near the Great Belt."

"The Great Belt's a long way away."

"But it's safe. The air's so fresh. Everybody goes there to get fresh air."

"Do you always go there to get fresh air?"

"Only with your type, of course, when there's no apartment available. I've a girlfriend who owns an apartment in Verdun, but her friend spends four nights a week there. We don't want to cause her any problems."

The car took off toward the Great Belt. By now Eros had been transformed into a human being behind the wheel of a car, proud as a peacock as he drove through the city streets. He stopped at a gas station to fill up. Urged on by Eros, the attendant roused himself with some difficulty. Sa'id could have woken up the entire neighborhood with his horn. The attendant filled up the car, then rubbed his eyes with the back of his hand before going back to sleep. Once the car had left, he turned off the gas station's lights so he wouldn't be disturbed again.

By now the car was making its way through completely empty streets. Some street-lamps were still on, which was unusual since they're normally turned off at midnight. The road turned dark. Some isolated buildings were just visible, while others had lights on; and there were probably still others that he couldn't make out in the dark.

"Turn right here," Su'ad said after a while. "There's the spot where we can get some fresh air. Have you been here before?"

"No."

"It's a beautiful place. You should get to know it. Everybody who loves fresh air comes here."

"This air is certainly different."

"Exactly. You can discover that for yourself."

The car was moving slowly along a dark road. In the dark everything seemed empty. Sa'id could feel his heart beating. He took out a small bottle of Black Label from under his seat and handed it to Su'ad. She opened it, took a swig, then handed it back to him. He took a swig as well so as to bolster his courage and rid himself of his worries about this empty road.

"We must stop," he told her. "Aren't there police patrols or Garde Mobile jeeps around?"

"No, I know this place very well."

The car stopped.

"I'm feeling very cold," Su'ad said. "Hand me the bottle again. I'm going to get out for some fresh air."

She had another big swig, then opened the door and got out.

"She's certainly no normal girl," he thought to himself. "Maybe it's the hashish. She certainly smokes it with relish."

After a while he became aware that there were four people around him. One of them wore a hat and had covered his face and neck.

"Don't hurt him, 'Abdelqader," he heard Su'ad say from a distance. "He's a nice, kind person. Just take everything and leave him his ID. Don't behave the way you did on that foul night with that other stupid man. And don't forget: if you want to get warm, he has a bottle of whiskey."

THE CART

(1993)

The Scavenger

One skinny cat was mewing behind the garbage, while another stretched out its front paws as far as it could to grab a stinking fish-head with flies buzzing all around it. Yet a third (maybe it was a kitten) was waiting by the other one's tail, sniffing and waiting for crumbs.

When a dog suddenly appeared, the cats reacted instinctively, startled. But the dog was not bothered about the cats. He seemed full; he had already had enough to eat, it seemed, which helps explain why he didn't bother with either the cats or the garbage. Now a man arrived, pushing a small cart. Kicking fat and skinny cats out of the way, he started poking through the garbage.

He found a cardboard box, a stiff plastic bag, and an empty bottle, and put them all into his small cart. He then moved on to scavenge in other garbage bins, hoping to find yet more boxes, plastic bags, and bottles.

Sometimes his hands came into contact with human excrement, as though human beings don't have such things as toilets. Truth to tell, there are still some houses that do not have toilets, even though the girls that regularly emerge from them look chic enough. They may not be all that beautiful, but they look smart and can speak broken French. All (or most) of them can talk about their grandfathers, the *Caid*s, during the colonial period, or about the fact that they are waiting for some imaginary inheritance or an eternal trip to Europe. Even marriage does not pay any more.

But none of that bothered the scavenger. He left, and the cats were able to go back to the garbage. Now that he had tipped out the entire contents of the garbage bin, they managed to grab a whole smelly sardine. For the cats, this was a real party. The kitten was the only one that didn't get anything. He stood apart in the space between the wall and the garbage, mewing. Even so, one of the cats seemed to notice his pathetic cries. Going back to the garbage, it jumped deftly right into the middle of the heap, grabbed something, and threw it to the skinny kitten. Then it went back and knocked a sardine head with its paw; sardines usually had no bones.

Continuing on his way, the scavenger came across a big garbage bin and told himself that here he might well find some real treasure. It was in front of a big apartment house. Never before had he seen such strange plants as the ones growing downward from its balconies. They all looked imported. He put his hook inside the bin and poked around, then inserted his long arm and pulled out some rags that looked like women's underwear. He put that carelessly into his bag; he would check it later. Sometimes he came across something valuable, but most of the time he was well aware that the things he was carrying were useless. The sweat and the swollen feet all day long were for nothing. Could it be that other scavengers had come by already? That was why he was eager to get up so early. But sometimes, when he had drunk too much bad wine, he only managed to get up in the afternoon, totally wasted. Even so, he would leave the house, determined to scavenge for whatever the others, the early risers, had left behind. Sometimes he picked up pieces of cardboard from the pavement; in winter they would be rain-soaked, while in other seasons they might be all dried out. Even cardboard could be sold, although not for much. In any case, he realized that he was living in a country where everything was for sale. People needed to sell everything. The rich could afford to buy everything, even bags of dry bread bits. From it they would either make something for humans or else sell it to cattle farmers with livestock. He realized that everything he picked up could be sold; it made no difference whether it was cheap or expensive—it was sellable. Actually, there were some things that no one wanted to buy from him, perhaps because they were completely useless. But at any rate, no one would die of hunger in Morocco.

An old scavenger had once told him that when he was young, he and his friends used to lie on the ground and lick up the honeyed alfalfa that dropped from carts transporting it for the colonists' cows. The alfalfa was sweet, the old man told him, and that filled them up. To finish their meal, they used to go to the sea to steal corn, which they would then grill on a vacant lot.

Honeyed-alfalfa carts didn't exist anymore, but cornfields certainly did. He saw them whenever he traveled to the countryside. When he got rich, he planned to buy a piece of land and plant corn, watermelon, melon, cucumber, mint, and tomatoes. People said you could sell them for a lot of money in Europe. But he had also heard that French farmers would block Moroccan trucks carrying tomatoes at the Spanish border, and the same thing with potatoes.

So, fair enough, there was no point in planting potatoes or tomatoes; he would make do with corn. It was only a dream, but it was one that could be realized. How many scavengers even had a chance of becoming rich? He might find something really expensive that had been dropped in the garbage by mistake. When he thought about it, he chuckled, because sometimes all he found was human excrement. Even so, he still believed that luck hadn't smiled on him yet, but one day it would. Who knows? Anything was possible. He had seen some films, especially American ones, where a lot of poor people became rich, even scavengers. Life was strange. If it smiled on you, it was a woman; if it ran away from you, it was the Devil's own wife; God forbid!

The scavenger's dreams were as plentiful as the garbage he rummaged through. He knew that many scavengers had become owners of companies and shops where they sold imported goods and consorted with government bigwigs who could facilitate the sale of smuggled products. With his own eyes he had seen how owners of luxury cars used to crowd the flea market in order to buy such products: electronic devices, Italian clothes, and so on. What mattered was that he would keep rummaging through the garbage till one day he too became rich like them. As far as he knew, tramps would inevitably either get to the top or else fall into the abyss, where he still was now.

As he pushed his wooden cart, he felt exhausted. Today had been a tiring trip. Never mind, one has to tolerate everything for the sake of living. God the Great and Almighty created us in order to discover how to live and scavenge in this world, even if it means soiling our hands with human excrement.

He praised God, then spotted a garbage bin a little distance away. He stopped pushing his cart and began to scavenge, holding onto the hook as he did so. He started poking at the contents: some paper, orange peels, and a yogurt carton. Then from the bottom the hook pulled out a wrapped black bag. Putting it down on the curb, he opened it carefully, convinced that there was a turkey inside because what was in it was soft. However, he was astonished to find that it was a dead baby. For a second he was stunned, then he started running, leaving the cart behind. He ran and ran till he fell down on the grass in a park, panting. He had no time to praise God.

Moral Crime

$\mathcal{T}$eakwood trees lined the curb a few meters away, each one placed in the middle of a ring of smooth rocks. Their leaves were pale, stiff, and curled up. Some had already fallen, while others hung in the air as though attached to an artificial tree in a New York storefront window.

An African American was leaning against a tree trunk, totally indifferent to people passing by. He had his hands in his pockets and was chewing something, as he calmly took in everything happening in front of him. On this particular night he'd left the air base, and now here he was, thinking about finding himself a woman to warm him up and keep him company; a woman who could make him feel that he really existed, just like this tree, this branch, and this curb.

"Smith told me I could easily get myself a woman if I wanted to. Just yesterday he said he regularly had fun with the most beautiful woman on earth. That's what Smith told me . . . ," and so on and so on. . . .

He stayed where he was and coolly placed a cigarette in his mouth. He lit it in the same nonchalant way and started smoking.

"If Maggie'd married me," he thought, "she'd have come with me. Then I wouldn't need to commit a sin. Oh Lord Jesus, don't let me sin! But here I am, doing it in spite of myself."

Maggie had treated him badly.

The smoke was seeping from between his lips, then drifting upwards toward his nose and his forehead before vanishing into thin air. He was still paying no attention to passers-by, but he did notice an American officer holding his wife's arm and gently pushing his son's stroller. He knew him. No, he didn't. His shoes were covered with the dust at the foot of the tree, and his frustration made him keep thrusting them still further into the dust. Snatching the cigarette from his lips, he threw the butt away.

His mood was neither happy nor satisfied. His body seemed somehow heavy and disconnected, and he kept having a strange sensation that bothered him. For sure his situation was not normal.

"My friends in Chicago must be happy. William and Henry may well be sitting in a café somewhere. I wonder if they remember me? Sorry . . . sorry . . . they may be on a plane headed for Vietnam."

Soft music was wafting out of a nearby café, obviously requested by someone with good taste. He paid no attention to the Moroccan man who started talking to him; the words were coming out of his throat, full of anger, pain, and hunger for something. The guttural sounds simply blended with the rest of the noise inside his head.

The young Moroccan in his *jallaba* was very insistent, but the American pushed him away, gently at first, but then much harder. In spite of everything, he refused to react to the Moroccan's insults.

"There are lots of bums," he thought. "Does this nasty Moroccan really think I own the Ford Motor Company?"

He swallowed in disgust. "Today the world's changing," he told himself, as he scratched his side. "It's assuming a totally different form."

He went into the café to his right and sat on a chair. His mind was wandering. He was not thinking about anything in particular; or rather, he was thinking, but about a whole load of meaningless things.

"What's your name?" he asked a girl.

"Khadija."

"And your friend?"

"Habiba."

(They were both ugly.)

"You're beautiful," he told Khadija.

"Really?!" she replied, feeling proud of herself.

"Don't you believe me?"

"I don't know." (Although deep down she did.)

"Then ask your friend."

"I have no opinion on the subject," Habiba said.

At this point the American felt a sense of victory as he drank his beer; he'd managed to get two girls instead of just one.

"If Smith saw me now, he'd die of jealousy. But he's still a good friend."

He was drinking to all his friends, present and absent, living and dead.

"Why aren't you drinking your coffee?" he asked Habiba.

"I don't feel like it."

"Aren't you happy?"

"Absolutely not."

"She's just lost a friend of hers," Khadija told him, "so she's feeling sad."

The American laughed, and that made him cough. "She's bound to find someone else," he said.

"You're both laughing at me, aren't you?" Habiba said.

"What do you mean?" Khadija asked.

"I think she's mad at us," the American observed.

He offered her a cigarette, which she grabbed eagerly.

"I think I'd better be going," she said, once she'd taken her first drag.

"There's no need to go," the American told her. "You can keep us company."

While he kept staring at Habiba, she let her mind wander. She looked out at the dark sky and the trees standing there, defiant and proud.

Khadija was thinking to herself that tonight's catch was going to be priceless. This black American was a nice enough male animal. So why on earth was this stupid woman filling the air with clouds of smoke?"

"Why are you acting like this?" she asked her friend in Arabic.

"I need to leave," Habiba replied.

"Look, you'll have to choose. Either leave or look happy."

"What do you mean?"

"Nothing, but you must understand."

"What are you both saying?" cut in the American. "I don't understand anything."

They didn't answer his question. Instead Khadija kept talking to her friend.

"Tonight you . . ."

But she didn't complete the sentence. She made do with leaning on the American's shoulder and rubbing her coarse hair on his chin.

"Can't we leave?" Habiba asked

"Let's leave in a little while," the American suggested.

A police car drew up to the curb, and two policemen got out; one was driving, and the other was his assistant. Both of them had the right build for the job.

"It's so demeaning to have to search cafés like dogs!" he commented to his colleague.

"We have to do our job," the second replied. "What would we be doing if we stayed at the station? Absolutely nothing."

"Working at night is very tiring."

"Oh, shut up and stop grumbling!"

One of them went inside the café. The other bent down to tie the laces on his right shoe, then caught up quickly with his partner.

The first policeman approached their table and touched his cap, although he did not take it off.

"May I see your ID?"

"Oh, please," Khadija begged.

Habiba and the American remained silent.

"Give me your ID!"

"I don't have it on me."

"And you?"

"Me neither."

"Okay, let's go to the station."

The second cop moved back as though the entire thing did not concern him. He was watching the waiter, who was wiping spilled coffee from his uniform.

"We'll have to take them both down to the station," he said, turning to his friend.

"Let's go."

The two girls stood up, huddled together. They kept glancing at each other, each one expecting the other to come up with an excuse for the offense they'd committed against public decency.

"Come on, move it!" the policemen yelled at them both.

By now the waiter had finished cleaning his pants and was watching what was going on. The policemen pushed him aside. The two girls walked out with their heads lowered. There were no other customers in the café.

The American stayed where he was, convincing himself that he was just plain out of luck.

"Another wasted night," he thought, "just like all the others before it. What do I tell Smith? Do I tell him I made out with a beautiful white woman, a very beautiful woman, all last night?"

He called the waiter over. "How much is the bill?" he asked.

"Three dirhams."

"What was that about?" he asked as he paid. "What do they want with those two poor girls?"

"What can we do for them?" the waiter responded, then walked away. He'd heard someone calling him from outside the café.

"What can we do for them?" the American kept repeating to himself. "What can we do for them? What can we do for me?"

Pushing his chair back, he got up to leave, with one hand crammed firmly in his pocket. Before exiting the café, he turned around and had one last look. The owner was still there, standing behind the cash register. He was giving him a languid look, his head tilted to one side.

A Tiny Kingdom

*T*o the right was a high mountain; to the left another mountain, less high and flatter in shape. All of which made the huts and mud-brick houses feel closer to each other. By contrast, other houses scattered all over the mountain on the right seemed almost suspended. However, the thing that linked the two mountains was the greenery in the valley below. For some time, inhabitants of the mountain villages had treated this valley as communal property, something that helped forge family alliances by marriage.

Takarmouss had married Fetoush, and his son Hadou, president of the rural commune on the second mountain, had married into the Bahoush family on the first. The relationship between the two mountains was thus of considerable vintage and had been cemented by the green valley below. Neighboring tribes were still embroiled in disputes, things that went back many years; the makhzan authorities were the only ones who had managed to resolve things by interfering at the appropriate point. But the tribes of these two mountains had avoided such hatred and conflicts. So it was that, while we learned about conflicts involving neighboring mountain tribes or even occasionally others in the plains and valleys, we never heard anything to suggest the slightest rancor between one mountain and the other.

Any such conflicts had happened a long time ago. In older times the pattern had often been repeated. Tribes had decided to side with one dynasty or another or one monarch or another. But when the tribes from the two mountains became linked by marriage, the valley turned into a genuine paradise. The trees had all looked dead, and the plants had died off as well, but the point was to give seeds a chance to restore life to the valley in between the two mountains that had been neglected. But from now on, it was no longer neglected as it had been before. Axes and hoes dug into its soil, duly followed by women, men, and small children, whose hands labored hard. Now the trees no longer looked dead. Seeds found their place in the soil, carefully tended by human hands. Dynasties, monarchs, and generations followed one another, and the valley began to blossom green, now that human will was involved.

The valley's trees and plants die away so as to allow for nature's patterns to be repeated, as axes and hoes dig their way into its soil. When both earth and sky are angry, we cannot know for sure what is the primary factor that motivates every member of the tribe to go down to the valley in order to restore life. Most likely, blood-ties are responsible. In fact, sometimes it seems that human blood has a bond to nature itself. It may well be that we won't be able to find one single cryptic explanation for the whole thing; and that is even after we have observed the tribes from both mountains leaving their isolated homes or their communities and carrying their tools down into the valley, while their wives and children dig here and there. After awhile, trees will start to blossom, buds will open, fruits and crops will ripen, and mankind will continue to defy nature. When the valley turns green again, there are lots of wedding celebrations and engagement parties that bring together the tribes of the two mountains. On such occasions dowries are not paid in cash, but rather in kind: cattle, sheep, and goats. Most of the time, at some point in the middle of the night, the celebrations move from the houses, be they small or large, down to the green valley below. People gather among the trees on the banks of the small river where two wooden bridges have been built.

Even though the river dries up sometimes, the valley stays green most of the time. The villagers know how to tap the soil and extract water. Only one thing has them beaten; it is something they cannot handle. Occasionally, wild boars will attack them and wreak havoc everywhere, but they're not allowed to kill the animals because the authorities punish anyone who kills a boar. The president of the rural commune has complained to the authorities, but in vain. The law is the law, they are told. Certain animals may not be killed in the kingdom, even though human beings may be (may God have his mercy on them. Amen!).

Legend has it that this valley and its surrounding villages, where the social structure differs from the rest of the Anti-Atlas mountain villages, were under the authority of a Berber woman. A long time ago she proclaimed herself queen and thereby defied the central authorities in Fez. Even though the king laid siege to the district, he was unable to subdue her. She was self-sufficient and did not need to import anything from outside the borders of her territory. The soil belonged to her, as did the water and sky. That explains why the tribes' inhabitants became renowned for their pride, happiness, and willingness to die for their honor. If they could not kill a single boar, it was not out of cowardice, but rather respect for the law. And that in itself was a kind of pride.

Then, one day in 1974, a new *Caid* was appointed in charge of the region. He did not realize that he had been given authority over a tiny kingdom with its own rules. In most cases those rules were not actually correct: things that people were not really responsible for and knew nothing about. Even so, the people had a vague notion of how they worked, just as they firmly believed that the law was paramount. And, since the law governed everyone, it could sometimes be trodden underfoot. That is precisely what happened when the new *Caid* whipped an old woman in the market because she had taken him to task for something. Whereupon a young man grabbed him, stabbed him with a knife, and left him drowning in his own blood till he breathed his last. However, this young man was cut down by a bullet as he stood alongside the newly appointed *Caid*. But, in spite of such a tragedy, the tribes held both religious and secular ceremonies to celebrate the honor of their pride and heritage. No one felt sad or wept tears. In this country they might not be allowed to kill a boar, but a human being, even a *Caid*, could certainly be killed, because the myth of the tiny kingdom's laws was sacred and could not under any circumstances be violated. Wild boars could do whatever they wanted, but no human boar could behave the same way, even if he were a tribesman. Tradition was tradition. Everybody would die at some point, and God alone determined a man's lifespan.

However, the tiny kingdom's laws were bound to change, because every robust system has to bear in mind that there exists a still stronger system. When the incidents involving the new *Caid* with the old woman and the proud young man occurred in the green valley, a strange, heavily armed force arrived the same night. I don't know what took place later in that small kingdom. Was anyone killed? Arrested? It was dark, and I could not make out anything. In any case, it's better not to know, because everyone needs to clean his own front door before cleaning his neighbor's.

The Street-Sweeper

There he was, sitting on the curb, his back leaning against the low wall from which branches hung down, laden with flowers and still-unopened blossoms. He'd left the trash-cart in a space between two cars. The broom was still swaying in the breeze; it was long and weighed very little, since it was probably made out of reeds.

He lit a cigarette, coughing all the while. Did he have pneumonia or just the flu? No one knew. When it came to old age, or let's say any age—middle-age, youth, or childhood—everything was possible. It didn't matter whether he smoked or not; he was coughing continuously. One of his daughters had offered to take him to the doctor, but he'd refused; he'd never been to a doctor before. He was just coughing, that was all. Perfectly normal; everybody coughs. It certainly wasn't anything to be bashful about; in fact, there might not be anything seriously wrong. At his age everyone coughed.

True enough, some people can die of it. He had had a friend who used to smoke *kif*, then one day he'd simply gone on coughing and coughing till he dropped dead right beside him. He probably didn't die of coughing, but something else: loneliness, perhaps. After all, he'd spent ten years living on his own in an isolated room. His children had moved away when they got married; they'd bought cars, become rich, and purchased apartments in other neighborhoods. Coughing probably won't kill you, and yet his friend had coughed and coughed till he passed away. He himself had watched it happen. He'd propped his friend up on a pile of dirt till some other people arrived. They'd all gathered round, chatting and sympathizing. Some of them had been coughing, as well. They'd taken him away and buried him.

234

Even though a breeze was blowing, it was still very hot. Birds were chirping in the branches that dangled over his head. A butterfly fluttered by in front of him, landed on the broom, then flew away; perhaps it didn't like the foul stench. He was still smoking and coughing. Stretching out his legs on the curb, he stared at one of his toes poking out of a hole in his shoe. Wearing a torn shoe didn't bother him. Even as a child he had usually walked barefoot, but one of his daughters had made him wear new shoes and occasionally a clean suit. None of that bothered him, but he really wanted to go to the local bath-house. After all, he'd now done the things he really cared about. He'd spent most of his life in a shack, but now he'd put up a two-story building. His daughters were grown up: one worked at the Social Security Office, and the others were in London. Some people suggested they were doing something bad. God alone knows—people talk too much. Every raisin comes with a stick in its butt. At any rate, they sent him money every month. He'd be able to put up another building for them to settle down in, once they decided to come back home. Home, sweet home! What you need to do in your homeland is build things—construct apartments, found companies, and make chicken coops. He may be just a street-sweeper, but street-sweepers collect everything. He was thinking about his daughters; he loved the broom just as much as them.

His daughters had tried to persuade him to get another job, but he'd refused. He was used to drinking the cup of tea that a woman would give him, or chewing the piece of dry bread handed him by a child. As far as he was concerned, that was a delicious meal, matched only by evening soup and the cup of coffee before bedtime. At times it was hard for him to eat his soup, because the old lady talked a lot and kept thinking about their daughters in London. She kept saying how much she missed them, living in a foreign country. They were like two complete strangers, people with no parents. He would respond by reminding her that they kept sending money every month. She should thank God they were old enough and knew what they were doing. Be quiet, woman, he'd tell her. And with that he'd go back to sipping the soup, then finish his coffee and go to bed.

Their mother used to talk to other people about the kind of work Moroccan girls do in England, France, or Italy. Many families have daughters in Europe, and sometimes in other countries they know nothing about. What really counts is that his job involved sweeping the ground, whereas they were sweeping pockets with the sweat of their brow. God Almighty, to whom be ascribed all perfection and majesty, knows how to distribute subsistence to His servants. For example, just consider the cases of the sweeper, the gardener, and the cabinet member.

"What if I were a cabinet member?" he wondered, then went on: "Why doesn't one of my daughters marry a cabinet member?"

He knew a girl in the neighborhood who'd married an important man. She'd been lucky because she wasn't anything like as beautiful as his daughters who were now working in England. Maybe she'd been lucky because her father wasn't a street-sweeper. He'd passed away a long time ago, leaving her mother to make alcohol, sell toothpicks, and dye her hair. Important people certainly admired mothers like her. But the more talkative ones, the kind that made soup and coffee for him in the evening, could even drive the very Devil himself away if he were to come and ask for the hand of one of her daughters.

In any case, the butterfly flew away, then came back. By now the wind had died down, and the broom was no longer swaying. After he'd smoked a couple of cigarettes, he glanced toward the end of the alley. He still had quite a distance left to sweep, fill his cart with garbage, and then empty it into the disposal bin. By now, the worker whose job was burning the garbage would have left; he usually quit work early because his boss did too. No matter; they could burn the garbage any time. But before that happened, whole armies of insects, of which he could only recognize flies, would have made a beeline for it.

There are other small insects that can sting and leave red marks in the skin; that's why they should really burn the trash immediately. Those particular insects are black, and look nothing like the butterfly that was landing, then flying away; landing, then flying. It was apparently disgusted by the stench of both the broom and the cart, so it landed instead on the roses and flower blossoms. Praise the Lord!

Some creatures like living in the trash, while others prefer roses and flower-blossoms. In creation there are both dirty black insects and beautiful butterflies; some live in the daylight, others prefer the dark. Humans are just like insects; some live like bats, others live like flies and butterflies.

He stood up and started pushing his cart along the alley.

"Hey, you!" a little girl called out to him.

He turned round wearily. She was carrying a tray with a pot of tea and some bread. He took a look at some of the trash piled in front of him, but left the cart where it was. He sat down on the curb near the spot where the girl had put down the tray in the sun. She went away, chatting to two other girls. Leaning against the wall and stretching his legs out wearily, he poured himself some tea.

At that moment, he remembered that his daughter who worked at the Social Security Office had asked him if he needed anything. "You embarrass us," she said. "The neighbors keep calling us the street-sweeper's daughters."

He also remembered how he had responded. "It's this broom that's turned you into real women. You used to sleep in a barn, but now you can sleep in a proper building."

"You have to stop sweeping."

"I'll retire in a year, then you can marry whomever you want, someone who's prepared to accept a street-sweeper as a father-in-law. Who knows? His father might even be a street-sweeper too."

"I don't meet street-sweeper's sons."

"How can you say that to my face without feeling ashamed?"

He took a sip of tea, lit a cigarette, and tried to forget everything. The little girl was still chatting with her friends. She moved away a little. One of them tried to stretch up and pick a rose on the wall, but in spite of several attempts, she couldn't reach it.

Just then the wind blew down a wilting red rose. The little girl was thrilled. She picked it up, smelled its scent, and held it under the other girls' noses. He finished his cigarette and the whole pot of tea. He called over to the girl, but she didn't hear him. He called again; this time she heard, but kept chatting with her friends. Maybe they were talking about what might happen to them in the future or what had happened at home yesterday. Standing up again, he grabbed the cart's handles and looked to the end of the alley. Many piles of trash were still waiting for him, but no matter; he had been doing it for a long time and was quite used to it. One of his daughters had told him that street-sweepers in London were well paid. In any case he was fine. Sweeping streets in Casablanca was better than sweeping London streets. God would reward you for sweeping Muslim streets and collecting their trash; it was better than collecting Christian garbage, even though some Christian trash was definitely better than that of Muslims. They could intercede with the authorities, get passports, and take some Moroccan girls back with them.

May God bless them! If it weren't for those Christians, we would not have been able to build even a wall, and his two daughters would not have gone to London. . . . Some of them are good, others bad. They aren't all the same; in fact, sometimes they can be better than the Muslims in Rabat. Yet Christians are still Christians, and Muslims are Muslims. God created them all and knows what's in their hearts. He knows who's a believer and who's a non-believer. Atheists are all one and the same.

The trash was still piled up at the end of the alley. He would listen to the usual chatter, eat the soup, drink coffee, and contemplate the walls which he had built with the sweat of his brow or armpits, or something else going on in London. He was still pushing his cart when a service vehicle passed by.

"Haven't you finished this alley yet?" the supervisor asked, peering out the window.

The driver was paying no attention as the supervisor looked out and issued this warning.

Meanwhile the street-sweeper kept on walking behind his cart, picking up pieces of paper and orange-peel, melon and watermelon rinds. He wondered if people on London streets discarded melon and watermelon rinds, or other things instead. He hadn't asked his two daughters that question, but if he remembered, he would certainly do so next time. All he could remember was that they told him there were Arabs living in London; they would certainly discard pieces of paper, melon, watermelon rinds, and banana peels. Some of the Christians living in London would slip on them. Since people always discard skins in this alley, others will certainly keep on doing the same thing; after all, Arabs will always be Arabs, whether they're from Casablanca or Mecca. That's the way God made them: they peel and eat, and others sweep. Even sweepers peel and eat; sometimes they slip as well. In the end we'll all slip our way toward God. No soul can know in which country it will finally slip nor on which curb or in which street. How many cabinet members have fallen from lofty heights and slipped to the ground, and how many sweepers? But once you've slipped, falling is not the same: the way a minister falls from on high is not anything like what happens to a street-sweeper. That, at any rate, is what he'd heard from his daughter who worked in the Social Security Office.

"Many employees fall down on our office-floor, Dad," she said. "The cleaner must use something slippery to clean it. That's just one possibility."

"The only thing I know of to make employees slip is homemade soap. For my part, my daughter, I'm anxious to keep the alley clear of orange and banana peels so that no one will slip. I've done it for years, and it's a job that's helped you grow up."

A boy now appeared out of a narrow alley and hit the street-sweeper in the face with a rubber ball. The kid started crying and ran away. The sweeper put his hand up and felt his face because the ball had hit him really hard. He sat down on the curb and started coughing again. This time, however, when he touched his lips, he noticed something red—blood. The ball had certainly hit him on a sensitive part of his face.

After a while he got up, then started pushing the cart again. The cut on his face was still bleeding. He still had a few meters of the alley left to clean, but behind him he was leaving a trail of blood for others to mop up. Before he reached the end of the alley, he totally collapsed. As he lay there spread-eagled on the street, no one could figure out what had happened.

The Baby Carriage

Everything was plunged in darkness as night descended from heaven to earth. No one was walking along the corridor-like alley. Streetlights were perched at intervals like evil goblins, trying to eradicate the darkness and stop its cancer-like spread. The wind had started blowing violently, and that made some partially closed windows bang loudly against the walls. But even though the wind was blowing, it wasn't cold; actually, it was quite warm. Even so, no one was out. It felt as if a war had started, or else winter had arrived early.

At times like these, Ibrahim would make just as much as he normally did. Passers-by would go to and fro as though wandering around a market. That may explain why he'd long since chosen this particular alley.

But tonight, things were different. No one was coming by or looking out windows, as though the world were no longer in existence. The wind was still blowing hard, but it wasn't chilly.

"Something must be happening," Ibrahim told himself. "This is impossible. Only three passers-by in two hours."

He stayed silently where he was, like an inanimate object. He felt utterly confused; a sense of bewilderment overwhelmed him, body and soul.

By now, fog had started to settle in as well, and that suddenly made the entire place look like a truck carrying tons of combed cotton. Blinding white light fused with the darkness. All you could see of the streetlight poles was a foggy yellow point at the very top. Ibrahim stayed right where he was, lost in the fog, and switched his brain off for a while. If anyone happened to pass by and stub their foot on the curb, he would come to.

"Something's got to be going on," he thought, "so what's the point of hanging around here?"

He felt the small baby carriage nestling by his side like a house-trained cat, then ran his hand over the piece of leather strapped to his backside, to which the bones that constituted what was left of his legs were attached. He put up his hand and felt the hat on his head; it was almost as though it didn't belong to him and someone else was doing the begging. There he sat on the curb by the alley corner, feeling his leathered backside, or, to be more precise, his sturdy pants.

"Why stay here?" he asked himself.

Picking up the piece of cardboard in front of him, he started combing the ground for coins he might have lost; he always put any coins he got between the cardboard and ground. Occasionally he would lose the pennies that he had counted when he received them from a generous hand. In fact, he would often stumble across coins in this particular spot because it was where he used to hang out every afternoon. He would stay there till nightfall, just like now. One day he'd made up his mind to get a leather purse to keep the money in, but the entire idea had horrified him. For example, what if a thief attacked him and made off with it? For that very reason he was quite happy to put the alms he received under the cardboard he was sitting on; that way, he could avoid the risk of encountering one of the nasty crooks that the city was spawning around here.

Everything was shrouded in fog. As Ibrahim sat there, glued to the ground like a tree trunk with the top half missing, he could feel the tension in his muscles. He tried to stretch in the narrow space available, but when he moved just a little, it felt painful and uncom-fortable. For a while he was lost in thought, so he did not hear the heavy steps as someone walked by, banging the ground like the tread of an exhausted soldier. It had to be a drunkard.

After a while Ibrahim noticed that, apart from himself and the outline of the trashcan facing him just a short distance away, the alley was completely empty. He thought to himself that he was no taller than the trashcan; actually, it was higher than he was. Just then a weird idea occurred to him, one that made him shudder. He cursed himself for coming up with such a notion—namely, that some scumbag would come, pick him up, take all his money, and then toss him into the trashcan. Seizing the small baby carriage resting beside him, he moved it back and forth to make sure it wasn't broken and would be able to take him back to his shack as usual. Shrouded in his blanket of silence and gloom, all he could do at this point was to think of Kulthum. It was as though she'd never had to deal with such heavy fog, along with the wind and bitter cold that was gradually getting worse.

You're late, Kulthum. Do you think someone else will come now and push the baby carriage if you don't?

There he stayed, scrutinizing the features of whatever happened to stop or pass by in front of him, but all to no avail. The light-poles could no longer provide enough light even for themselves. He decided to crawl a little, leaning on his hands and pushing the small carriage ahead of him. Eventually, he reached a light-pole where the darkness was less intense. He started to take deep breaths, as though he'd just climbed a high mountain. Now, he told himself, I can watch for Kulthum's shape to appear.

The alley remained immersed in silence. No passers-by, no motorcycles; just a few children playing around somewhere in the distance and yelling. If I were them, he thought, I'd go to bed and enjoy the warmth, rest, and sleep. You little rascals, you keep looking for trouble, no matter what.

By now there was no hope of Kulthum coming. If this had been the first time she was late, he would not have believed she was not coming; but, as it was, she had left him many times sleeping in the alley and resting his head on his small carriage. The last time it had happened, he had woken up at dawn to find himself spread-eagled in the middle of the road with no money. That tragedy was not going to be repeated tonight, but what actually would happen?

He didn't spend much time thinking about it. Instead, he suddenly started yelling at the children who were passing by and jumping around here and there.

"Who wants to earn thirty cents?"

"Me . . . Me . . . Me," said the children in a chorus.

"Good. There's a job I want you to do."

"I'm ready," one of them said.

"You can't do it, you're too young. I want that older boy."

"Me?" asked the boy.

"Yes."

"Thirty cents isn't enough."

"But you don't know what you're going to do for me."

"Yes, I do. But it's very late. Night work is different."

"I'll give you thirty-five centimes."

"Forty."

"Are you out of your mind? I can take a taxi for that."

"A taxi! I see, you want me to push your carriage."

"Yes."

"Fifty centimes then."

"I can take a taxi."

"Take it then! Let's go."

The children started running away. He was afraid they'd go home to sleep, so he yelled out to them again. Reluctantly he agreed to pay fifty centimes, even though his daily take had not been that high. The children helped him get on to the carriage. Once there, he looked just like a sack of potatoes.

"Can I come with you, Ali?" said a child to his friend.

"But you have to push too, okay?" Ali replied immediately.

"Okay!"

They started pushing him, while he swayed precariously from side to side.

Now he was lying there in his shack, spread-eagled in a corner. His eyes kept staring and looking around like a chameleon. Eventually he decided to move. After shifting a bit, he stopped in the middle of the shack and started rubbing his eyes, forehead, and face. Crawling over to the water jug, he filled a jam jar that he used as a mug, drank his fill, then washed his face and hands. He went back to the spot where there was a pile of threadbare rugs, and shook them out so he could locate a piece of dry bread. He started nibbling at it like a household pet that can neither speak nor express emotion. He stayed where he was, motionless and quiet; only his hands and jaws were in motion. After sitting there for a long time, he finally mumbled, "She's late this morning, too."

He didn't regret her absence as much today as he had the day before. There aren't any thieves around now, he told himself, ready to steal anything. I'm in the shack, not the street. It's daytime, not night, and the money's well hidden. No one knows where except me. Yesterday, the carriage was the problem, but now the situation's different. I can leave it in the shack and crawl my way to the alley. But what if it rains, and the ground gets wet and waterlogged? It isn't winter, but this weather may well bring some rain. It isn't cold, either, but it'll probably rain. That's why the baby carriage is crucial, and I need someone to push it. Kulthum hasn't shown up this morning to get the lunch ready, the way she usually does. We usually wait till the afternoon so we can head for the alley.

Scooting on his backside and leaning on his arms, he left his shack. Looking out from the doorway he found that the weather was reasonable; it was not threatening to rain the way he'd imagined. He decided to go to Hamadi's place to find out if he'd seen Kulthum around either today or yesterday. As he crawled, he left behind a long trail in the dirt, just like a dog. He told himself that he could do with a cup of mint tea, and had the comforting thought that he could buy a pound of sugar from Hamadi. He still had some tea in his shack, enough for two or three days. But Hamadi wasn't there, and the shop was closed. Maybe that morning he'd overslept.

Ibrahim went back to his shack, thinking all the while about the trail he had left behind him a short while ago.

"It looks as if I'm a plow," he thought to himself. "Or maybe a train."

When he reached his shack, he turned around and examined the two almost parallel lines he had drawn, one going and the other coming back. He gave a sardonic smile.

"It looks just like a train," he thought.

He waited till afternoon, but Kulthum still did not come. It was at that point that he decided to crawl all the way from his shack to the street. But the problem that preyed on his mind till just before sunset was the following: Should he wait for Kulthum, or leave? Even if she were to come now, what would she do? Would she push the baby carriage? But I wouldn't have it with me. Would she carry me on her back? That would be impossible.

The darkness and fog began to take hold; the night seemed just like previous ones. Ibrahim may have realized that when he didn't have the carriage with him he didn't need Kulthum, but he was still inclined to hang around, even for a little while. Why? He didn't know. Perhaps Kulthum would show up, and they could go together. He would scold her for not coming and would have a lot of other things to tell her, as well.

So Ibrahim decided to wait, but all in vain. This night was like other nights: the alley was empty, and the fog shrouded street-lights and buildings. However, he wasn't worried. He decided to crawl as far as the bus stop. Since the night was still young, he assumed buses would still be running. But once he reached the bus stop, his endless wait began. He decided to put an end to it by flagging down a passing taxi. The driver picked him up with evident disgust and tossed him inside.

When the taxi stopped by the shack, Ibrahim swore to the driver that he did not have a penny to his name. With a torrent of curses, the driver took him out, got back in the car, stuck his head out the window, spat at him, and mumbled some obscenities. That made Ibrahim feel happy. He could certainly tolerate all the insults; they were much easier to bear than having to pay money.

Just then, he had an idea. How about finding someone else to push his baby carriage instead of Kulthum? But is there anyone else in this world who would do it, he wondered? Of course there is, came his own reply. But Kulthum didn't just push the baby carriage; she gave him warmth at night as well, and slept with him for free. That's all fine, he thought, but she stays away a lot. What about Ahmed, he wondered. His son doesn't go to school or do anything else. Why don't I go and ask him if his son could push my carriage twice a day? I'll pay him. That's a good idea, isn't it? But then, what if Kulthum comes back? If she does, her only function will be in bed. She's homeless and likes to sleep a lot. We can both get our fill of sleep.

So Ibrahim went to see Ahmed and talk to him about his son. Their shacks were not far apart. Eventually they reached an agreement.

Next morning Kulthum did come back after a full two-day absence. Even though she had no home, she still managed to disappear for days on end, only to come back to the shack. Ibrahim didn't bother to ask her about her two-day absence; the question-and-answer session had become a routine. He simply told her that from now on, she would only be sleeping with him; she wouldn't be pushing the carriage anymore.

"Why don't we get married?" she asked.

His response was a guffaw with no clear answer.

In the afternoon, when the time came for him to go to the alley and beg, Ahmed's son didn't show up to push the carriage. They both seemed to have forgotten about him. Without any comment Kulthum helped Ibrahim get into the carriage, locked the shack door, and started pushing him as usual. Not a word was spoken on the way, but the baby carriage kept on squeaking.

THE FLOWER-SELLER

(1996)

The Flower-Seller

 $\mathcal{T}$ he flower-seller was killed by her servant-woman. She was so old, she could not defend herself.

Before the servant-woman killed the flower-seller, she had already locked the door and started pilfering whatever she could. Then she tried to escape out the third floor window, hoping she could gain access to the apartment next door. But she fell to the ground; she died, as well. Scattered alongside her body on the sidewalk were all the things she had managed to steal. So the flower-seller and the other woman had both died, one in the apartment, the other on the sidewalk.

People clustered around the corpse on the sidewalk. Some of them stared up at the apartment. No one knows if any of them stole what was there to be taken.

Of course, the emergency services all came—firefighters, police, and ambulance. They removed both corpses, one from the apartment, the other from the sidewalk, and took them away to the morgue, where autopsies could be performed if needed. But even though they took both corpses away, the crowd of people still did not disperse; maybe they had nothing else to worry about.

"The flower-seller was from Senegal," one of the men said. "She grew up in a convent. That's why she only spoke French."

"No, that's wrong," said another. "She spoke Arabic. Even though she was black, she wasn't Senegalese. Her mother was a Moroccan from Ouarzazate. After her mother gave birth, she left the baby girl with a nun at the convent. She was older than me, true enough, but I've heard about her. Her mother worked as a housekeeper in foreigners' houses. No one ever found out who made her pregnant."

249

"Blacks are everywhere," said another. "They work as masons and gardeners in villas. Maybe one of them got her pregnant."

In fact, no one knows anything about the flower-seller. She was a withdrawn, chic woman, who used to walk her dog on Sundays and talk to it.

She owned a flower shop opposite the church that had been abandoned by its worshippers; a solitary monk still occupied one part of it. The monk knew the Qur'an by heart and did bad things with young Moroccan men in exchange for helping them get passports and work contracts in France.

The black flower-seller lived on the third floor over her shop. Her window overlooked the now-deserted church. Sometimes you could see a cross on a golden chain dangling from her neck. She did her best to keep it hidden; she may have been afraid someone might steal it, or else she was worried that she might be called a Christian. Nobody knew whether she was Muslim or Christian; she never discussed such things. She was black, and that was it. She used to walk her dog and give alms to beggars, even when they did not even ask her. She seemed to know the real significance of almsgiving, just like her mother when she had handed her over to a nun, and the monk handing out passports and other things. The church's door, it seems, was not narrow, so alms would emerge from within.

The flower-seller's door was open, too, but it was narrow. It was not open to everybody, only some old foreign women from Spain, Italy, and France, and some Moroccan women married to Europeans. Their husbands were all dead, but the women all stayed in this neighborhood, visiting each other and bitching. Not only that, but they would frequently change servants as though they were changing their underwear—and all out of an irrational fear of some imaginary disease usually associated with old age.

They are all as keen on cleanliness as they are on changing servants. The servants are keen on stealing, too, but some of the really crazy ones go so far as to kill. That is how the servant came to kill the flower-seller. She may well have stolen from her many times before she actually killed her.

So, the black florist is dead, and the servant-woman as well. Before the two of them, a Spaniard had also died. He used to buy flowers from the shop once a week. He was in his seventies and had never married. He used to drink all day long and pass by the florist's shop almost every morning. He would talk to her for about half an hour, but never ask her if she had been married before. No one asked her about that. However, she used to talk about a deceased male person, but nobody ever knew if that person was her friend, husband, brother, or one of her relatives. What is significant is that whenever women talked about men, she always mentioned this deceased male person. He seemed to have been both elegant and polite and to have had a government post during the French colonial period. From such conversations, it emerged that the deceased used to drink a kind of light wine, adored dogs, and loved bowling, especially in the evening or on weekends. The florist did not like changing servant-women the way her old-lady friends did, to such an extent that she even pretended to forget other household expenses. Even so, servants would decide to leave, some of them to get married, only to be divorced later on, while others would completely disappear. Apart from that, prison was always open to all comers. So were mental asylums, if there were any. Speaking of which, no one knows for certain whether they took the bodies of the florist and the servant-woman to the hospital or somewhere else. However, everyone knows there's a place in 'Ayn Chuq where they regularly perform autopsies.

It is a Frenchman who is in charge of opening up dead people's skulls and doing autopsies. He's always getting drunk at the Capitol Bar. He drinks alone, as though he can vividly recall all the skulls he has opened up and the body parts he has dissected and abused. The florist died; so did the servant-woman. The other deceased male had died, as well, but he was elegant and polite, and loved this and that. Of course, everybody loved this and that, and then either died or was killed, just like the black woman and the servant-woman. In death there is no real difference between being killed or dying a natural death. Humans die so that others may come after them. For example, someone will buy the florist's shop, and someone else will either rent or buy her apartment. Another servant-woman will certainly come to clean the house again. The flower shop will be reorganized; other flowers will be displayed instead of the ones the black florist used to buy.

Some things disappear, others remain. Some things replace others. Flowers fade; so do souls inside human bodies, migrating perhaps to other bodies, whether white, black, or yellow. Now the black woman has died; so has the servant-woman, the deceased man, the Spaniard, and the others as well. Their souls have wilted like flower blossoms. When flowers and souls dissolve, they will first have wilted, then died. But they all look for a successor. No one knows if the black florist's soul was looking for a successor. She used to live with the flowers, her dog, the deserted church, the old women, and the deceased soul. Has her soul now met his?! No one knows. Everybody clings to the idea of staying in this world; that is their absolute right, because they have no idea of what lies beyond that curtain. If they found out, they would surely all commit collective suicide in order to escape the murder, starvation, mocking looks, and scorn.

"I wish we didn't have eyes and ears!" the black florist once told one of her friends.

"With eyes we see," replied the old Italian woman. "And with ears we hear."

"Not only that," commented an old Moroccan woman who was married to an Austrian Second World War veteran. "But we also have noses so we can smell fragrant scents, rotten odors, and other things, too."

Even so, the florist did make an effort to examine, smell, and listen to her own flowers. Although she often heard things that interested her, she would never make any comment. She was always silent and never said much. Maybe the servant-woman who killed her took her silence to be a kind of stupidity or dullness. But she was by no means as stupid as people imagined. The nicely displayed flowers in her shop window were an apt reflection of her personality.

She did not like to talk much. When the women started talking about men, she would speak about the elegant, polite deceased man, or about her dog and flowers. She knew the names of so many flowers. Actually, she was not as good at remembering her friends' names as she was the names of the flowers she sold. She never mentioned the deceased man's name. Once, one of her friends heard her say "Pedro," so the old woman told her friends that the florist had been married to a man called Pedro. They all had comments to make.

"Maybe her father was a black man from a Spanish colony."

"From Latin America. My poor husband was born in Andalusia, but spent his childhood in Honduras. When his father died, he returned to Spain and joined the Rojos Army, then fled the war and married me. His name was Pedro, Pedro Gonzalez."

"Was he black?" another woman asked.

"No. Not at all. He was dark and handsome. His only fault was that he was a womanizer. Even so, I loved him. He was a courageous man, but he loved women. I believe that any courageous man must love women."

"The deceased was a brave man, too," the florist had said on one occasion before she died, "but he did not like women too much. He loved light wine, bowling, and hunting boar. He stayed that way till he died."

"Was he your husband?"

She would fall silent and start trimming the flowers, looking out the window at a few passers-by. She let her eyes wander far away toward a strange world that only she knew. A tear might fall from behind her spectacles. Anyway, to all those nosy women who did their best to find out all they could about her, the identity of the deceased man remained a mystery. She died without anyone knowing anything about Pedro. Nobody ever saw Pedro. Even though they had known her for a long time, nobody had ever entered her house. She once said that he was good at cooking boar's meat; the meat was so good, especially the piglets. Pedro was a master-chef.

When the florist died, none of her relatives came to visit her house, nor did anyone pretend to be interested. What is strange is that no black man, child, or woman came by her shop. A few days ago, four people arrived and opened it up. Some of the flowers had wilted. The

people closed the iron grill, locked it, sealed it with wax, wrote something down on a set of forms, had a brief discussion, then left.

Is this the way life begins and ends? A teacher who lived on the
same street had such a thought, but he had no connection with either
flowers or animals. No one went to the florist's funeral. No one found
out how or where she was buried. What matters is that they took her
away in an ambulance and came back later to seal the shop. No one
knows if they buried her in a Muslim, Christian, or Jewish cemetery.
From a distance the teacher told himself that the important thing is
that death is one and the same. Some people are buried, others are
cremated, and still others are consumed inside the fish's belly. But
death is one and the same. Who cries for whom? Those who cry for
the dead today will die tomorrow. If anyone leaves something behind
after his death, someone else will come along and adopt it without
any effort.

"I'm not going to leave anything for heirs," the teacher told himself. "But then, what can a teacher leave behind, if he refuses to take
bribes?!"

Now that the black florist has died, something about the street
has changed. In spite of that, her shop was reopened later on. Another
woman may have bought it. She talked in a Fassi accent and kept
looking up at the sky as though there were no ground under her feet,
the very ground where she herself might well be buried at some point
in time.

The shop will probably be closed and sealed again, at least tem-
porarily. That is the end for all of you.

Walking

$\mathcal{I}$t may have been 1950, '51, or '52; I don't remember the exact date. The only thing I remember now is the tiny shacks scattered far apart and a few camelhair tents, also scattered and far apart. The tents were bigger than the shacks. The shacks were spread out along the left-hand side of the road toward the port of Mahdiya; the tents were pitched on an incline; at the bottom was a small lake where we used to play or swim, or else watch barefoot women wailing in a funeral cortege. I had no idea why so many of the people who lived in those camelhair tents on that incline below the road died in spite of having so much space. When it came to our shacks, the only people who remained in them were older children and a few women who bewitched men, women, and children.

But, as the saying goes, the one who bewitches the most is always the closest to death. Many are the witches who died for bewitching lots of men and women whom they'd never even seen. It may well be that some women living in the tents on the incline below the road used to do the same thing, and that explains why so many of them died and so few survived. At any rate, they'd all die just like their forebears.

We may die because of magic or for other reasons. Many other things can be deadly; people talk about them—something called cholera or plague. In 1950, '51, or '52 (as I mentioned above, I can't remember which year it was), we'd hear women yelling at their children, "May God give you the plague!" It sounded like a nasty disease that killed people and livestock. For sure, the people from the incline by the lake-shore, behind whose coffins the women were wailing, had

255

died of magic, plague, or the other thing that people called cholera. It was scary for us to watch barefoot, half-naked women slapping their thighs and faces as they walked behind the coffins. Some of them ripped their clothes apart until they were almost naked; others rolled in the dust or the mud by the lake. Their lamentations sounded like howling wolves (although I must admit, at the time I'd never seen a wolf in that region. However, when I grew up and you could hunt wolves in the forest, I ate wolf-meat grilled. The meat didn't smell as bad as I'd been told; in fact, it was delicious. I'm convinced that, if people hadn't eaten wolves' meat, they would have died).

Hunger could kill too. In our house, for example, we only had plain bread and tea, and, if we could find any, herbs. We rarely saw sheep grazing on the slope by the lake on the other side of the road. Most of the time, if a lamb, sheep, or goat appeared, there was bound to be someone behind it, or else in front of or close by it. No animal could possibly graze on its own without someone to watch it; someone would be bound to steal it either to sell or slaughter. If you don't keep a close eye on your animals, someone may come and steal them. It's the same with women: if you don't watch your wife carefully like an animal, some other man may come along and take her away. And that's the way it is. You have to take care of your property, both livestock and humans. When I grew up and learned things, I became very fond of this hadith: "Everyone is a caregiver, responsible for his flock." Since the Prophet was himself a shepherd, he knew what he was talking about.

For that same reason, it seems that the people who lived on the slope on the other side of the road knew how to graze their cattle. But on our side of the road, where the scattered shacks were, all we had was a skinny cow. Needless to say, it didn't belong to all of us; the owner was a crazy man from Bani Hasan who never talked to anyone. No one knew where he'd got the cow from. So we had dogs barking, frogs croaking, flies buzzing, and the cow mooing, along with the continuing silence of that crazy man who owned, fed, and guarded the cow—and once in a while even talked to it. Here again, when I grew up and understood things a bit more, I read a story by a Russian writer named Chekhov, about a coachman who used to talk to his horse, but I can't say for sure that he was insane. So, who knows? Maybe the cow's owner wasn't insane, either. I can't remember. It was back in '50, '51, or '52. In any case, at that time the cow was alive and living on the left side of the road leading to the port of Mahdiya on the Atlantic Ocean. It kept on mooing, while beneath the snow in White or Black Russia the horse might be neighing.

Anyway, there were shacks and camelhair tents, separated from each other by a road leading to the port of Mahdiya, and there was a small lake. Some people died, others survived. Wailing women slapped their thighs and cheeks and tore their clothes.

In life, all this will come to an end one day, just as many things have ended and others have started. For example, war may start, only to stop one day; then another will start, and it will come to an end, too. Someone may be born, while someone else dies. Livestock may be slaughtered, while other animals may be born, only to be slaughtered later; someone else may show up to slaughter, skin, and eat them. If he's generous, he'll donate some of the meat to his neighbors.

I realize that such things are rare, but it can happen. It certainly did when someone donated wolf-meat, and many people were disgusted. I heard my mother and aunts who came to this region Moroccans call "the West" talking about the number of animals that were slaughtered at one time; they also mentioned hunger and men joining the French army; some of them came home injured and ailing, while others had died. Their wives are still waiting for compensation from France.

In our shacks at least, we don't have any war-wounded, but there may be some in those tents. By the roadside nearly two kilometers from our shacks there's a French officer's tomb built with cement and encircled by a chain fence; we would jump over it to get on top of the tomb and play on it. We had no idea why that tomb was there, all alone and solitary on the ocean beach; whereas the Christian cemetery was only about ten kilometers away. To tell the truth, the Christian cemetery was very beautiful; there were flowers and roses on each tomb, and at the iron gate, a living Moroccan was posted to stand guard over the dead. When we were children, we wanted to get into the cemetery, but that very alive Moroccan would threaten us with a big stick. He would be fully alert, even when he seemed to be fast asleep under the hood of his *jallaba*.

It is really nice to have a living Moroccan guarding dead Christians. Later I discovered that Islam is a religion of tolerance; but the Christians attacked us and kicked us out of Andalusia. According to what I've read, not one Christian stood guard over Muslim tombs; in fact, they actually exhumed the bodies.

We certainly didn't do that to the French officer. All we did was play on his tomb. We'd find empty wine bottles. It was a lonely, isolated tomb with a tall tree behind it and the Atlantic Ocean beyond. How did this man come to die here? Nobody knows. He's dead; that's it. We're all going to die, and nobody gets to choose his own tomb. Even if there's a will, they'll still choose it for him. The people on the other side of the road who've died probably didn't leave a will, but they've certainly left dozens of children. They'll be buried somewhere, will or no will.

Anyway, some people will be born and others will die, the way this French officer died. Instead of putting up this tomb, they could have hung his photograph somewhere. If he's managed to do something with his life and wasn't just "hardhearted," he could have had a whole bunch of medals and decorations on his chest. But no matter.

So, once more, there were shacks and camelhair tents; and the road that led to the port of Mahdiya. It was a long, long way, and the she-donkey kept on walking. Where to? No one knows. Some people used to walk and live in shacks by the Atlantic Ocean; others walked and lived in camelhair tents. The French soldier was fated to remain isolated and alone, with children playing on top of his tomb.

Then one morning, I spotted some men, both Moroccans and foreigners, walking around; they were checking the shacks, talking and pointing, but not toward the camelhair tents. At noontime I saw women slapping their thighs and faces. The men had gathered under a fig tree and were talking. What were they talking about? No one knew.

Next morning, carts and trucks arrived and transported us all to the city's suburbs. When I'd grown up and learned enough, I found out that they were intending to build a French naval base—which they did. Even so, they didn't know what they were doing. They hadn't put up a school by the shacks or camelhair tents, but they did build one in the city's suburbs, and that's where we all studied. If they'd never walked, talked, and built a naval base, we would never have left that place and studied. You only walk to the place that God has chosen for you.

There are those who walk to tombs. There are those who go on the pilgrimage by foot. But I took another path. When they evicted us from our shacks, I grew up and started learning things. I learned how to write stories like this one. So you should all start walking. It's a long road, and the she-donkey. . . . And so forth.

At the Genoa Beach

*L*isten, I said, the sea view here is really beautiful. It's pretty well unlike anything I've ever seen. The waves aren't high, it's true. But then there are short green trees all along the edge of the beach, with flowers of various colors hanging from their branches. They take good care of the beach here. You've come in spring. If you come back in the summer, you'll see something else. Everything will look different. You'll see beautifully sculpted female bodies sunbathing on the golden sand. The small beach-bars will be packed with customers thirstily downing beer, as though Doomsday's arrived and they'll never get to drink again.

You want to see such scenes in our country as well, you say. No. No. That's impossible. We need too much time for our women's bodies to become slender and for children and drunkards to stop breaking branches off small trees. You're right: their physique is just like ours. Didn't the Arabs come to Genoa a long time ago? It's an ancient but beautiful city. Did you look at that huge church we passed the other day? Great architecture, isn't it? I've seen other churches in Europe, but the Genoese one looks beautiful and different.

Do they pray?

Yes, they're religious, but there are some atheists and fatalists as well.

Don't be surprised. It's seven in the morning; that's why you can see so many cars. They work like ants. Yesterday you may have seen them drinking in bars, but they still manage to wake up early. What matters is that they work in order to be able to eat, drink, wear nice clothes, and talk about soccer results. You said they don't read.

That isn't important; they don't pay any attention to what's going on. They voted for the prime minister even though they're all against him on buses and in cafés. They are a people that like to eat, drink, and wear nice clothes. And they make wonderful shoes.

Italy isn't Morocco, you have to understand. When all is said and done, this country doesn't resemble yours. They go to bed late, but still manage to wake up early.

When it's time for elections on Sunday, some Italians go to the polls, but others choose to stay at home, with either their dog or their sleep-mate in bed beside them. That's why the election results can be so unexpected. They sleep a lot. They've no excuse. They work all week long. It doesn't matter who wins the elections as long as everything stays the same and American air bases still exist. Do you realize that, after Moroccans, the largest foreign community in Italy is the Americans, followed by Filipinos? By the way, when you go back to your country, tell them that when an Italian gets drunk and starts fighting his friend, he'll say, "Shove off, you dirty Moroccan." What a surprise! A Moroccan woman who used to work in Saudi Arabia once told me that when Saudi women fight, they insult each other by saying, "Beat it, daughter of a Moroccan!" Isn't that cute?

But none of it's surprising. You've seen for yourself naked Moroccan girls on the streets in Milan, Genoa, and Rome. It's the same in other cities, too. In a just a few months they can make a lot of money, then they go back to Morocco to buy houses, shops, and unemployed men. Don't act surprised if I tell you that even married Moroccan women behave that way with the complete acquiescence of their husbands.

That's a disgrace you say. I agree, it's a disgrace for people in Morocco, but not here. After all, what could such women do if they stayed in Morocco? They have to prostitute themselves for a piece of bread. Sometimes they even have to pay the unemployed man who protects them; if they don't, he slashes their faces with a razor. Here, they don't slash women's faces; they either slash their bodies or kill them. However, they don't rob them of the fruit of their labors. The profession has its own morality.

That girl who's trying to use the underpass to get to the other side of the highway is really pretty, you tell me. She is indeed, but when she grows up, she may turn ugly and mean. Who knows? Maybe she'll practice the same profession, or become a great scientist. She's young and pretty. She's trying to use the underpass by those short trees with dangling blossoms. When she's older and those trees lose their blossoms or die, she may have to use that same underpass on a cold rainy day like this.

Are you afraid of death? You're stupid. People here aren't scared of death. That's why they eat and drink a lot. They say that since life is short, flowers die, and rivers dry up only to fill up again later, they must eat, drink, and do all those other things. Go to Sicily, and you'll see. There they go home at eight p.m. They have no idea how to argue and quarrel the same way we do over there. If there's a misunderstanding between two people, you can be sure that one of them will be dead by the next morning. The other one will keep on eating and drinking till his turn comes. Then flowers will start growing on his tomb, and a woman will come with her lover to cry over him. Those flowers will fade, and others will grow.

Now there's the girl disappearing behind those flowery trees. Who knows which direction she's going to take now? That underpass has four exits; nobody can guess which one she'll take. What matters is that, as far as you and I are concerned, she's disappeared. For sure that doesn't apply to other people. She will cause them problems just as they will her. Actually, she may even have a problem before she exits the underpass.

Yes!! What are you saying? Life itself is like an underpass! I'm not sure; I may agree or disagree. The underpass will sometimes be dark, and at others, properly lit. That's okay, as long as you insist that life is an underpass. The girl has gone through that underpass the same way other people are doing right now. Look, they all go in, but no one has any idea where they'll come out. It has four exits; Genoa has many entrances and exits. What's important is knowing where to enter and exit.

Do you smell that strange odor?! It's the wind blowing in from the sea. It always has a special smell to it. If you walk away from the beach a little, you won't be able to smell it any more. Maybe the Genoans' ancestors decided to build their houses here so they could savor that special smell. People have the right to choose where they feel at ease, even if it's a basement or a tomb. . . .

You don't need to tell me you agree. I am well aware that if you didn't agree with me about many things, we would not be sticking together so much. You are feeling particularly happy, you say. Why not? Just looking at this calm sea and ancient castle right in front of you, and dreaming about the beer you're going to be drinking in a minute or two at the "Gira La Terra" bar, that's enough to make you feel even happier.

No one seems interested in that girl, you say. I see her sometimes; maybe she's the girlfriend of someone who works here. Every morning she comes here, reads the newspaper, gets in her car and drives away without ordering anything. I've no idea what she does. She doesn't say a lot; that's what makes her really attractive; she prefers to remain silent. Occasionally she'll say a few words to one of the workers, and flip through the newspaper or read it more carefully, but then she gets into her car and drives away. All over the world, women aren't the same. I don't know whether that girl's from Genoa or not. What I do know is that she's female and certainly doesn't resemble any other woman.

Moroccan women are all the same, you all say. I don't agree. No woman resembles any other; nor does any man. God created each person with a particular temperament.

The flowers are beautiful, you say?! Of course they are. People here love beautiful things, but they don't know how to talk about them. Their poets do it for them. Speaking of flowers, I once went to a bar in Casablanca with a friend. A girl came over, kissed us and joined us for a drink. She was already kissing us even before she had a drink, but once she got really drunk, she wanted to kiss the other people who kept staring at us, not at her. The flower-seller came in, but no one bought a single flower. They're not interested in flowers. Even so, my friend bought a very expensive one and gave it to the girl. She looked at it, smelled it, drank her beer, and put the flower on the bar. She was the kind of girl that any prisoner would crave. We left the bar and decided to head for a night club. The girl took the flower with her. She stared at it for a while and then was about to throw it away.

"What do you want me to do with this flower?" she asked my friend. "Shall I cook it for my nine brothers?"

Dropping the flower, she stomped on it as though it were the body of an enemy. She stomped on that beautiful flower, but here people don't even dare cut them. They love flowers, the same way they love other things, like killing people, for example. That's the way they are; they'll kill someone in an instant, whereas we only kill slowly.

You understand me, you say. That's great. We have to understand each other before we start fighting. Just look how crammed together their cars are. But they still don't run over pedestrians, because the latter have a sense of self-preservation, except when they're drunk. Some Moroccans don't have any sense of self-preservation; they cross the road without bothering to use the underpass. Maybe there's a reason for that, some instinctive urge. What's life worth when compared with a large sum of money to pay for an apartment building with a garage, or shops that sell spices, rats' tails, frogs, and just-culled orphan baby tortoises?

People die in Morocco just as they do here in Genoa. There's no difference. People seem to forget that there's something called death. The way they choose to marry, procreate, live, deceive, squabble, or settle down: none of that really matters.

You don't like talking about death? That's only natural. But you know more about it than I do. Oh, we shouldn't be talking about it this early in the morning!! So when should we talk about it, bearing in mind that it's with us at every single moment? Even while I'm talking to you now, many people have died and others have been born.

You're watching those cars speeding. Don't be surprised. Other people are doing exactly the same thing somewhere else. Still others are still asleep. It may be just past eight a.m., but no one knows where all those cars are going. They certainly aren't hanging around here. Even some Moroccan women aren't wasting their time here either. That's their right and duty, as long as they don't catch that incurable disease.

But wait a minute. Can there be a disease more foul than poverty itself? If it weren't for poverty, they would never have to come to Italy. Those poor women, they're decent and clean. Any Moroccan man needs to watch what he says about this subject. If he isn't happy about the situation, then he should support his sister or his Hajja mother and stop them taking the trip to this Christian country. What will the girl who trampled on the flower do if she comes here? Will your government (sorry, our government) appoint her ambassador? Don't get angry. It's just my opinion. Be open-minded.

Yes, I'm an Italian citizen, but I'm still Moroccan. Otherwise, the Argentinians would be able to expatriate Carlos Menem and send him back to Syria. You can use that as a point of comparison. I'm sorry, don't worry about me; my nerves may be on edge because I drank a lot yesterday. You too? In that case, you have the right to do whatever you like in this world. It's worth living, because we were not created of our own will. What's the use of existing without knowing how to live? You say there are obstacles in our path. I don't disagree, but we have to use our minds a little in order to overcome such roadblocks.

You don't seem to understand me. I say one thing, and you say something else. I'm talking about human relations, and you're talking about the airport. Genoa airport is very close. You'll travel and return to your country. The taxi won't cost you very much. It's a pretty airport that extends into the sea. When you get on the plane, you'll be able to see Genoa; how beautiful it is, built around a lofty fortress just like Chaouen in your country. . . . There are lots of cities in Italy built close to mountains and valleys, and sometimes seaside beaches and rivers, as well. Wherever they feel good, they set up camp, even in Mittenwald (the Bavarian village). It's built on a mountain, the way Genoa is in a valley, as you'll see.

I can't hear you very well. What are you saying? Oh, it's a garbage truck. Look, it is about to pick up the trash dumpster, empty it, then put it back in place. When you go back to your country, please don't tell anybody about it. Unemployed Moroccans are already spending the night in these dumpsters. After they've cleared them out, they use them to sleep in. But other people have discovered a different solution. They buy a broken-down car and use it to sleep in until they can find a place of their own; I won't call it a home. Sometimes they even occupy the offices of bankrupt companies.

They come back to their country with gold chains around their necks, you tell me. That's possible. They'll do absolutely anything here. Some of them do nothing at all. Just look at that boy, for example, the one cleaning the car window. He's from Morocco. His mother may well be working somewhere else. Many children are doing the same thing as this boy. Over there, paralytics rent children; here they rent window-cleaners. You're wondering how they get here. I have no idea, but they do. I know they have to pay a lot of money to get a visa.

I arrived here years ago. I may go back or may not. That doesn't matter. I'm alive. I feel I have to talk to you about these Moroccans here. You don't know them. I've lived here for many long years and have no problems, but I feel sorry for them. Some get rich quickly. No one knows how, but things are clear enough. They trade, whether it's drugs, humans, or something else. Only God or the Devil know what . . . as we all say, assuming that the Devil exists in human form. In the morning the child window-cleaners are all over the place; they're rented out or sold like retail cigarettes. Their sisters or mothers do other things at night.

You're yawning. Obviously you didn't get enough sleep. I know you need a beer. The "Gira La Terra" bar's open. Once you've had a drink, you'll understand what I've been telling you better. The problem is that any conversation about what's happening here is bound to go on for a while. I hope some Moroccan journalists will come here on a visit and see the dumpsters, the women, everything, for themselves.

We can cross to the other sidewalk now; we'll use the underpass. Don't bother; I'll take care of the bill. We can finish our conversation about what goes on at the Genoa beach sometime later. When you get back there, tell them that he didn't have enough time. He was taking care of me because I'm one of you. Tell them, too, that he's still one of you, even though he's become an Italian. He's not the exact image of Mu'awiyah Ibn Hady, the first conqueror of Italy, when he destroyed the gates of Sicily.

Okay, let's use the underpass. Are you listening to me?

The Rat and the Birds

*T*here were no pedestrians on the street, just a few cars parked bumper-to-bumper. In the space between the cars little Fattah seemed to be playing with something. At first, the man didn't notice as the boy came rushing out from between the cars, yelling and looking behind him.

"Hey mister!" the boy shouted when he saw him. "There's a huge rat over there. It went into that storm drain. It was about to eat me."

"It can't eat you. You are a human being. Rats are afraid of them."

"It went in there. It's bound to come out again. It may bite my sister Kawthar's toes. She's asleep. She's scared of mice, cats, and dogs. Cats are beautiful, but the black ones are bad."

The man looked at the boy, then at the storm drain between the cars. There was no sign of a rat, just rubbish, piles of magazines, and an empty bottle of wine—all perfectly normal. The street is always full of trash, and lazy trash collectors always come late. There are lots of cars, but not many rubbish collectors.

Fattah moved back a few steps and pointed toward the storm drain. "It's disappeared," he said. "If Kawthar had woken up and come outside, that rat would have bitten her toes. It's fat; but I couldn't find a stone to kill it. Here's where it went in."

Fattah went back to his spot, rubbing his eyes. The man put one hand on the car and threw away the thing he was holding in the other; it might have been a piece of paper or something else.

"Is your brother Nawfal still asleep as usual?" he asked.

"No, he got up early this morning."

"Did you wake him up, or was it your mother?"

"When I woke up," the boy replied, "I didn't find him beside me. There was only Kawthar and Faysal, who was snoring. It's Sunday; so we don't have class. Nawfal got up early to bury the bird in the yard."

"Did you have a bird?" asked the man.

"Yes. Nawfal bought it the day before yesterday. It was a pretty little bird, but it died. Nawfal dug a hole and buried it before a rat or cat could eat it. There are lots of cats and rats. This one's hiding in that storm drain."

He moved back a bit and pointed to the storm drain. As he bent his thin body between the cars, he looked like a piece of threadbare cloth that had been discarded and was waiting for a trash collector. He rubbed his groggy eyes again.

"The bird was beautiful," he said. "We wanted to keep it as a pet. Actually, we didn't buy a cage. It may have died because Nawfal tied its leg with a piece of thread. Kawthar tried to feed it bread, but I don't think it eats breadcrumbs. But we don't have any seeds in the house. My mother sent the wheat we had to the mill, so there's nothing left, not even a seed. That's how that poor bird died, so Nawfal got up early and buried it. It's better that it died and was buried before a cat or something else came and ate it. You know, Nawfal sleeps a lot, but he got up early to bury the bird. Nawfal almost burst into tears."

As the man was listening to him talk, a small jeep drove by behind him, honking its horn to get him to move out of the way.

He lit a cigarette. He may well have been moved by what he had heard, especially since he didn't usually smoke in the morning.

"I'll buy you a bird and a cage," he told Fattah. "Tell Nawfal. Tell him so. He shouldn't cry. Tears won't bring the dead back to life."

"Where's the bird gone now? Does it have a soul like us? Teacher tells us we all have a soul. When we die, we'll find beautiful things if we don't behave badly during our life on earth. Is that true?"

"What teacher told you is true. If your bird dies, you must bury it so that no other animal can eat it. Some kids don't bury dead birds;

they just throw them into the street. That's bad. Those children won't find the things your teacher told you about. You and Nawfal aren't bad boys. You'll find those beautiful things in a place called Eden."

"Where's that?"

"It's in the hearts of believers," replied the man.

"Who are believers?"

"When you grow up, you'll know them. They're in Rabat."

"When I grow up, I'll travel to Rabat to meet them. I'm sure they bury birds there and don't throw them into the street."

"They grill men instead of birds."

"I don't understand."

"When you grow up, you'll understand. What's important is that you and your brother have buried the bird. You did well to chase the rat. Otherwise, it would have bitten Kawthar's toes."

"At first, I was afraid of it, but when it stared straight at me I tried to kick it. Eventually it ran away and went into the storm drain. It must have a family there."

"Sure. Have you had your breakfast yet? Or is your mother still asleep?"

"No, I haven't had any breakfast. My mother always gets up early. She used to do that even when my father was with us; that was before he went to France to work there. He sends us money and clothes. When he comes back, I'm sure he'll buy us birds and cages."

The man thought he had talked to the boy too much. He took a handful of coins from his pocket, gave the kid a dirham, and left. Fattah went back into the house. The door was half open.

The man walked along the narrow sidewalk toward the news-stand, hoping to find a newspaper before it sold out. The street was totally empty. When he had almost reached the pharmacy, he sensed a strange movement, but it was only Nawfal, sitting on the curb between two cars. When Nawfal saw the man, he ran towards him.

"It's dead," he sobbed. "My beautiful bird has died."

Nawfal tried to dry his tears.

"Don't cry," the man said. "Men don't cry. You're a man. Tears won't bring the dead back to life."

"It was a beautiful bird."

He took out a handful of coins and gave them to him without even counting them. "Here, take these," he said, "and go buy another bird."

With that, he turned away and made his way along the street leading to the newsstand, but from a distance he could see that it was closed. He decided to go back home and have a second cup of coffee without his newspaper. It is often sold out, in any case.

Ward #36

$\mathcal{I}$ won't lie to you. My father never taught me how to lie. He passed away without teaching anyone how to lie, whether to himself or anyone else. My grandfather did not know how to lie either.

He was a quiet old man who always used to sit by the tree to smoke his pipeful of *kif*. The tree is still standing in our yard, by which I mean the courtyard of the nuns' school where my grandfather used to work as a guard. When he grew old, my father took his place. Now I live in a house next to the school.

Forgive me for speaking in French. I can read Arabic, but I'm used to speaking French, since I grew up at the nuns' school. They are really good at Arabic, but they generally speak French and sometimes another language as well, probably Latin. I said I live in a house there, but not alone. Again, I won't lie to you. I live with my mother, and I have a married brother who sometimes visits us. He comes on his own because my mother doesn't like his wife.

That's all there is to it. I remember how often my brother and I used to play around the tree; in summer we used to spread out a straw mat under its branches and get high on hashish. I'm not shy in front of my brother; he is just like a friend. My father and grandfather used to smoke *kif* by the tree trunk too. Maybe you'd be surprised if I told you that my grandfather used to bury lumps of sugar around the tree trunk and water them. I've no idea why he did that. When my grandfather died, my father kept doing it. Now that my own father is dead, I'm still doing it.

I wish you would come to the nuns' school with me, to our house. Then you'd see the tree. Every evening I put sugar there and water it; I've no idea why. It was just my grandparents' idea. They always had great ideas, things we didn't understand. They knew better than we do, that's for sure. It's true that people used to fight a lot . . . at least that's what I read at the library of the nuns' school. The world has seen so many wars in which everybody died: people who fought, people who got in fights, and even people who didn't fight at all. And you know that we're all going to die eventually, even if it's not by being stabbed with a knife or shot at. We're all going to die. You can be sure of that.

I'm not lying to you. My father never taught me how to lie. That's what he didn't learn from my grandfather, nor did he learn it from his grandfather. There are so many liars in this life, but I'm not one of them. As proof, I told you yesterday that I had sold my bike so I could buy a golden bracelet as a present for one of my female friends who got married recently. I still have some money left. I'm going to buy two bottles of wine, and we'll get drunk together. Actually, I don't like getting drunk. It's just that I like to drink, especially with someone like you. They say that drinking wine is forbidden in Islam, but I've watched so many people drinking!

I got used to drinking wine at the nuns' school. They can drink, but they don't get drunk. You have seen for yourself how Muslim women drink. They drink, then start fighting each other, smashing bottles and glasses and tossing chairs at each other's heads. Rest assured, I'm not one of them; I could never do anything remotely like that. . . . They even fight their friends. You're my friend, but I would never think of behaving like that. Besides, I'm always at your side. It's true that I am taking care of that patient, but I care more about you. To be honest, there is a big difference between you and him.

He's nice, but he's stupid too. I get a decent salary. I'm well aware that his illness is caused by his parents' separation. His father's a surgeon who's living in France now, but his mother still lives in Morocco. She swore on her grandparents' graves that she would never go back to France. She's a teacher with lots of friends, but I can't even remember them all. They drink a lot; it's almost as if the entire house is a whiskey store.

You know better than I do. Her son has stopped shooting up, but I still have to give him tranquilizers whenever he starts hallucinating. He is nineteen years old and keeps accusing me of having an affair with him. He has a Jewish girlfriend. Sometimes after I've given him a few pills, I kiss him just to calm him down. He falls asleep in my arms. I'm not having an affair with him, the usual kind of thing anyone could picture. You know full well that people can imagine anything, whether it's about themselves or others. Take me, for example. Sometimes I see myself as his mother. I forget about my only son who was taken from me by his father when he left Morocco. What's important is that my son is living with his father in the country that can provide many things for him. Don't think I'm talking this way because I'm drunk. I'll tell you everything. Why should I keep anything hidden? Other people can hide their own stuff if they want. To each his own life. What counts is that I have only one concern, and that's you.

I'm not lying to you. My father never taught me how to lie. . . . I chatter too much, but you must forgive me. I keep on listening to him. He says a lot of things without actually saying anything, yet I still put up with it. You told me once that people need to be tolerant; that's the only way of dealing with a life that none of us chose to enter. Do you remember? Of course you do. You remember everything. That's why I love you. For sure, I'm going to teach you how to put sugar lumps around the tree trunk, then we'll water them together, just the way my father and grandfather used to do and maybe others before them. I don't need to say it again: we need to follow the example set by grandparents, whether they were stupid or wise. I understand you very well. You don't like hearing the word "love," but I do love you. You know that love isn't affection. I feel as much affection for that young man as I do for his mother, who is busy drowning herself in alcohol. Sometimes I wonder why she's doing it, slowly killing herself. They've put her in hospital many times, but she always starts drinking again. Her son managed to stop drinking and shooting up, but, as I've told you, I still give him a few pills and keep lulling him until he falls asleep like a docile child.

I feel for him. When my husband left me and took my only son away, I was in the same predicament. I was committed to Ward #36 in the psychiatric hospital; I overheard the doctor telling the nurse that I was psychotic. I don't know anything about this illness. I can feel something hurting me, but I can't tolerate anyone who doesn't understand me, even if it's my own fault. Think of it as a kind of egotism. But in the long run, one can still be held responsible for one's own temperament and behavior. You told me once that there are things we can't understand, things far beyond our mental capacities. So don't think I'm being selfish if I happen to make a mistake and reject the idea that people cannot bear something. That's my nature, some things are beyond my mental capacity. In the same way, the things that have pushed that young man and his mother towards addiction are beyond their mental capacity, too. I know that very well; I learned it from you. I sympathize with him just as much as I love you. I loved my husband as well, but then he did what he did.

A woman just can't trust men—pitiful, these men! Every time she trusts one of them, he gets all puffed up like a turkey and struts around like a peacock. You're claiming just the opposite. I'll agree with you that what applies to men also applies to women. I used to know two cats, a male and a female, that lived in the yard at the nuns' school. They were inseparable. However . . . another female cat showed up from somewhere—over the fence, perhaps—and the male cat fell in love with her. Do cats fall in love?! Yes, you say. I agree with you. The first female cat meowed for days, became weak and skinny, then died. Good heavens! I didn't die when he took my son overseas. I stopped eating for a while and cried a lot. The cat meowed, and I cried.

When I met you, I forgot everything. As I told you, I was in the same situation as the young man, except that his mother is still drinking and crying all the time. She has not even tried to forget what has happened to her. She may have made some mistakes of her own, or she may have been wronged, but she hasn't even tried to forget.

What are you saying? I can't hear you very well. Oh, you're saying that life itself is a mistake. So who made a mistake by creating it?

Sometimes I don't understand you. You're also saying it's a mistake for some people to be born. I hope I'm not one of them. As proof, I'm looking after that young man. If I hadn't been born, who would be taking care of him? And if doctors weren't born, who would be looking after both him and his mother? Some people, you say, are born to correct other people's mistakes. That I can understand. But you keep insisting that life itself is all a huge mistake. It's great to hear you talking, even if I don't understand what you mean. Not everything that is said is understandable, but it's still nice to hear it coming from someone you love. When we love someone, we understand things he says that would otherwise be incomprehensible. To us, at least, it all sounds nice and logical, so we try to interpret it. A lot of it sounds right.

Anyway, those are your words. Sometimes you seem unclear to me, and yet I understand you. That's why I love you. Don't blame me if I cry sometimes. I burst into tears whenever I remember things that previously seemed foggy in my memory. Even so, they make me cry. Sometimes I burst into tears for no reason. You have told me it's strange, but then you have also told me many times that nothing in life is strange. I have often regretted knowing so many men before you. All they ever did was repeat the same phrases—things like, "You should be inside a home, not in the bar."

Why are all men so much alike?! Why are you different?! You say it's God's will. So why does God want something for one person and not for others? You tell me that such talk is heresy. No, I'm no heretic. All I want is to know. To prove that I'm not a heretic, I am thinking of going to Mecca when I'm older; then God will pardon all my sins, won't he? You say we're all sinners. I haven't done anything, so I'm the least sinful of all. Even when they put me in Ward #36, I had no idea why. They could have taken somebody else who needed tranquilizers. Of course, I needed tranquilizers as well. Whenever I take them, I manage to relax.

Can you believe I saw angels once? Have you ever seen angels? What are you saying? You tell me you've seen devils in human guise. Oh, my God! That's very strange. I hope I never ever see a devil, even if it's disguised as a human being. But I think I understand what you mean by devils. I often hear the young man and his mother saying, "Let go of me—leave me alone," even though there's no one there. You're saying that actually Satan was there with them, but I didn't see him. If I had seen him, I'd have escaped through the window or some other opening. Don't scare me! You say he can follow me. He rebelled against God, so why can't he chase human beings?! But I know that God is powerful. He can put Satan in a cage and keep him there till the Day of Judgment.

Listen, my dear. You're telling me lots of things that may send me right back to Ward #36. They are beyond my capacity, and I can't understand them. I'm not going back to Ward #36, that's for sure. Now I've understood the game. I'm not crazy, so I'm not going back there. They put me there because they didn't realize that I don't understand them. You have to be aware of how crazy they are; otherwise they might consider you crazy too; either that, or that you're psychotic.

Oh! As usual I've kept on chattering. You don't mind my talking, do you? That's what I like about you. I wish all men were like you and didn't steal their wives' children and take them away to a distant country. But it's fine. All I can tell you now is that we'll talk again till Death comes. I believe our destiny will be one and the same. Of that I'm sure. Actually, I've dreamt about it many times. You don't believe in dreams, you say. But my father told me that dreams are mentioned in the Qur'an, and you like the Qur'an a lot. Many times you've told me what a wonderful book it is.

Oh good heavens! I've learned so much from you. Forgive me, my dear, but the talk never stops. The young man must have woken up by now. I have to give him some tranquilizers. His mother will have fallen on the floor and broken the utensils and the whiskey bottle. I must go now to put things right. It's all beyond me. Don't pay for what we've drunk. You always pay, and it's too much for you. Goodbye. "Bye"-bye. *Fais moi une bise.* Give me a big kiss.

Afterword

This anthology is intended as a tribute to one of Morocco's greatest writers of narrative, Muhammad Zafzaf, a pioneer of the modern Moroccan short story. The present collection makes a significant contribution to a literary genre whose roots can be traced back to the Arabic oral tradition, a genre usually translated as "tale." The Moroccan context for both tales and short stories is little known in the Western world. Nevertheless, in recent years a few useful attempts have been made through the translation of selected works into English by Roger Allen, Denys Johnson-Davis (*Arabic Short Stories*, 1983), Malcolm Williams and Kevin Waterson (*An Anthology of Moroccan Short Stories*, 1995), and Jilali El Koudia (*Moroccan Short Stories*, 1998). Otherwise, the Moroccan short story has barely managed to emerge from the narrow circle of academic research papers, newspaper articles, and magazines.

Muhammad Zafzaf was born in 1945 in Suq al-Arbi'ah, a town in the province of Kenitra. After receiving his high school diploma in Kenitra he attended Mohammed V University in the capital city of Rabat, where he started a degree in philosophy but never finished. He then left for Casablanca, where he lived for the rest of his life, teaching high school. In 1968, he became a member of the Moroccan Writers' Union.

Zafzaf's work, which includes poetry, novels, translations, and short stories, encapsulates his long, fruitful experience with life. Writing was very difficult for him, involving four decades during which he strove to present the best of himself, reinventing his artistry several times.

According to Ahmed Bouzfour, a fellow Moroccan writer of short stories, Zafzaf's career can be divided into three distinct phases: the Moroccanization of writing ("Al-Didan Allati Tanhan" [The Worms That Bend], 1970); the depiction of social misery ("Al-Aqwa" [The Strongest], 1978); and a concern with the more stylistic aspects of writing ("Al-Shajara al-Muqaddasa" [The Holy Tree], 1980.[1] At each stage his work manages to reflect both socio-cultural and political events taking place across the globe, and reactions to them. The essence of each era is mirrored in his story collections; the social, political, and cultural influences involved shaped, redefined, and enriched his narrative method.

As a writer, Zafzaf was considered a rebel, someone who never knew (or wanted to learn) how to play the game of the "court," and whose work was labeled as "pejorative." From early in his writing career, Zafzaf strove to establish his own particular craft and identity. Zafzaf's writing possesses a particular essence that makes him unique among modern Moroccan writers, one that has earned him the respect of writers and critics, both local and international. His use of the older Arab tradition of oral tales, when colored with the tints of everyday Moroccan Arabic dialect, makes his storytelling style very simple (perhaps deceptively so), one that is easy to read and close to the expectations of the ordinary reader.

Like the stories of many Moroccan writers, Zafzaf's are set within a variety of contexts. They portray a slice of life, a simple struggle for survival in a challenging world that is changing at a rapid pace. Narrative time is reduced to a single glimpse, full of irony, sarcasm, and sympathy. He covers all aspects of Moroccan life, from the most remote rural villages and "douars" (districts) to modern cities, and especially Casablanca, the city that he adored and had no desire to leave. It is the city of Casablanca that most influenced his decision to focus on the individual's subjective experience, something that is clearly illustrated by his extraordinary sensitivity to the most

1. See *Afaq* [Horizons], vol. 61/62 (1999).

mundane and trivial aspects of everyday life. Actions and situations, ranging from sheer human stupidity to extreme cruelty, naiveté, callous indifference, abject suffering, and tragedy, all are described in the richest detail. The innermost thoughts of Zafzaf's characters are depicted with enormous precision, and his short stories thus become vehicles for searching criticism, expressions of wide social divisions and cultural nonconformity.

During his own lifetime, Zafzaf took upon himself the task of criticizing his society's social norms and values. In order to represent them accurately, he selects a variety of characters, ranging from rebel to defeatist. He writes about the behavior and customs of people in his society, especially those from the lower and middle classes, and focuses his attention on relationships rather than on specific situations. Within such a framework he manages to present portraits that blend social misery and injustice, patriarchal society, and political questioning.

Throughout his career, Muhammad Zafzaf explored the various myths, beliefs, and traditions that operated within his culture, questioning them from a distance. He always insists on the storyteller's involvement in, and shaping of, his surroundings; and, while he may utilize a neutral and distant narrator, he is still personally involved as a writer to such a degree that his work can almost serve as an anthropological adjunct to Moroccan social history.

As already noted, Zafzaf favors an easy, conversational style—what has become known as a Zafzafian style. All his short stories include either dialogues, internal monologues, or stream-of-consciousness. The series of sentences depend on each other as part of a whole, a connected and interlinked chain, constituting a sort of eruption: an almost frustrating narrative mode that makes it hard to separate the autobiographer from the writer of fiction. A degree of ambiguity persists between writer and dispassionate narrator. Zafzaf is continually more interested in *how* to write, rather than *what*; in how he narrates, and not what. Throughout his career as a writer of narratives, he managed to exert a huge influence on an entire generation of storytellers.

The stories in this collection were not chosen at random; they are intended to present a comprehensive picture of Muhammad Zafzaf's work throughout his career. The collection is arranged in chronological order so as to demonstrate the various transformations that his writing technique underwent. We have to admit here that it was no easy task to select a sampling of his works from a plentiful corpus that is so valuable and diverse in nature, one that manages to provide its readers with an accurate artistic portrait of Moroccan culture, itself.

Most of Zafzaf's work has been published in newspapers and magazines all over the Arab world, and his stories have been translated into many languages. One of his early short stories, "Al-Didan Allati Tanhan" [The Worms That Bend] (1970), immediately established him as a prominent short story writer, one who could be placed alongside such illustrious names as those of the Egyptians (Yahya Haqqi and Yusuf Idris, to name just two). Even before his death in Casablanca on July 23, 2001, the Ministry of Culture in Morocco had published his collected works, an unprecedented gesture and one that gave due recognition to his status as "the Tolstoy of Morocco." It is from that collection of his complete works that the stories included in this anthology have been taken.

Why have we chosen examples of the short story genre in order to represent Zafzaf the writer? One reason is that he managed to elevate the Moroccan short story to the level of a self-conscious art. His contributions to this genre are generally regarded as the cornerstone of his journey toward creativity as an avant-gardist. The second reason is our admiration for a great master who was to have a major influence on a whole generation of Moroccan writers. This collection of his stories, translated into English, thus aspires to bring this important writer to the attention of a wider readership.

Glossary

Amazigh: the indigenous people of North Africa, often referred to by the pejorative term "Berber."

Anouilh, Jean (1910–87): a renowned French dramatist.

bedaia: a Moroccan garment.

Ben Barka's murder: Mehdi Ben Barka was a prominent left-wing Moroccan politician who disappeared in Paris in 1965. The factors involved have never been explained.

Bidaoui: from Casablanca.

Bni Yessef: a small village in Morocco.

Bouhmara: also, Bou Hmara. His real name is Jilali ben Driss Zirhouni al-Youssefi. A contender to the Moroccan throne by claiming he was the prince Moulay Ahmad, the eldest son of Sultan Moulay Hassan, and that he should be king of Morocco instead of Moulay 'Abd al-Aziz. He established a kingdom in the East and the North of Morocco. He was later arrested and executed in Fez in 1909.

Caid: the term used to describe the governor of a particular district within Morocco.

cherbel: traditional Moroccan women's shoes.

choro: churo, a Spanish fried-dough pastry.

comptoir: counter, bar.

dama: checkers.

doum: chamaerops, a kind of flowering plant, sometimes called "dwarf palm."

fqih: a Muslim jurisconsult.

Garde Mobile: Moroccan Auxiliary Forces, a paramilitary group that supports other branches of the security forces and operates under the interior ministry.

Hajj, Hajja: the honorific title given to Muslim men and women who have performed the pilgrimage (hajj) to Mecca. Usage: al-Hajj, "the Hajj."

Yahya Haqqi (1905–92): a prominent Egyptian short story writer and critic.

harira: a characteristic Moroccan soup dish, made with lentils and spices

Hawziya: a Moroccan singing style.

Ibn Abi Dunya (823–94): a prominent Muslim scholar, renowned for his prose style.

Ibn Masoud (7th cent.): a companion of the Prophet Muhammad.

Yusuf Idris (1927–91): a famous Egyptian writer of short stories.

jallaba: the ankle-length garment worn by both men and women in Morocco and elsewhere.

jinn/jinni: supernatural beings prominent in both Islamic and pre-Islamic myth. Often mentioned in the text of the Qur'an, they can be forces for good or evil.

ka'b al-ghazal: (gazelle's ankles) crescent-shaped Moroccan cookies.

kas'a: a terracotta dish for Moroccan couscous.

kif: a product of cannabis resin.

Carlos Menem (b. 1930): the former president of Argentina (1989–99) is of Syrian extraction. Following his presidential term (2001), he was arrested and charged with corruption.

mokhazni / makhzan: a member of the Moroccan Auxiliary Forces. The "makhzan" is the general term for the Moroccan government and its organizations.

Mu'awiyah ibn Hady: also known as Mu'awiyah ibn Hadaij, a governor who was sent by the Caliph Mu'awiyah to conquer Sicily.

Muslim ibn al-Walid (c. 748–823): one of Arabic's most famous love-poets, often known as "sari' al-ghawani" (victim of beautiful girls).

General Muhammad Oufkir (1920–72): initially a confidant of King Hassan II of Morocco and appointed minister of the interiors, he led a plot against the king in 1972 and was assassinated. His entire family was sent to a desert prison, described by his daughter Malika in the book *Stolen Lives: Twenty Years in a Desert Jail.*

Rojo: a member of the Republicans who were called Los Rojos (the Reds) during the Spanish Civil War.

saykouk: a Moroccan cold dish usually for summer heat, made of buttermilk and small-, medium-, or large-grained couscous.

shikhat: Moroccan female singers and dancers.

tajine: actually the name of a cone-shaped cooking dish, the word is also used to describe a characteristic dish of Moroccan cuisine, involving a mixture of meat (chicken, lamb, or fish), fruit or vegetables, and couscous.

Tamazight / Tashelheet: two of the local dialects of the language-family of the Amazigh (see above).

'Uthman ibn 'Affan: the third Caliph of Islam, who headed the Muslim community in Arabia from 642 until his assassination in 656.

zakat: the Arabic word for "almsgiving," it being one of the five "pillars" of the Muslim faith.

Zammori: a Moroccan singing style.

Mbarek Sryfi is a lecturer in Arabic at the University of Pennsylvania. He is also an adjunct assistant professor in English at Mercer County Community College in New Jersey. His translations have appeared in *CELAAN* (2008), *Metamorphoses* (2011), meadmagazine.org (2012), *World Literature Today* (2012), and *Banipal* (2013).

Roger Allen won the 2012 Saif Ghobash–Banipal Prize for his translation of *A Muslim Suicide* by Bensalem Himmich (Syracuse University Press, 2011). Allen retired from his position as the Sascha Jane Patterson Harvie Professor of Social Thought and Comparative Ethics in the School of Arts & Sciences at the University of Pennsylvania in 2011. He is the author and translator of numerous books and articles on modern Arabic fiction, novels, and stories.